MISCHIEF FOR MISS CHARTLEY

Miss Omega Chartley tried to be a proper young country schoolteacher after her fall from grace as one of the dazzling young beauties of the London *ton*.

But there was nothing proper about her position now.

A runaway little boy was in her charge. A Bow Street runner was on her trail. And a man whom she could neither trust nor resist had reentered her life—revealing the shocking secret of his past—and threatened to complete her ruin.

Omega knew what a sensible young lady would do. But she had left good sense far behind—and had only love to guide her. . . .

CARLA KELLY lives in Springfield, Misso a public relations writer for a local hos

Miss Chartley's Guided Tour

Carla Kelly

A SIGNET BOOK
NEW AMERICAN LIBRARY
A DIVISION OF PENGUIN BOOKS USA INC.

For Rosalind Barrow,
my sister-in-law

NAL BOOKS ARE AVAILABLE AT QUANTITY DISCOUNTS WHEN USED TO PROMOTE PRODUCTS OR SERVICES. FOR INFORMATION PLEASE WRITE TO PREMIUM MARKETING DIVISION, NEW AMERICAN LIBRARY, 1633 BROADWAY, NEW YORK, NY 10019.

SIGNET TRADEMARK REG. U.S.PAT OFF AND FOREIGN COUNTRIES
REGISTERED TRADEMARK—MARCA REGISTRADA
HECHO EN DRESDEN, TN, U.S.A.

SIGNET, SIGNET CLASSIC, MENTOR, ONYX, PLUME, MERIDIAN and NAL BOOKS are published by New American Library, a division of Penguin Books USA Inc., 1633 Broadway, New York, New York 10019

First Printing, July, 1989

1 2 3 4 5 6 7 8 9

PRINTED IN THE UNITED STATES OF AMERICA

Prologue

If he were a wagering man, he would have bet houses, lands, horses, and hounds that he was the first of his line to ride to his wedding in a hired conveyance.

The thought afforded no pleasure, only a deep washing of shame that flooded his body from face to toes. He closed his eyes against it, only to see himself again as though it were early morning, stumbling into the alley off St. James Square and falling to his knees on the cobblestones, overcome by the enormity of what had happened.

"My God, what have I done?"

It was the first thing he had said aloud in hours, and his words made him jump and then grasp the hanging strap in the hackney. He gripped it tight, retracing in his mind the long walk back to his own flat on Curzon Street, well-wrapped in his opera cloak, head down, praying no one would know him, or speak to him, or wish him congratulations.

He opened his eyes and sobbed out loud, seeing again the pile of bloody clothes he had ripped from his body as if they had burned him, standing naked in front of his mirror and not having the courage to look himself in the eye.

The cold that covered him then, covered him still. He was still shivering, still trembling like an old man with palsy. After he had dressed himself he had tried and tried to pick up the little wedding ring on his bureau. It had taken both hands, and then he had dropped it twice before seeing it into his pocket.

The clothes jumbled about him on the floor he wrapped in his opera cloak and carried down the stairs and into the alley. A quiet walk behind the row of flats and then the bundle was stuffed deep into someone else's ashcan.

There was no time to speak for his curricle from the

stables. He had hailed a hackney and directed the Irishman sitting on the box to St. Alphonse on Wadlington Lane, his fiancée's special choice because she loved the stained-glass windows and the choir screen.

The driver looked at him carefully, and his heart dropped to his shoes and stayed there. "Are ye all right, sor?"

He had nodded, too devastated to speak. If I open my mouth, I will tell him everything, he thought. No one must ever know.

The journey that he wished would take years was over in a matter of minutes. The hackney stopped and the driver sprang from the box and stood by the door, hand on the latch. "St. Alphonse, sor," he said.

"Oh, drive on, please. Just a little farther."

After another careful look and a shake of his head, the driver returned to the box and clucked to his horse. When they were beyond the church, he slowed again, and rapped on the roof.

He had no idea how much money he gave the driver. The man sucked in his breath and bowed, so it must have been more than patrons usually flicked his way. He turned to go, and the man grasped his arm. Again the chills traveled the length of his body.

"You'll not be calling the constable and telling him I robbed you, now, will you, sor?"

He waved the driver away and started back toward St. Alphonse. The clock in a tower several blocks distant chimed twice; he was already half an hour late. He wiped the sweat from his face, unmindful of the cold wind that blew off the river. At least all the wedding guests would be inside. He would be far to the front, next to the altar, and if he looked a little pale, his friends and relatives would put it down to wedding jitters.

He forced himself to hurry. His best man had never been distinguished for his patient temperament and was probably even now wearing a rut in the carpet. And his fiancée?

He broke into a run which ended on the bottom steps

leading to the massive front door of St. Alphonse's Church. Already a crowd had assembled, a collection of children and poor people from the neighborhood, who knew that the gentry inside were inclined to be generous when they came out after a wedding. And failing that, there were pockets to pick.

But the people on the steps were talking among themselves, casting a glance at the church now and then, and laughing behind their hands. Some were already beginning to move away.

He mounted the steps, two at a time, and stood by the entrance with another crowd of more brazen folk, bits of London chaff blown there by news of a wedding. He stood next to a man who balanced on one leg and a peg, a man who nudged him and winked.

"I disremember when ever I saw *this* happen before. And what a crime, I say. Look there at that pretty little lady."

"Yes, look," chimed in the woman on the other side of Peg-leg. "You should have seen her skip up the steps. And such a smile on her face! You could have lit lighthouse lamps from that smile."

He could only groan inwardly as another great tide of shame washed over him.

Peg-leg shook his head. "And now her face is whiter than her dress. There's one gentleman ducking and running in this city who ought to be pulled up sharp-like. See her there?"

He looked where Peg-leg pointed. The doors were open and there she sat in the vestry of the church, flowers drooping out of her hand, her face a study in shock. Her brother was speaking to her, kneeling by her, his hand on her back. She drew away from him. When her father squared his shoulders and started up the aisle toward the altar to make an announcement, she burst into tears, helpless tears that he knew would ring in his mind and soul for the rest of his life.

The clock in the tower chimed the half-hour. From habit he pulled out his pocket watch and clicked it open. Two-thirty. He snapped it shut and shoved it back in his pocket, feeling as he did so the wedding ring.

He couldn't leave London fast enough.

1

When the coachman blew on his yard of tin and signaled their approach to King Richard's Rest, Omega Chartley pulled her mother's watch from her reticule, snapped it open, and examined it. They were precisely on time. The thought pleased her, as all perfect things did, and she smiled to herself.

The loudly dressed fribble sitting opposite her mistook her smile for approval of himself. He sat a little straighter and tugged at his wilted shirt points, smiling back and revealing a mouthful of improbable porcelain teeth.

Omega snapped the watch shut with a click that made the vicar next to her sit up and peer around in fuddled surprise. She fixed the forward young man across from her with the same quelling stare that had reduced many an unprepared student of English grammar to visible idiocy. The man gulped and looked away as the color drained rapidly from his face.

It was high time she squelched his pretensions. Earlier that morning, when she was dozing off as a result of her sleepless night in the last inn, someone (she suspected the man with porcelain teeth) had prodded her feet in a scarcely gentlemanlike manner. It would never have done to call attention to the matter; how nice that she could put him in his place now.

"So the rain has finally stopped," remarked the clergyman on her left as he pulled himself awake and tried valiantly to fill in the awful silence caused by Omega's set-down.

She returned some suitable, if vague, answer, and looked out the window. The rain had stopped, but there was no lifting of the gray covering that had settled over the gentle hills and valleys. All was gray. It was not a propitious beginning to her holiday.

Throughout Plymouth's dreary winter and spring, when each day was done and she had corrected papers until her eyes burned, she had treated herself each night to a few moments with *Rochester's Guidebook of England for Ladies*. By the sputter and stink of the work candles that Miss Haversham grudgingly provided for her teachers, Omega Chartley had plotted out the journey that would take her from Plymouth on holiday.

At first the holiday had no plans beyond an excursion to Stonehenge on the Plains of Salisbury ("Entirely suitable for ladies not easily exercised by thoughts of druidical rites," according to the *Guidebook*), and then beyond to the Cotswolds and back again. When, in early spring, a letter had arrived from St. Elizabeth's in Durham with a coveted contract to teach English grammar in the wilds of north England, the holiday turned into a move.

Other than a brief trip to Amphney St. Peter for Alpha's wedding, she had not left Plymouth in eight years. Omega could claim no attachment to the damp seacoast town other than the fact that it was far removed from anyone she once knew. Miss Haversham's Academy for Young Ladies would not bring her face-to-face with any bad memories.

For several years, Alpha Chartley had tried in vain to draw her from Plymouth to Amphney St. Peter. Omega would have none of it; she had chosen her exile and there she would remain. And so she would have, had not the letter come from her own former teacher, advising her of the vacancy and requesting that she apply for it.

And so Omega had applied. She was weary of the gray ocean. She could hide in Durham as well as Plymouth and teach mill owners' daughters instead of the offspring of sea captains. The money was better too. She was on the shady side of twenty-six, and needed to think about her future.

But there was the present to contend with now, and the clergyman who bumped her as he gathered together his belongings.

"Pardon, miss, pardon," he said, his face as red as Mr. Porcelain Teeth's waistcoat.

Omega smiled to reassure him, and made herself small in her corner of the mail coach. She sighed inwardly and wondered if the time would ever come when she would feel at ease traveling on the common stage.

The pretentious young man left the coach as soon as it rolled to a stop, not glancing her way again. The vicar followed and then stood by to give her a hand out.

As she was bending out of the coach and reaching for his hand, a traveling coach rolled into the innyard and dashed past the Royal Mail, spattering the vicar with mud. Omega leaned back inside to avoid the mud, but she was sure she could hear people laughing inside the closed coach.

The vicar sighed a prodigious sigh and extended his hand again. Omega took it and stepped lightly to the soggy ground. Without a word, she helped the clergyman brush the mud off his coat. She was used to tending young girls in similar circumstances and thought nothing of it.

"You are too kind, miss, too kind," said the clergyman, his face redder than before.

"It is nothing," she replied.

The vicar directed his gaze at the traveling coach, which had swung to a stop by the inn door. "You would think that the better classes would set the example for the rest of us, miss," he said darkly.

"Yes, you would think that," she agreed. No purpose would be served for the clergyman to know that when she had been a member of the "better classes" she had never thought of herself as an improving example. Better to let him labor under the misapprehension that his betters really were better.

When the largest chunks of mud had been returned to the innyard, she retrieved her traveling case from the coachman and followed the vicar into the taproom. The inmates of the private coach were nowhere in sight, and the landlady was just returning to her guest register.

Omega spoke for a room, but turned down the offer of a private parlor. Too many of those would end her trip far south of Durham, as much as she would have enjoyed the comfort.

"And may I have my dinner brought to me?" she asked.

"Of course you may, Miss Chartley," said the landlady. "Only you must please wait until I have served the members of that private coach and four."

"I understand," Omega replied. Her head was beginning to ache, but it would hardly have been fair to blame it on the private coach and four.

The room was small and cool, with the lingering scent of cigar smoke. After the landlord deposited her trunk on the floor with a thump, Omega went to the window and opened it, leaning out and breathing in the fresh smell of countryside after a rain. Her room fronted the street, but beyond the busy thoroughfare were the haying fields. She could make out sheep on the hills, and as the wind blew, she caught the sound of their bells, one here, one there, almost an echo.

"I will not miss Plymouth," Omega said out loud, and smiled to herself. If she never again saw the mesmeric swells of greasy ocean or breathed in the pungency of tar and hemp from the ships, she would not mind.

Omega rested her elbows on the windowsill. As she watched, the sky reformed itself, the clouds parted, and the watery sun shone through for the first time since the Plains of Salisbury. The sky lightened, almost as if dawn were approaching, rather than dusk. People on the street hurried home to their dinners, and mothers called in their children.

At the end of the street, where it divided into two roads, men were dismantling a tent and folding it away into an already overloaded wagon. Another Waterloo fair, Omega thought.

She remembered the Waterloo fairs around Plymouth in the early weeks of July, the mad, joyous parades celebrating Wellington's victory in Belgium. Miss Haversham had permitted her to take some of the older pupils into the streets, where they all gazed in wide-eyed wonder at the French eagles and bloodstained battle flags of both sides carried through the shrieking crowds.

After that first night, they did not return. The spontaneous parades where children skipped alongside their parents gave way to vulgar burlesques of Napoleon and Marshal Ney with their trousers down around their ankles, as Wellington beat them with a broken sword.

Here it was, late August, and still the fairs continued, the sideshows moving from town to town, and people in villages more and more remote turning out to hear the stories of the Thin Red Line and the orchard of La Haye Sainte.

Omega refreshed herself with a splash of lavender water on her wrists and forehead, and then sat down with a book to wait for her dinner. Tonight, when the plates were removed and the fire was lighted, she would pull the lamp closer and work on her course outline in English grammar.

Her good intentions slipped away when the empty dishes were withdrawn and she was left alone with English grammar. After all that rain, it was too fine a night to be wasted on the subjunctive. The sky continued to lighten as more and more clouds scudded away like the Waterloo fair.

Omega pulled on her shoes again, gathered her shawl around her, and left the room, tucking in her curly hair where it always seemed to fly out from under her cap. She whistled to herself, looking around to make sure no one was within earshot, and pulled on her gloves as she hurried down the stairs.

She had no knowledge of the village, so she resolved to walk only to the end of the street where the road forked. The wagon was gone now; there would be no fair again until Harvest Home. She sniffed the air. It was late summer, but already there was something in the wind that smelled of winter. And then in January, when the dreariness of winter threatened to overwhelm, there would be that faintest hint of spring in the cold air. Another year would pass.

And I will be one year older, she thought.

She reached the fork in the road, stood there a moment,

and was preparing to turn back when she noticed a boy digging about in the garbage heap left by the Waterloo fair. Surely her eyes were deceived by the dusk. She looked again, squinting against the coming darkness.

The boy, scratching about in good earnest, did not pause in his rapid search through the rubbish. He couldn't have been more than ten years old. Omega stepped closer and watched him. His clothes were grubby about the knee and elbow in the fashion of little boys, but they were of excellent cut and fine cloth. His black hair was trimmed smartly, even modishly, in imitation of his elders. Her eyes caught the sparkle of the buckles on his shoes.

As Omega watched and wondered, the boy stopped and turned around. He looked at her in silence, as if wondering what she would do. Omega was too well-bred to show surprise, but she knew that the face was familiar.

It might have been the way he held his head slightly tipped to one side, or the way he pursed his lips. Whatever it was, she wondered if somewhere she had seen this boy before, or someone very like him.

He smiled at her, the uncertain, tentative smile of someone who knows he should not be pawing about in a midden.

"I thought I could find something to eat," the boy said at last.

He made a motion to leave, so Omega sat down on a tree stump. She did not want him to run away. "When did you last eat?" she asked, leaning forward and clasping her arms in front of her knees.

"Yesterday I found some apples." He grimaced. "They were too green by half, and my breadbox hurt for hours."

"Apples do that to me too," she said. "And do you vow never again to eat a green apple, and then break your promise next summer?"

He grinned. "Something like that," he agreed.

They regarded each other in silence. Omega heard voices; people were coming up the street from the direction of the inn. She did not recognize them from the mail coach. They must have been the contents of the coach and four.

The boy eyed them too. "You see, I am not good at this," he said at last.

"Are you running away?" she asked.

He measured her with his eyes for a moment, as if trying to gauge her response, and then nodded. "And I won't go back," he said. "No one can make me." He scrambled to his feet, as if fearful he had said too much.

Omega put out her hand to reassure him. "How can I help you?" she asked.

When he said nothing, she continued. "Would you like some food?"

He fixed her with that penetrating, naggingly familiar stare again, and then smiled in some relief. "I would like that above everything else," he admitted, "but it did not seem polite to ask."

Omega rose to her feet slowly so he would not bolt. "Then come with me to the inn, and let us find something."

"I should not," he said. "I think my uncle has set the Runners on me."

Her eyes widened. "The Bow Street Runners?" she asked. "Good God."

He realized he had said too much, and began to edge away from her.

"Oh, please don't run away," said Omega as the boy darted away from her.

He did not get far. He ran directly into the arms of the gentleman strolling with his companions toward the fork in the road. The man was thrown backward several paces by the force of the boy against him, but he did not fall, and did not lose his grip on the child, even as the boy struggled.

Omega hurried toward them.

"Was this snatch-gallows bothering you, miss?" asked the man, a bit breathless from the encounter. He gave the lad a shake.

"Oh, no, no, nothing like that, sir," Omega replied. "Please let him go. He means no harm, I am sure."

The man only tightened his grip, whirling the boy about and grabbing him by the hair. He pulled his head back for a good look, and jerked his head from side to side as the boy struggled.

"You'll hurt him," said Omega.

"You can't hurt scum like this," said the man to his companions, an elderly lady who stood a little back, and a younger woman who ignored the boy and stared instead at Omega Chartley.

The man took a firmer grasp on the boy's hair, making him cry out.

"Oh, please stop!" cried Omega, and took the man by the arm. He shook her off.

"And did you say something about the Runners, boy? Did you?" he asked again, shaking the boy. "Answer me!"

The boy sobbed, but he would not speak.

"I'm going to march you back to the inn and we'll see what we see," said the man.

Before he could act on his threat, the boy raked his heel down the man's shin. The man threw him off and into Omega's arms. Without even hesitating, Omega grasped the boy firmly by the shoulders, whispered "Run!" in his ear, and gave him a shove in the direction of the forked road.

Whatever possessed her, she could not explain even to herself, much less to the man who stood glowering at her. For all she knew, the boy was a desperate felon, wanted for crimes she couldn't even imagine.

In her heart she knew this was not so. Omega recognized the look of terror mingled with humiliation on the boy's face. It could have been her own face eight years ago, chalk white and on the edge of tears. No one had helped her then, but that had not stopped her now.

The man could scarcely speak. He worked his mouth open and closed a few times like a hooked fish. "You . . . you let him go!"

"She did more than that," declared the young woman, who had watched the whole incident. "She gave him a push. I saw her." The woman looked back at Omega again. "And *wherever* do I know you from?"

Omega said nothing to her. She squared her shoulders and looked the man right in the eye, even though her knees trembled. "Yes, I let him go. You had no right to treat him so roughly. If the Runners want him, they can find him."

Pulling her skirt closer to her and settling her lips in what Alpha called the "Chartley schoolteacher look," she shouldered her way past the trio on the sidewalk and walked toward the inn. She wanted to break into a run, as though she were pursued by barking dogs, but she did not.

"Did you ever?" she heard the old woman say.

At the woman's words, Omega squared her shoulders again and gave her head a little toss. Instantly she regretted the gesture. She heard the young woman behind her gasp. "I know her now!" she said. "Oh, Mother, do you not remember? I have been puzzling and puzzling where I have seen her before. Oh, Mother! How could you forget? Remember the Bering-Chartley wedding? Oh, Lord, the wedding of the Season!"

Omega sucked in a ragged breath and hurried faster, lengthening her stride and putting distance between herself and the voices and stares. Another hundred feet would put her back at the inn. She could walk calmly inside and then scurry up the stairs and hide in her room until the morning, when the private coach and four would depart. Omega gave herself a mental kick for succumbing to the blandishments of a fine evening and forsaking the safety of English grammar.

A hand reached out and touched her sleeve as she entered the inn, her eyes on the stairs. She whirled around to see the landlord, who stepped back, frightened momentarily by the look in her eyes.

"Miss? Miss? Did you not hear me? I must request your presence in the taproom."

She shook her head. "I have a headache," she managed.

There was another, stronger hand on her elbow, and she found herself propelled into the taproom. "Sorry, Miss . . . Miss . . ."

Omega did not enlighten the man who bullied her into

the taproom. She did not even glance at him as she found herself pushed gently down into a chair.

"I really must protest," she said faintly to the landlord. To her own ears her voice sounded no louder than a cricket sawing on the hearth. Miss Omega Chartley, who by the mere shifting of her eyes could send a whole rank of fourth-form students to the brink of the valley of the shadow, was reduced to complete submission.

Omega stared straight ahead, and a red-whiskered man intruded upon her view. He smelled of cigar smoke and horse sweat, with the odor of greasy leathers thrown in. She could not bring herself to stare at him, but abandoned herself to the perusal of his muddy boots, which, from the looks of them, had never met the acquaintance of a blacking rag.

When he spoke again, his voice was kind enough. "I did not mean to give you a start, miss, but I'm speaking to everyone at the inn, ladies not excepted." He sat down directly in front of her. "It has been my experience that ladies are more acute observers than toffs, any road."

"How, sir, may I help you?" she said in a frosty voice that would have sent her brother, Alpha, into a fit of giggles.

He said nothing, only watched her. It was not an unkind stare, merely a businesslike one.

Omega folded her hands in her lap. "What is it that you wish from me, sir?" she asked again.

He leaned toward her, resting his elbows on his knees. "I'm a Runner, ma'am, from Bow Street. Have you heard of it?"

She nodded and looked down at her hands, unclenching them slightly when she noticed how white her knuckles were. He followed her gaze, but made no comment.

"You have the advantage of me, sir," she said. "What is it that you wish?"

"I'm asking all the patrons at every inn, lodging house, and flea palace between here and Oxford. Have you see a lad about ten with black hair and brown eyes?"

She had. "Sir, you could be describing half the little

boys in England. Does he have a name?" she temporized, not wishing to answer him if she could help it.

"Answers to Jamie. James Clevenden. He's a runaway, miss."

The sap in a log popped on the hearth and Omega jumped. The Runner watched her. "Have you seen the lad, miss? Answer me, now."

She opened her mouth, but someone else's voice came out.

"Yes, she knows him. Ask her how she let him escape from me."

It was the man from the road. Omega didn't bother to glance around. She wasn't sure that she could have. Her body felt as though it had turned to ice.

The Bow Street Runner said nothing to her, only looked at her. Everyone in the taproom was silent. The occupants of the room did not look at her, but she knew they were listening, judging, forming their own opinions.

"I came across the boy where the road forks," she said in her quiet voice. "He was scraping about in a midden."

"Tell the Runner how you gave that cutpurse a push and told him to run when I tried to do my citizen's duty and stop him," insisted the man.

"You were hurting him," she protested. "I would do the same for anyone."

The silence thickened like pudding. The Runner slapped his knees again and stood up, towering over her. "Could you tell me where he went?" he asked.

She shook her head.

"Does that mean you don't know, or you won't tell me?" persisted the Runner.

Omega stood up to face him. On her feet, she felt as though she were standing in a hole in front of him. What would a big man like this do to a boy like Jamie if he found him? She didn't want to consider it.

"It means, Mr. . . . Mr. . . ."

"Timothy Platter, ma'am."

"It means, Mr. Platter, that I do not know where he went," she said steadily. "It also means that even if I did know where he was, I am not sure that I would make it my earnest desire to enlighten you. He was terrified of something, or someone, Mr. Platter. And now, if you will excuse me, I really have nothing more to say."

The Runner adopted a more placating tone. "Miss, it is my charge and duty to return him to his uncle, who misses him surely. He means the boy no harm; nor do I. This is my job, and it keeps my wife and kiddies from eviction."

She could not doubt the sincerity in his eyes. For the smallest moment, she felt a wavering of her own conviction. But only for a moment. "I still have nothing to say, Mr. Platter. Please excuse me."

The Runner put out a hand as if to detain her. She stared him down, grateful that he could not see how her knees were trembling. Omega turned and swept out of the taproom, pausing in the doorway and gazing for a small moment at the two women who stood between her and the stairway. Head high, she stalked past them.

"Omega Chartley," said the younger woman. "Omega Chartley."

"Yes," Omega Chartley whispered back, and fled up the stairs, her courage gone.

In the safety of her room, she could only lean with her back against the door. Omega listened for footsteps, but no one followed. Gradually her breathing became calm again. With steadier fingers she undid the ribbons of her bonnet and set it carefully on the bureau. She looked in the mirror and sighed. Her brown curls were all wild around her face. Absently she twisted one curl around her finger and let it spring back.

"Botheration!" she exclaimed out loud, touching her curls again. There had been a time at the opera when Matthew Bering, bored beyond belief, twisted her curls around his fingers until she was in whoops and the Prince Regent himself stared at them from the next box, his quizzing glass raised.

"Botheration," she said again. Botheration that after eight years, one little difficulty could set off a flood of memories. Omega could still remember his fingers gently twisting the curls on her head. She remembered how she had gone so peacefully to sleep that night, sniffing the odor in her hair of the lemon-scented Spanish cologne that he always wore.

Omega moved away from the door and sat down at the table. The English grammar she had abandoned was open on the table. She lit the lamp and pulled it closer, feeling as put upon, tried, and tested as one of her own pupils.

"I wish people would leave me alone," she said, and copied that sentence in a neat, round hand onto the page in front of her. She put down the pen and looked at her handiwork. A reluctant smile came to her lips, and then a chuckle. "Omega, you are a goose," she said. "You would have your holiday, so you had better enjoy it."

In another moment she would be telling herself to write fifty times, "I will not think about Matthew Bering anymore."

"Or, at least, only five times a day instead of ten," she amended. "That would be progress."

She went to the open window and leaned her elbows on the sill. The sky was dark now, and all was quiet on the street. "Jamie Clevenden, where are you?" she wondered to herself. The evening was fine enough, but it would be cool before morning.

"Do look out for the Runner, lad," she said quietly.

As she spoke, someone lit a match below her window. Soon the smell of cigar smoke drifted to her nose. She looked down. She could discern the bulky shape of the Bow Street Runner, standing under her window as calm as a deacon.

She leaned out further and grasped the shutter. "You will likely rot your lungs out with that foul weed, Mr. Platter," she said quite distinctly in her best educationist's voice.

Omega Chartley pulled the shutter closed with a bang, but not before she heard Timothy Platter laugh.

Omega took off her dress, shook it out, and draped it over the chair. Already it was sadly wrinkled from only two days of travel. Tomorrow she would trade it for her other traveling dress, and when she arrived in Oxford, would pause for a general laundering, if the inn was respectable and the price not too dear.

She pulled on her nightgown and tucked her wayward curls under her sleeping cap. On her knees, she clasped her hands and rested them on the edge of the bed. On a typical night she prayed for the poor mad king, the prince regent, the armies of Wellington, the Archbishop of Canterbury, Alpha and Lydia Chartley, and the little Chartleys.

Tonight she began with the Chartleys and then proceeded directly to Jamie Clevenden. "Keep him safe, mighty God, and for goodness' sake, direct him to return home before he gets all of us in trouble."

Omega paused for a long time and then rested her cheek on the bed. She couldn't bring herself to say it out loud—she never did—but she thought it. And, Lord, please bless Matthew Bering, wherever he is.

2

The sun woke Omega the next morning. She burrowed deeper into her blankets for a moment, and then reached for *Rochester's Guidebook of England for Ladies*. She turned to the chapter on the Cotswolds, running her finger down the list of villages. Bisley, Sapperton. Cirencester, Siege of 1643.

Omega slammed the book shut. How singular it was that the tempting vision of sieges and castles that had kept her going throughout Plymouth's gray winter had so little attraction for her now. She put her hands behind her head and stared at the ceiling. "You're being out-of-reason foolish, Miss Chartley," she scolded herself. Jamie Clevenden was probably curled up in a warm hayloft right now.

She picked up the *Guidebook* again, resolutely shutting out of her mind the picture of a hungry boy scratching about in a garbage heap. She would travel as far as Cirencester today, replaying in her mind the battle of the

Cavaliers and the Roundheads as she wandered through the town. The next day it would be Chedworth, and perhaps a glimpse of the famous Roman mosaic floor. And so on to Oxford, to Amphney St. Peter to visit the Chartleys, and eventually Durham, and then the term would begin.

Omega presented herself in the taproom to request a small breakfast in her room. Timothy Platter was there, dirty boots propped up on the table, head well back, mouth open, snoring.

"Will he *never* leave?" Omega whispered.

"Exactly what my wife is saying, miss," the landlord said. "And he told me he wants to see you again. I told him, 'What can a lady have for you?' and he gave me such a wink. Miss Chartley, we'd all prefer to see his back." He brightened. "Can I have my wife fetch you some breakfast?"

She had been hungry before she spotted the Runner. "No, no, I think not. Tell me. When does the mail coach arrive?"

"Give it a few minutes, Miss Chartley." The landlord glanced over at the snoring Runner. "We'll see you make it."

She thanked him and wandered outside the inn, hoping that Jamie Clevenden would be long gone. The air was cool and Omega wondered if the boy had a coat somewhere.

She turned the corner and found herself nose to nose with the Bow Street Runner. He had come so silently that she had not heard him. How such a big man could move so quietly on his feet provided a moment of marvel that was quickly replaced by anger.

"*Who* would set a Runner on a small boy?" she cried.

"You'd have to ask Lord Rotherford," snapped the Runner, obviously as tired of her as she was of him. He touched her sleeve as if to detain her. "If you have something to tell me . . ."

She shook him off. "You're the last person I would ever tell, even if I did know anything, which I do not!"

She stomped inside, up the stairs, and slammed the door, hoping that Timothy Platter would hear it. Omega sat down on the bed and waited for cold reason to wash over her.

It did not. The more she thought about Jamie Clevenden, the more she wanted to march back down the stairs and slap Timothy Platter silly. And that would never do.

She had seen beggars before. Plymouth was full of them, old sailors too fuddled to climb a ratline anymore; young hard-faced women reeking of gin; children scarcely old enough to walk, sleeping in doorways. Omega had closed her eyes all her life to England's little miseries. Why was Jamie Clevenden so different?

"Because he has a name," she answered herself, "and he reminded me of someone."

And what on earth was such a well-dressed boy doing rummaging through garbage? And didn't that dreadful Mr. Platter mention something about a Lord Rotherford? The name was vaguely familiar to her from those days before she became a teacher.

Omega's agitation increased. She stalked about the room until the landlady scratched at her door.

"My boy will come for your baggage."

Omega nodded and dismissed her.

She was still sitting and staring at nothing when the innkeeper's boy tapped on the door. She nodded to him and he took her baggage downstairs. After another look around the room, Omega settled her bonnet on her riotous curls and stuffed the *Guidebook* in her reticule. She waited in the innyard while her baggage was tied on top of the mail coach.

She happened to glance up at the open door to the hayloft over the stables. Jamie Clevenden crouched there, looking down on the Runner. Timothy Platter stood below, hands in his pockets, rocking back and forth on his heels, puffing on his cigar until his head was wreathed in blue smoke.

Jamie shuffled his feet, and bits of straw drifted from

the open hayloft. She glanced quickly at Platter. The man remained with his back to the stables. Omega stepped away from the coach and made a shooing motion with her hands. Jamie ducked inside.

And then Omega Chartley's mind was made up. Cirencester and the Siege of 1643 would have to wait.

"Remove my bags, please," she said in her clear voice.

Platter turned around, his eyes filled with surprise.

"But they're already tied down," the coachman protested.

"So they are. And they can be untied just as easily," she said. "The yard boy can take them to my room again."

Omega went inside the inn and retrieved the key that still lay on the desk. As she hurried upstairs, the coachman blew his horn and the mail coach left the yard. When her bags were back in her room, Omega retied her bonnet and left the room again.

She knew that Timothy Platter would be waiting for her, and she was not disappointed. With a nod in his general direction, she left the front entrance and walked at a spanking pace up the street. She was certain that Platter would follow her, and again she was not disappointed. Her irritation lessened as she heard his ragged breathing behind her. I told him those cigars would rot his lungs, she thought with some satisfaction. A little smile played about her lips as Timothy Platter began to cough and slow down.

Omega let up her relentless pace and stepped smartly into the little bakery she had noticed last night during her twilight stroll. "I'll have four of those rolls, a loaf of bread, and a pork pie," she said, taking the coins from her reticule.

The proprietor wrapped her order in brown paper and tied it with a flourish. Omega took it from him and went into the street again. Platter stood there, red-faced and out of breath.

"Sir, are you following me?" she asked him point-blank.

He blinked and had the good grace to blush. "Do you need to be followed?" was his recovery.

"Of course not," she said briskly. "I am twenty-six

years old, an educationist, and quite capable of taking care of myself."

"From the looks of that package," he growled at her, "you have a prodigious appetite too."

"Prodigious," she snapped, and set off at a rapid stride.

Without lessening her pace, Omega continued up one street, and traveled down the next street. She settled down finally in a small park and unwrapped the package, eating one roll and stuffing two others in her reticule.

She sat there until she was sure Mr. Platter had gone. If he were truly, seriously, looking for a runaway, he would not waste much time on her. He can call me an eccentric and tell his colleagues on Bow Street that he has finally met England's gorgon, she thought.

When the sun was high in the sky, she left the park and strolled back to the inn and went to her room. Leaving her bonnet on, she pulled a chair up to the window, but not too close, and sat watching the field where the roads forked. Nothing moved, and then she saw Timothy Platter, standing next to the entrance of the lending library, out of sight of anyone observing from the empty field.

"Drat you, Mr. Platter," she said. "Why won't you go away?"

She watched him a moment longer. He went inside the library. She stayed at the window, but he did not reappear.

Omega waited several more long moments and then went quietly down the stairs and into the yard, careful not to be seen from the street, where Mr. Platter inside the library might see her. She went into the stables, standing by the entrance until her eyes were used to the gloom.

No one was in sight. Gathering her skirts close around her legs, she climbed the ladder and found herself looking into the grinning face of Timothy Platter. Beyond him, his hands tied together, was Jamie Clevenden, his eyes red from weeping.

Platter held out his hand for her. Wordlessly she took it and he hauled her up into the hayloft. In silence she dusted off her dress and knelt by Jamie.

"Are you all right?" she asked, and brushed the tangle of hair back from his forehead.

The boy nodded. His lips were set in a firm line that again made her think she had seen him before.

"Sit down, Miss Chartley," said Timothy Platter. "You are not quite ready to take on Bow Street."

She couldn't disagree with him. She sat down.

"I could have you arrested, you know," he continued, "for interfering with the law." He took a deep breath, warming himself to the task. "You *knew* he was here, didn't you? And still you marched me all around Robin Hood's barn!"

Again Omega could not disagree with him.

Platter permitted himself a smile. He took out a cigar and stuck it, unlit, between his teeth. "I have the boy, and that's all I want. You can go now; I am prepared to be generous."

Jamie Clevenden began to cry, great gulping sobs that went right to her heart. Omega rose to her knees and turned toward him, taking him in her arms. She patted him, looking beyond him to the ladder, wondering how she could get them both away, when she noticed the ladder moving. Someone else was climbing up.

Omega prayed that it was the yard boy, and burst into noisy tears of her own. Out of the corner of her eye she watched Platter rise to his feet, shift the cigar from one corner of his mouth to the other, and come toward them. Omega cried louder as he approached masking the creak of the ladder.

The yard boy moved fast. Before the Bow Street runner could even turn around, the boy had brought down the muck-rake handle on his head. The cigar flew from Timothy Platter's mouth and he dropped to the hay with a thud.

"Here, untie the lad," said the boy, handing Omega a knife.

She did as he said, and in a second Jamie sat rubbing his wrists. The boy grabbed him by the arm and tugged him to his feet. "I hit that cove smartly, but he won't stay down," he said. "Hurry up!"

Jamie scrambled down the ladder, followed by Omega and the yard boy. Omega thrust Jamie at the boy. "Keep him close a moment more," she said, taking a swipe at the hay on her dress. "My money is with my baggage."

She forced herself to walk into the inn, sighing with relief to see the taproom empty. She walked quietly up the stairs, alert for every squeak and protest of the wood. Her key seemed to scream in the lock as she let herself into the room.

Her luggage was gone. She uttered a cry of dismay and whirled to the door again.

The landlord stood there, his eyes wide. "Mr. Platter ordered us to put your luggage on the noon mail coach that just left," he said. "He told us to address it to Bow Street."

She could only stare at him as her face drained of all color. "But everything I own is in those bags," she stammered.

"He said he was 'authorized,' " explained the landlord. "I'm sure if you explain it to him . . ."

Omega brushed past him. For all she knew, Mr. Platter was even now sitting up in the hayloft with an aching head. She ran down the stairs and into the yard again, grabbing Jamie Clevenden by the hand. She waved her thanks to the yard boy, who was again raking muck from the open stalls, the portrait of innocence.

Jamie needed no urging to keep up with her. Omega gathered up her skirts and ran for the woods, Jamie right next to her, matching her stride for stride.

She ran until her side ached. She stopped and sank to the ground, pulling Jamie with her. He made no objection. The only sound was their breathing. Jamie stretched himself out on the grass and stared up at the sky. He turned to look at Omega, a hint of brightness in his eyes.

"Oh, did you see how his cigar flew across the room?"

She nodded and laughed, taking off her bonnet and fanning herself with it. "I wish he had swallowed it."

Omega handed Jamie one of the rolls she had stuffed in her reticule. As he ate quickly and tidily, with the economy of the hungry, she opened her coin purse. The sight was daunting.

He finished the roll, carefully corralling the crumbs on the front of his elegant, dusty jacket and rolling them between dirty fingers into a little pill, which he popped in his mouth.

"Who are you?" he asked.

"Omega Chartley," she replied. "I am a teacher."

"Oh, you can't possibly be," he disagreed. "You're too pretty." He smiled. "I'm not sure that I would mind you."

She laughed out loud."Oh, you would! I'll have you know I was the terror of Miss Haversham's Academy in Plymouth."

The dimple showed again. "Are you what my father would have called a 'prune-faced bluestocking'?"

"Most assuredly. Your father is right."

Jamie got to his feet then, as if reminded of the situation. "My father is dead," he said quietly. "We'd better go."

Omega held out her hand. "No, wait. You need to tell me what is going on." She stood up when he did not stop. "Jamie Clevenden, I just helped get you out of an awful scrape, and I've lost all my luggage *and* my money, and goodness knows, Mr. Platter may be preparing a rope for me at Newgate!"

He stopped then and hung his head. "I'm sorry. I never meant to cause you trouble."

A week ago, even last night, the loss of her money, clothing, and grammar books would have sent her into a fit of the megrims that would have consumed the remainder of her summer. Why isn't this bothering me? she asked herself as she came closer to Jamie and touched his shoulder.

"I know you didn't mean to cause me trouble. But please tell me . . . tell me what is going on?"

He did not answer her, but looked over his shoulder. "Do you think he will follow?"

"Oh, yes," she replied. A small shiver traveled the

length of her spine. Timothy Platter was not a man easily dissuaded.

"Then let us walk. I . . . I will talk then."

They walked on in silence. "Is your mother alive?" she asked finally, when he seemed disinclined to talk.

"No. She is dead too."

"And where is your home?"

He would not answer.

"Why are you running away?"

No answer.

Omega stepped in front of Jamie and put her hands on his shoulders. He shuddered at her touch, but he stopped walking. He looked her in the eye, raised his shirt, and bent over so she could see his back.

It was covered with welts, some raw, red, and weeping, others fading to a duller red. The skin was drawn and puckered, as if gouged and left to heal on its own.

"My uncle beats me," Jamie said, his voice calm, as if he were describing someone else. "I will not go back, even if he is my father's brother. He can send everyone on Bow Street after me, but I won't go back." Jamie tucked his shirt in again.

He had allowed her only a quick glimpse of his back, but as Omega walked beside him, she knew she would retain the ruin of Jamie Clevenden's back in her mind's eye longer than she would remember the ruins of Stonehenge or any other amazement listed in the *Guidebook*.

"Then where are you going?" she asked quietly. She brushed off a tree stump and sat down on it.

The boy continued on several paces and then looked back to see her sitting. He waited a long moment, and she held her breath while he considered his strategy and wrestled with the panic within him. To her infinite relief, he walked back slowly and sat down next to her.

"I have another uncle . . . Mama's only brother." He spread his hands out in a gesture of helplessness that lodged in her heart. "Mama said he lives somewhere in the Cotswolds." Again he made the gesture. "I just don't know where, and I'm hungry," he finished with all the logic of a ten-year-old.

She handed him the last roll. "Do you know his name?"

He shook his head. "He is the Viscount Byworth. Mama . . . Mama always called him B, but that can't be his name, can it?"

"No. It must be her nickname for him." Her face brightened. "Oh, but what was your mother's name before she married? Surely it would be the same as your uncle's."

Jamie's face fell. "I was four when they died, and my Uncle Rotherford never spoke of her. I mentioned my Uncle Byworth to him once, and he just laughed."

Omega sighed. "That's hardly a gentlemanly thing to do."

"I looked in my Uncle Rotherford's atlas one night when he was drunk, and found this." He pulled a page from his pocket.

Omega smoothed it on her lap. The page had been folded and unfolded so many times that the creases were starting to rip, but she looked where Jamie pointed.

"See there, it says 'Byworth.' At least, I think it does." Jamie took the page from her lap and cupped it in his hand like a living thing and then folded it. "That is where I am going." The assurance left his voice then, and for the first time he sounded as young as his years. "Do you know how far it is? Is this the right direction?"

"I . . . I don't know," she confessed. "And see here, you have torn the section from the book and not left any references."

Jamie sighed and put the scrap of paper back in his pocket. "I was so excited just to see 'Byworth' that I didn't think about that. But I have to find it, don't you see?"

Omega nodded. She took out *Rochester's Guidebook* and thumbed to the section on the Cotswolds. Jamie gave her the paper again and she turned it this way and that, comparing it with the tiny map in the book. "Doesn't that read 'age'? There, where you have folded it so many times?"

Jamie squinted at the little paper. "It could."

"Perhaps it is Wantage," she said. "And if it is, then your Byworth is about ten miles beyond."

"And if it is not?"

She rose to her feet. "We'll just have to try. And when we find your Lord Uncle Byworth or whoever he is, perhaps he'll have some ideas about retrieving my baggage from Bow Street."

"I'm sure he will. Mama was always used to say that there wasn't anything her brother couldn't do." Jamie darted ahead of her on the path.

Let's hope you are right, Omega thought grimly. Maybe he can also tell me what on earth I, a spinster educationist, am doing traipsing about just a jump ahead of the Bow Street Runners.

The thought made her giggle. She crammed her bonnet back on her head and hurried to catch up with Jamie.

3

If Omega Chartley had ever spent a more miserable night, she didn't know of it. They consumed the afternoon and early evening walking in a northeasterly direction that paralleled the main highway but did not come too close to it. Several times they heard the mail-coach horn. Each time, Omega wondered if her money and baggage had arrived in London yet, to be investigated and pawed over.

She had addressed her baggage to St. Elizabeth's in Durham. Suppose one of the Runners went there to await her arrival? The thought of a man like Timothy Platter invading the rarefied atmosphere of a very correct girls' school to inquire after the newly hired English teacher nearly made Omega gasp out loud.

I must devise a wonderful lie, she thought as she trudged along beside Jamie. That thought made her blanch again. It is amazing how rapidly one well-brought-up person can go to the dogs, Omega thought.

Only a day ago she was a proper, well-mannered lady of advancing years. In the course of twenty-four hours Omega Chartley had prevaricated, attempted to outwit an officer of the law, obstructed justice, permitted a wanted person to escape, and done nothing to prevent an assault. The rapidity of her decline made her blink. I have only to steal, commit murder, and perform a treasonous act to be perfect in my ruin, she thought, and smiled in spite of herself. Absurd.

The source of her misery was an unprepossessing barn, constructed perhaps during the late Ice Age of some nameless stone and roofed over with a sieve, which would have been wholly adequate before the rain started. By then, darkness was coming, and no other likely-looking possibilities for shelter sprang into view, which was just as well. An inn would have overdrawn the modest coins that she had in her reticule, and would have meant the scrutiny of a landlord. The barn it would be.

Omega took exception only when Jamie looked at the leaking cavern with a professional eye and then started for the loft ladder. She put out a hand to stop him.

"See here, Jamie," she protested. "Do you not think we would be drier on this lower level, with the overhang of the loft to protect us from that lamentable roof?"

Jamie appraised her with the look of One Who Knows. He shrugged. "I have found that there are more mice on the lower levels, where there is often grain spread around," he commented.

"Dear God," said Miss Omega Chartley faintly, and followed Jamie Clevenden up the ladder, already imagining little cadres of mice snapping at her heels. The prospect of sharing her chamber with rodents was even more daunting than the prospect of teaching gerunds to little girls who wished themselves elsewhere. Had there been room on the ladder, she would have passed Jamie.

They found a corner where the holes had not totally taken over, and settled in. There were vague rustlings in the hay, but Omega resolutely ignored them as she removed her bonnet and placed it in the driest corner she could find.

As the rain pelted down, a chill settled over the loft. Jamie edged closer, until he was leaning against her arm.

He was silent for the longest time, and she thought he had drifted to sleep, when he spoke.

"I like that," he said, and burrowed closer.

"What?" she asked.

"My mother smelled of lavender too," he said.

She smiled into the darkness. "I am surprised you can still catch the fragrance of it."

"Mama kept her dainties in lavender," Jamie said, his voice small under the pelting of the rain on and through the roof. "She would hand me her sachet bags and I would pummel them about until the lavender was properly stirred up." He sighed. "I kept one bag, but it doesn't smell anymore."

He was silent then. Omega wanted to put her arm about him. At Miss Haversham's, there had been numerous occasions, at first, when she had wanted to console a pupil, some of them scarcely more than babies, it seemed to her, but she had been dissuaded by Miss Haversham. "It's a hard world, Miss Chartley. The sooner they realize it, the better for their souls." And so Omega had not cuddled those little ones. Soon she never considered it. She was considering it now.

"I have—had—a pressed flower from my papa," she ventured tentatively. Papa had handed her the half-open bud during their last walk together about the gardens before she made that dreadful trip up the altar. The bud had never opened, but she had saved it.

"Where's your father now?" Jamie asked. He spoke a little loud, and she wondered if he was repeating himself because she had not responded the first time. How easy it was to forget oneself in this place.

"Oh, Jamie, he's dead."

He put his hand in hers.

The rain continued and the cold settled in. Why the rains of August were gloomy, Omega did not know, but it was so. Maybe it was because soon the birds would be flying south to the Azores and the leaves would droop and die.

Jamie sat in silence, doing nothing to solicit her sympathy, but Omega put her arm around him and drew him closer. He sighed and leaned against her, closed his eyes, and slept.

Sleep did not visit Omega so swiftly. No matter how devastating had been some of the events of the past eight years, this was the first time she had been wet, cold, and hungry. Her stomach rumbled, and she shifted slightly, so as not to awaken Jamie. She carefully pulled him over until his head was in her lap, and rested her hand on his arm.

Omega no longer mourned the loss of her trunk; she had no possessions that were irreplaceable. Everything of any value had been auctioned off after Papa's death. Even the loss of her money was less onerous than anyone could have told her it would be. She had only to apply to Alpha for a small loan, and he would find a way to cover it. And knowing Alpha, she believed he would chuckle over her mishap.

But what was she to do about St. Elizabeth's? It was the middle of August. Omega had a month until she was due in Durham. If none of the constabulary from Bow Street contacted the headmistress seeking her whereabouts, perhaps she could contrive to slip through this little detour of her journey. As she leaned over Jamie to protect him from some of the rain, Omega told herself that in the course of a day or two Jamie would be with his uncle the Viscount of Byworth, and the whole adventure would be something to laugh about with the Chartleys.

Provided they found the uncle. Provided Timothy Platter did not sniff them up first. Omega closed her eyes. I *will* sleep, she told herself. Things will appear in a better light in the morning. Omega did sleep then, her head nodding over Jamie.

What it was that woke her toward morning, she could not say. There was no sudden noise, no alarm, no indication of any disturbance. If anything, the night was quieter. The rain had stopped, and it was too early for the birds of dawn.

But something had wakened her. She sat silent in the cool darkness as some strange sense told her that the barn was occupied by others. She could not see them, but they were there. She made herself small in the corner and surprised herself by going back to sleep.

She woke when morning came, woke to find that Jamie had shifted and was curled up next to her, his head resting on his hands, a beatific smile on his lips that belied the dried streaks of tears through the dirt on his face. She listened to the rustle of mice about the vicinity of her bonnet and almost rolled over and went back to sleep again before she remembered the other occupants of the barn.

All was still. Surely her fears of the night were only a dream. She listened and heard nothing, but the feeling settled over her again that someone waited below.

Carefully, cautiously, Omega rose to her knees and stretched herself close to the edge of the loft, mindful not to waken Jamie. Holding her breath, she peered over the edge and into the eyes of a little girl, who lay on her back, looking up directly into Omega's face.

Omega's eyes widened. She watched in amazement as the little girl smiled at her, put her finger to her lips, pointed to the man sleeping beside her, and shook her head.

The man lay stretched out on his back, one arm under the girl's head and the other one placed on his chest. Omega looked again. He had no hand on the end of his wrist. His shirt sleeve had been pulled back, and his arm ended abruptly above his wrist in a mass of scars and rough-looking flesh.

How singular, thought Omega, too surprised to be repulsed by the man's deformity, or amazed by the girl's calm acceptance of her. Omega rested her chin on her hands and stared below. The girl had closed her eyes, her long black lashes sweeping against her cheeks. She appeared perfectly relaxed and not at all nervous under the scrutiny of a strange woman in the hayloft. How singular, thought Omega again, and redirected her gaze at the sleeping man.

He was tall, with several days' growth of beard on his chin. His hair was curly like her own, and richly black. He was dressed in soldier's breeches. His jacket lay nearby, draped on a piece of farm equipment, and he wore a frilled white shirt.

Omega peered closer. The shirt had been torn, bloodied, washed, and carefully sewn together again, but it was undeniably the shirt of a gentleman. Odd indeed, Omega thought as she raised up on her elbows and observed the scene below. She felt no fear, none at all, from these strangers. Omega smiled at the girl, who smiled back, sighed, rustled down further into the straw that was her mattress, and closed her eyes again. The man slept quietly.

That he was a soldier, there was no doubt. Whether he had only recently returned from Waterloo minus his hand, Omega did not know. And the little girl? Omega could only speculate.

For a woman who has spent considerable time in recent years avoiding people, you are surprisingly curious, Omega Chartley, she told herself as she settled her chin on her hands and promptly returned to slumber herself.

She woke with the sun in her eyes, dust tickling her nose. Omega sneezed enormously, prodigiously, making the kind of racket that would have caused her to rain coals of fire on the heads of her students committing such a solecism.

"Jesús, María, y José," said the little girl, who was wide-awake now and sitting up.

"Bless you," said the man, his voice a deep baritone.

"Goodness," said Omega. "Thank you," she continued, remembering her manners.

The little girl regarded Omega a moment and then dipped her fingers into a tin bowl. She took two more small bites, chewing thoughtfully, and then handed the bowl to the soldier. He gestured toward Omega.

"We saved you some. That is, if you'll be coming down . . ."

His voice had a singsong Welsh texture to it that was pleasing to the ears. Coupled with the deep tones that seemed to swell upward from the soles of his feet, the effect was altogether enchanting. Omega waited for the man to say something else, and then realized it was her turn.

"Oh, thank you," she said again. "But there is someone else with me, a boy. I'm sure he won't eat much," she added.

The man smiled. "Boys always eat too much." He cocked his head toward the girl. "Angela, what do you say?"

The child looked up at Omega. "We would not be good soldiers if we did not share," she replied quite seriously.

"Well, then, come down," said the soldier, getting to his feet and extending the bowl toward Omega.

Before she could speak, a shadow fell across the barn's entrance. Omega drew back, praying that she would not sneeze again. There was a space where the boards in the loft had warped and separated slightly. She put her eye to the hole.

Timothy Platter stood below in the entrance, holding the reins to his horse. He dropped the reins, but the horse followed him into the barn and stood cropping wisps of hay. Rumpled and dirty, Platter looked as though he had slept in his clothes. He walked the halting gait of someone who has spent the night in a most uncomfortable place. Nothing about him spoke of ease or contentment. He looked like a man thoroughly annoyed by failure.

Never taking her eyes from him, Angela scrambled to her feet and stood beside the soldier, who tucked the bowl in the crook of his arm and dipped in with his good hand. When he finished, he proffered the bowl to Timothy Platter, who waved it away.

"I'm from Bow Street and I'm looking for a runaway boy and a woman."

Omega held her breath.

Platter continued, coming closer to the soldier, who stood his ground. "The woman is short, with wild-looking curly hair."

Wild-looking? Wild-looking? thought Omega. How dare he?

"But she's not an antidote," continued Platter, "not entirely. She has a trim figure and a brisk way of walking, but she's a bit grim about the mouth." He laughed suddenly. "And such a sharp tongue! You'd know her if you saw her." He chuckled again, but with little mirth. "Or heard her."

"And the boy?" asked the soldier.

"He is ten, has black hair, well-dressed, brown eyes. Small for his age. Name of Jamie Clevenden.

Timothy Platter looked around him, scrutinizing the loft, looking up at the boards until Omega wanted to scream. "Well, my man, have you seen these two?"

"What did they do?"

"Oh, Lord, man, have you seen them? There's a reward," said Platter, softening his voice a bit as Angela moved behind the soldier. "A big reward from the runaway's uncle." The Runner adopted a wheedling tone. "You wouldn't be sleeping in barns anymore. No more soaked corn. That's food for swine."

The soldier was silent for a long minute. Omega felt the tears starting in her eyes. Oh, please, she said silently. Even though you do not know us. Please.

"I haven't seen them," the soldier replied. He rested his good hand on Angela's shoulder and she drew in closer to him.

"You're sure?"

"Didn't you just say to me that I could not forget such a woman?" countered the man. "I lost my hand, not my brain."

Timothy Platter was not satisfied. Omega slowly let out her breath and peered down at him. The Runner took out a cigar and clenched it between his teeth, a gesture she was familiar with. "I know they're around here somewhere," he insisted.

"Then you had better look for them," the soldier murmured. "We swine have to eat now."

Platter looked at the soldier. " 'Twas only a figure of speech, lad," he said more softly. "I meant nothing by it."

"Still and all, you'll be needing to hurry on."

"If you see such a woman and boy, would you let me know?"

"No," said the soldier, and nothing more. He sat down again and crossed his legs.

Timothy Platter said nothing, only looked daggers at the

soldier and chewed on his cigar. He gave a mighty swallow, and Angela gulped.

"I don't know that you're anything you say you are," the soldier explained quietly. "And I'd rather sleep in a barn and eat corn than betray people."

Timothy Platter stomped out of the barn. Omega held her breath a moment, listening, and then heard the sound of a horse riding away. She let out her breath and rested her cheek for a moment on the floor of the loft.

Jamie was awake. With wide eyes he watched her. "Is it over?" he whispered.

Omega nodded and stood up, shaking the straw and chaff off her dress. After another moment's look around, she descended the ladder, careful to keep her skirts tight about her. At the bottom, the soldier helped her down. She looked into smiling gray eyes and had to smile back.

"He offered you a reward," Omega murmured.

Angela still stood with her face turned into the soldier's shirt. Omega touched her gently on the shoulder and she looked around.

"Thank you for not telling him," she said to both of them. "Jamie and I would have been in a real broth then," she added, not even flinching at her own use of slang. How low can I go? she thought as she watched Angela, and smiled at her.

Jamie came down the ladder then, coming no closer than the bottom rung.

The soldier eyed him a moment, and made no move to come closer. Instead, he lowered himself to the ground and sat cross-legged. He handed the bowl of corn to Omega.

"We found a little corn in the feed bin and soaked it last night," he said. "Angela put in a pinch of salt. You'll find it better than you think."

After a slight hesitation, Omega put her hand in the tin bowl and tasted the corn. She chewed it slowly, and then took another bite, and handed the bowl to the soldier. "I am Omega Chartley," she said. "I really don't have a sharp tongue."

"Omega?" asked the soldier. "And were you the last child?"

Omega nodded. "My mother died when I was born. And I actually have an older brother named Alpha. We are both teachers. And this is Jamie Clevenden."

Jamie said nothing, only remained where he was, eyeing them all with suspicion. The soldier held out the can to him and gradually Jamie came closer, sitting down finally to eat.

"Well, I am Hugh Owen, late of His Majesty's Fifty-first Rifles. And this is Angela."

The little girl smiled and curtsied, but all the time her eyes were on Jamie Clevenden. Omega watched, amused and a little touched, as Angela eyed Jamie as though he were some rare species. Omega would not have been at all surprised if the girl had not circled him about.

What is she thinking? Omega wondered as the child continued to stare at Jamie. Finally Angela cleared her throat.

"Pardon me, please," she began, her English heavily accented. "Did that *hombre odioso* say that you were a runaway?"

Jamie eyed her suspiciously. "Yes," he admitted finally.

"You had a home, and you ran away?" Angela persisted.

Jamie nodded, intent on finishing the corn in the tin bowl.

"And you had a bed and more than one meal a day and you ran away?"

The boy nodded again. He put down the bowl and regarded her, trading stare for stare. In her turn, Angela blushed and moved back beside Hugh Owen. She continued to watch Jamie from the soldier's side, as if she could not believe that he was real. She looked to the soldier for reassurance, but the man said nothing.

The awkwardness of the moment did not elude Omega. "We must be on our way," she said crisply, filling in the gap of silence with her schoolteacher tones. "Jamie, be a friend and fetch my hat from the loft, will you?"

Jamie did as she asked, scurrying up the ladder again and rummaging about in the corner where she had stashed her precious bonnet.

"Oh, Miss Chartley," he said at last, "I do not think you want it."

"Of course I do," she replied. "Hand it down now, there's a good boy."

Jamie's head appeared over the edge of the loft. "Miss Chartley, a mouse has delivered ten babies in the crown of it."

Omega sighed. "Well, then, perhaps we should leave the rodents in possession. Come down, then, and we'll be off."

"Where to?" asked the soldier.

"Perhaps it would be best if you did not know," she said. "Then if you should meet with the estimable Mr. Platter again, you will not have to tell him a lie."

Hugh Owen did not persist. "We're glad that we could be of some assistance to you," was all he said as he extended his hand.

The absurdity of the moment overwhelmed Omega, and she didn't know whether to laugh or cry. She shook his hand. "Good luck to you and Angela," she said. Omega felt stiff and formal again. "Your kindness is so appreciated."

The soldier touched his hand to his forehead in a salute.

"Mr. Owen, is Wantage nearby?" she asked.

"We came from there two nights ago. It is about ten miles to the east of us." He smiled, but the smile held no warmth. "If you are a one-armed man, there are no jobs in Wantage."

"And is there . . . is there a place near Wantage called Byworth?" Omega asked. "I do not know if it is a seat of peerage or a village. Have you heard of it?"

"Byworth. Byworth. It sounds familiar . . . but I do not know. Mind you stay off the main roads."

"We shall," Omega said. "Good-bye."

They set off at a brisk pace, heading east, avoiding the roads again and tramping through fields full of the fruits of late summer and enclosed neatly about by stone walls. They skirted a small village and Omega ventured in long enough to buy four rolls with the last of her money. Her eyes were wide open for Timothy Platter, but the earth must have swallowed him whole.

She gave Jamie three rolls, thinking to herself as she nibbled her roll that the extra avoirdupois she had accumulated during her sedentary stay at Miss Haversham's would soon be gone. Her skirt already felt agreeably loose. Hmmm, thought Miss Chartley, this adventure could yield unexpected results.

They ate in the shade of a stone fence, glorying in the coolness of the stone at their backs. As was his custom, Jamie said nothing. His eyes were troubled, but he did not speak.

"And what if you do not find him?" Omega asked at last. She had plied him with several questions, spaced out over the length of their luncheon, and he had responded to none. Her upbringing dictated that she toss in a comment occasionally to fill up the void of profitable mealtime conversation. He surprised her this time with a reply.

"Then I will take the king's shilling and go for a drummer boy," he said, his voice firm with resolution.

"Surely it would be better for you to return to your uncle?" she ventured.

For answer, Jamie gazed at her in that oddly familiar way of his. "I told you that I will not go back."

They were still short of Wantage when night fell, coming swiftly upon them even as they were deciding which road to take.

"If I had a coin, I would flip it," Jamie said.

"Silly, you might lose it," said his companion. "I recommend that we walk toward the river. I am thirsty."

It was more than thirst. Omega wanted to wash her face and see if she could repair some of the damage to her hair. And if she could take off her shoes and just dabble some water over her toes, how good that would be.

There were men fishing along the riverbank. Jamie and Omega sat in the bushes until the men gathered their strings of fish and walked away, talking and laughing, and heading for their homes and dinner.

"I could eat those fish raw," declared Jamie.

Omega shuddered. "I am not that hungry."

"It's not civilized, but we won't tell anyone," the boy joked, and then gasped, pointing to the bushes they had just vacated.

The Bow Street Runner burst through the underbrush, a most determined look on his face. He stood still a fraction of a moment and shifted his cigar from one corner of his mouth to the other.

Omega felt her stomach sink to her shoes and then float free up toward her throat. "Run, Jamie!" she urged, as the boy hesitated, not knowing which way to turn.

And then he was all motion, darting away from the voice, running along the riverbank. Omega started after him, took only a step, and realized to her horror that Timothy Platter had a firm grip on the back of her skirt.

"Let go!" she gasped.

"Oh, no, Miss Chartley," he roared, and took a firmer grip on her dress.

Omega struggled toward the water, tugging Timothy Platter after her, even as he dug into the soft bank with his feet and hung on. She struck at him with her hands, but he had only to lean back to avoid her flailing attempts.

Platter tightened his grip on her skirt. She kicked him in the shins, but the Bow Street Runner hung on like a bulldog.

"I'll see that you're transported for obstructing justice." He made a grab for her waist. "Without you, I'll have that little snip in no time!"

The thought of being shipped to Australia galvanized Omega. She grabbed her reticule by the strings and swung it at him. The paperweight inside—the one Alpha insisted that she carry in her bag—connected with a satisfying thud.

Platter's eyes fluttered and rolled back in his head. He pitched forward against her, his hand still tight in the waistband of her dress, and they plummeted off the bank and into the water.

4

All was dark, all was black, but the pungent smell of woodsmoke convinced Omega Chartley that she was still alive. Mixed with the fragrant smoke was the warm, earthy smell of cow. No, this was not heaven; not even one of its environs. There was nothing to do but open her eyes.

"*Mira*, Hugh," exclaimed a clear, small voice that Omega remembered. "They are blue. You have won the wager."

Omega looked into the brown eyes of Angela.

"But I always wanted brown eyes, Angela," she responded. Omega's voice sounded rusty and ill-used to her ears. No matter; she was grateful she could still talk.

"You must trust me, Angela," said the other familiar voice. "English ladies with that particular shade of brown hair always have blue eyes."

"I have already agreed that you won." Angela pouted.

Now there were two heads leaning over her. Omega looked from one to the other, Angela with her thick black hair and Hugh Owen with his long, friendly face.

And then Omega remembered. "Good God, where is Jamie?" she exclaimed as she tried to struggle into a sitting position. Hugh Owen pushed her back down. She felt his hand on her bare shoulder and realized that she was wrapped in a heavy cotton blanket and nothing more. Her face reddened.

"Easy, Miss Chartley," Hugh said. "Jamie's over there, asleep. As to your clothes, they're drying by the fire. Angela saw to your welfare."

"And Mr. Platter? I think I killed him with my reticule."

Hugh laughed out loud, and then covered his mouth with his hand so as not to waken Jamie. "*Why* on earth do you carry a paperweight in your reticule?" he asked.

"It's Alpha's idea," she admitted. "He says that any

female traveling alone should have some protection. I . . . I couldn't think of anything but a paperweight. It contains bits of shot from the Yorktown Batteries, baked in glass. Papa was there," she added, as if that explained her choice of weapons.

"Well, it certainly gave Platter the rightabout," said Hugh.

Omega reached out for him impulsively. "But tell me, please—that wretched man is not dead, is he?"

"Oh, no. The last we saw, he was floating downstream clinging to a tree branch. He still had his cigar."

"Odious, odious man," muttered Miss Chartley.

"The only real casualty of the encounter appears to be your guidebook," said the soldier. "We're going to dry it out, though, because it could prove useful as tinder for fires." He held up the book with its bloated and wrinkled pages.

Omega settled herself more comfortably. "Well, I wasn't finding much use in it anyway. I seem to have strayed somewhat from my itinerary." Her head ached abominably. She reached a hand around to the back of her neck and felt a rising lump.

"You would not quit struggling, *señorita*," said Angela. "How was I to get you to shore?"

"How, indeed?" murmured Omega.

"Such a useful paperweight," agreed Angela. She rose to her feet and rearranged Omega's clothing by the fire.

"And did she . . ." Omea looked at Hugh Owen.

"Pull you from the river? Indeed she did."

"And Jamie?"

"Oh, you should have seen him racing along the riverbank, calling for help. He ran smack into us."

Omega's brain was spinning. "But whatever were you doing? I thought you were going in the other direction? Oh, I don't understand."

She yawned a mighty yawn then, to her vast embarrassment. To her further chagrin, water dribbled out of her mouth.

Hugh dabbed at it with the corner of her blanket. "You also swallowed half of the River By." He intercepted her sudden look. "Yes, the River By. The farmer whose cattle byre this is told us." He continued to interpret her expression. "And don't worry! He'll not betray us. His son died at Vimeiro. We're practically mates; he won't give us up to any Runner."

"I truly don't understand," Omega finished weakly. She wanted to close her eyes again, but it seemed scarcely polite.

"Just sleep now, Miss Chartley," said Hugh. "If you need anything, Angela is close by. I'm going to reconnoiter."

Against her will, better judgment, and sharply honed sense of propriety, Omega yawned again and closed her eyes.

When she woke, there was food, hot porridge—an island of it in a sea of cream, with a dollop of butter on top—and a mug of tea smelling discreetly of rum. Hugh Owen and Jamie were nowhere in sight, so Omega draped her blanket about her to better effect and rested herself on one elbow as Angela handed her a spoon.

"It's very good," said Angela, who sat cross-legged in front of her. "Hugh told me to see that you eat all of it."

She did as she was told, spooning down the porridge, which settled around all the river water in her stomach and made her burp.

"Goodness," murmured Omega, her face reddening. As Angela did not appear offended by such rag manners, Omega reached for the tea and sipped it slowly, relishing the way it burned down her throat and into her soggy insides.

"My papa used to call tea 'English manna,' " said Angela.

"Where is he now?" asked Omega, handing back the empty mug.

"We buried him at Toulouse," was her reply. Angela took hold of Omega's hand, and they sat close together, watching the cows watching them.

Omega was back in her clothes again when Hugh returned, Jamie close behind him. Jamie brightened at once to see her.

"Miss Chartley! This is famous! We are practically on the River By!"

She sat down again and he sat beside her. "I'm sorry that I could not rescue you, but I do not swim."

"Never mind about that," she said. "When you reach your uncle's estate, you must learn. We are both woefully ignorant and have only to be grateful that we fell in with smarter heads than our own. But, sir, where are we?" she asked Hugh. "And should we not look out for Timothy Platter?"

Hugh sat beside her, resting his maimed arm in his lap. "We have executed what General Picton—God rest his soul—would call a 'damned fine tactical maneuver.' I think Platter will not find us immediately."

"You see, we swam the river," said Angela.

Jamie clapped his hands together. "I tell you, it was famous! Angela hoisted you onto Hugh's back, and over you went, and then they came back for me! We're on the other side of the river from where Timothy Platter saw you come out."

It all made sense, and yet it didn't. "I still don't understand," insisted Miss Chartley. "What were you doing following us? I thought you had only just come from that direction."

"It's true," agreed Hugh. "But Angela was worried about you. And . . . and I own, I was too."

The self-sufficient Miss Chartley had no comment, other than the private consideration that the Lord blesses teachers and runaways, even—especially—when they are stupid.

"We've also marched a considerable distance back along the road we followed this morning," added Hugh. "That confused the Frogs any number of times in Spain, and so it should do for a Bow Street Runner."

Omega regarded Hugh with some admiration. "And you carried me on your back all this distance?"

"You're not very heavy," he said, and blushed under her scrutiny. "In fact, ma'am, do they let you out in high winds?"

Omega laughed. Her stomach rumbled, and even Angela

had to smile. Omega tried to suppress another burp and reddened in embarrassment. She began to cough uncontrollably.

"You're going to be doing that all night, Miss Chartley, so you had better get used to it. That's what happens when you swallow a river and live to tell about it. Angela and I have burped up our share of rivers, have we not, *niña*?"

Angela nodded and settled herself next to Omega, who put her arm around the girl's shoulders and pulled her closer.

"Thank you," Omega whispered, and kissed her cheek.

Jamie cleared his throat. "I told Hugh how we came to be together," he said. "I . . . I had to trust him. I showed him my back."

No one said anything for a moment. Hugh Owen's face was serious then. He leaned back against the stall and Omega noticed for the first time how tired he was, how deep the lines in his face. Clearly the effort of her rescue and their march, coupled with his own injuries, had exhausted him. She almost said something to him about that, but thought better of it.

"I don't hold with grown men giving little boys stripes like that to wear around," he said, "but never mind. The farmer says we're still a day or more away from Byworth . . . except he didn't call it Byworth. It was Byford. At any rate, if we follow the river, we'll find it. We will just squirrel away here until you feel like walking, Miss Chartley."

She smiled at him. "My discomfort is little compared to yours, sir. And I wish you would call me Omega. Miss Chartley is a schoolteacher, but Omega is on holiday." She sighed. "And she's a bit of a scapegrace, I fear. Such a holiday!"

She wanted to talk then, wanted to hear their stories, and even wanted to tell her own, but her eyes were closing again. As she drifted off to sleep, Hugh covered her with the blanket and she felt Angela cuddling up close to her. The warmth of the child's body took away the chill of the river, and she slept.

When she woke, the birds were singing, the cattle had

been turned out. Angela was braiding her hair, humming a little tune Omega had never heard before as she pulled her hair back and plaited it carefully.

Hugh came in then, Jamie at his heels, and smiled to see her sitting upright and finishing her breakfast. "Do you think you can walk?" he asked after she finished her tea and dabbed at her lips with the corner of the blanket.

"I can certainly try," she said, and then eyed him in the manner of the suspicious Miss Chartley. "But I'll be keeping my eyes on you, Hugh Owen. You tired yourself dreadfully yesterday, and I refuse to be party to your complete ruin."

"I was tired," he admitted, "but I am fit today. Jamie and I have scouted our march. We will do famously if we march among the trees, stay off the road, and avoid the river." He nodded to Angela. "Does this sound like our Spanish campaigning?"

"You told me England would be different," Angela accused.

"That was before I met Miss Chartley," was his prompt reply. "And her famous paperweight."

"Am I never to be forgiven my paperweight?" she asked.

"No," he said. He picked up the reticule by the fire and hefted it before handing it to her. "Mind you keep that to yourself or we'll all end up on a transport ship, watching the sun rise over the Great Barrier Reef. Come to attention, Angela. We must march."

Jamie stood a little straighter beside Omega and watched as Hugh Owen stood in front of them.

"Old Hookey called us an 'infamous army' not long ago,"he said, speaking more to himself than to them. "That was only because he had never seen this file."

"Lead on, sir," said Omega.

They walked into a beautiful Cotswold morning, where dew still decorated spiders' webs and the very ground smelled of summer. Every now and then the sweet, sharp scent of roses teased them as they passed crofters' cottages and skirted tiny villages that probably had not changed measurably since the days of Queen Elizabeth. Hugh ambled into several villages to inquire about Byford. The closer they came, the more information he gleaned.

"Well," he began after his latest side trip, "we now know that Byford is home to well over one thousand souls, is famous for its needlework, and has a church housing the relic of St. Stephen's little finger. Our latest piece of news is that the Viscount of Byford is also the justice of the peace."

"Is that good?" inquired Jamie.

"I hope so. Let's assume that he has a sharp sense of justice, but maybe not too much nicety about law by the books," said Hugh. "Jamie, have you considered what you will do if your uncle turns you over to your guardian? He could, you know."

The mulish look returned to Jamie's face. "I will not stay," he said.

Hugh Owen had the wisdom not to continue the conversation.

Still short of their destination, they paused for the night in an area of heavy woods. "From what I have learned, we could perhaps be there around midnight, if we continued," said Hugh, "but I do not think that rousing the viscount from his bed will further our cause any. Besides, I am hungry."

They all were, but no one complained about the short rations; Hugh and Angela were obviously used to doing without, and Jamie and Omega were too polite. Omega did find herself staring with some longing at a rabbit that watched them from the protection of a bramble thicket.

Hugh must have seen the same rabbit. He halted his little army. "Angela, could you work some Spanish magic?"

She grinned. "*Claro que sí*, Hugh. Come, Jamie."

He hung back. "I've never caught a rabbit before."

Angela stamped her foot. "*Fulano*! And how will you learn if you do not try?"

Jamie could think of no argument to counter Angela's logic. He followed his mentor into the brush by the tall trees.

Omega watched them go, and then seated herself on a

fallen log. "You do not think Angela will go too far away?" she asked.

"She knows what to do."

Hugh's short reply told Omega how tired he was. Without a word he sat down on the ground beside her and rested his back against the fallen tree. He raised his knees and propped his injured arm up on one knee.

"I do not know how it is possible for my hand to hurt when it is not there," he said at last. He shrugged. "And to think I ran away from Wales so I would never lose life or limb in the colliery."

"How did you lose your hand?" Omega asked, cringing inside as she considered all the governesses who had raised her to never ask any question more forward than the time of day.

If Hugh thought her encroaching, he gave no indication. He sighed again. "I'm almost embarrassed to tell you, Miss Ch . . . Omega. I mean, it was a chuffle-headed thing, the merest quirk." He looked at her in embarrassment. "You'll laugh."

"Most assuredly I will not," Omega replied. "This is hardly a laughing matter."

"No," agreed Hugh. He settled back against the tree. "It was about two hours before Boney's Imperial Guard turned about-face and ran from us. Or it might have been ten minutes. Time has an odd way of taking on new meaning during a battle."

He paused and looked off in the distance, hearing something she could not hear, seeing sights she did not want to view.

"Anyway, the Frenchies' cavalry swirled around us, and then they would back off and their guns would roar." He straightened out his injured arm and stared at the hand that wasn't there. "I was so tired. A ball from one of Boney's 'beautiful daughters' rolled into our square. It was just rolling along the ground, moving straight toward my captain's head."

"Your captain's head?"

"Yes. He was dead already and lying on the ground,

half-buried in the mud. We were so muddy. I reached out to stop that ball from slamming into him. Well, I was tired or I never would have done that."

"Good God," murmured Omega. She touched Hugh on the shoulder. He looked up, as if remembering where he was.

"I didn't even feel anything at first, until I tried to reload my piece and the only thing left was a bone sticking out. Oh, I'm sorry."

She knew from the look on his face that she was ghastly pale, even under her sunburn. She took a deep breath. He was still looking at her.

"Do you know, Omega, when you turn pale, those little freckles on your nose are quite, quite green?"

She nodded and managed a shaky laugh.

"I was lucky," he continued. "I was able to walk off that battlefield. Some of the wounded . . . some of them drowned in puddles of rainwater." Again he looked into the far distance. "I lost all my friends in that day's work. Every one of them."

Angela was waving at him from the edge of the clearing. He waved back. "And that is how I came to have Angela."

"Eh?" asked the articulate educationist.

"Her mother was a Spanish camp follower. She came to us with a small baby—Angela—and my best mate, Thomas Llewellen, took up with her. She drowned crossing the Duero. Thomas died at Toulouse, and our sergeant and his woman watched after Angela. The sergeant died at Waterloo, and I'm the only survivor of our file. Angela's my charge now."

"Surely she has . . ."

"Other relatives?" Hugh shook his head. "Her mother was an orphan. I could have left Angela in an orphanage in Brussels, but that would have been my last night of peaceful sleep."

Omega understood. If she had gone ahead and boarded that mail coach and left Jamie to his fate, she would have seen his frightened eyes every night she closed her own.

"Besides that, Angela searched every bed in Brussels

until she found someone from the file. I couldn't leave her behind."

"Most assuredly not," agreed Omega. "And I do understand. I seem to have declared myself Jamie's protector, whether he wanted me or not."

Hugh got to his feet. "You've discharged your duty well. Soon we'll be at Byford, and he'll be the viscount's worry."

"I suppose," she said, and wondered why she felt so little enthusiasm for what would have been a wonderful relief only yesterday.

Angela came dancing back into the clearing, followed by Jamie, who walked head down, the picture of failure. When he was quite close, he whipped out a snared rabbit from behind his back, a smile splitting his face from ear to ear.

"Omega, it was famous! The rabbit didn't have a chance. Angela has promised that she'll teach me how to do that."

Omega laughed out loud and clapped her hands together, delighting not so much in what he said as in the joy in his voice. That's what was missing before, she thought to herself as she grabbed Jamie, ruffled his hair, and kissed him on the cheek. He wasn't a little boy before. Now he is. Thank God and Angela and Hugh Owen.

Angela took the rabbit from Jamie. She set it on the ground and extracted two nails from her leather pouch. She looked around for a big rock, and pounded the nails close together into the nearest tree. With quick, sharp motions she forced the rabbit's hind legs into the nails.

Omega watched openmouthed as Angela took Hugh Owen's knife from him. A few quick cuts, a deft slice from vent to breastbone, and in a moment the pelt came off in one wrench. The naked rabbit glittered in the afternoon sun. Omega turned her head.

"Famous!" breathed Jamie. He put out his leg and made a sweeping bow. "Angela, you are a complete hand."

Angela laughed behind her hand like a proper Spanish

lady. As Jamie gawked in admiration, Angela gutted the rabbit and scurried to the river and cleaned her catch. She laid the rabbit carefully on a tree stump. With flint and steel she started a fire. Omega coaxed along the little fingers of flame with selected pages from *Rochester's Guidebook*, while Jamie added twigs. By the time the fire was of respectable dimensions, Angela had divided the rabbit into four parts, like Gaul, and skewered each section onto a green stick. She handed a stick to each diner and motioned them closer to the fire.

"I just hold it in the flames?" asked Omega.

"Up a little bit," cautioned Hugh, "or you will eat more charcoal than rabbit."

The four of them sat companionably close to each other, Hugh making an occasional comment to Omega, Jamie teasing Angela and being rewarded with her bell-like laugh. Mostly they were silent, listening to the wind in the trees and the hiss and pop of rabbit fat on the fire. Soon they were concentrating on the magnificent odor of rabbit almost done.

"I've never been so famished in my entire life," Omega said finally, to no one in particular, as she turned the stick over and over and wished the rabbit would hurry up.

She watched the flames again, wondering at her growing uneasiness in relinquishing Jamie Clevenden to someone else, even if it were a relative. For all his silence and stubbornness, she knew that she would miss Jamie. How much, she would likely discover tomorrow.

But right now, sitting in the little clearing surrounded by people who had become surprisingly dear to her in a short time, Omega experienced another sensation, sharper than hunger. It pierced through her worries about the morrow, and her fear of the future. It was a feeling she had not encountered since the morning of her wedding eight years ago, when she woke up and knew that before nightfall she would be in Matthew Bering's arms.

She felt happy.

5

During her one London Season, Omega Chartley had attended banquets, routs, teas, small dinners, large dinners, picnics al fresco, and elegant luncheons too numerous to mention. She never enjoyed any of them as much as the rabbit she ate under the trees along the River By in the company of Jamie Clevenden, Hugh Owen, and Angela.

They tackled the rabbit with little nicety, but much enthusiasm. Omega tucked her last clean handkerchief under her chin, grateful for the soberness of her dark gray traveling dress which defied the most obvious stains.

"Angela, have you any salt?"

Hugh paused in his attack on the morsel before him and wiped his chin on his shoulder, holding out the rabbit. Angela dug about in her leather bag and extracted a piece of salt the size of a thimble. Carefully she scraped her fingernail over the gray lump, as Hugh moved the rabbit underneath it. He winked at her and tasted the rabbit.

"Angela! Magnificent!" exclaimed Hugh.

Jamie held out his dinner for a minute scraping of salt. "Angela, this is famous!" he exclaimed.

"It is only salt," said the girl in her realistic Spanish fashion, but her eyes shone with the pleasure of the compliments.

"What else have you in that bag?" Jamie asked, more inclined to talk, now that the sharpest edge of his hunger had been distracted by the rabbit.

Angela took another bite, chewing thoughtfully. "I have a needle and thread—"

"Which has mended trousers and shirts, bullet holes and bayonet wounds," interrupted Hugh. "When the little wounds heal, she pulls off the thread, washes it, and winds it back on the spool."

Jamie made a face.

"I have a rosary."

"Put the cross in your mouth and bite down hard, and then the needle and thread glide along easier," Hugh continued.

"I have a medal of St. Christopher, blessed by the pope," she said imperturbably.

"How else could we swim rivers with swooning schoolteachers?"

Omega laughed.

"Hugh, you should not make a mockery of the pope," reproved Angela.

"Or of schoolteachers," added Jamie, getting into the fun of it. "Especially schoolteachers with prodigious paperweights."

"And I will not tell you what else is in my *bolsa*," said Angela severely, "not even if you have need of it, Jamie Clevenden."

"Fair's fair," agreed Omega. "Angela, let us withdraw now and leave these gentlemen to their port and cigars."

Angela shuddered. "Do not remind me of that mean Señor Platter!"

The two of them went to the river and sat there in pleasant companionship, watching the water and the occasional sparkle as a fish jumped. Angela sighed, and edged closer to Omega.

"Soon we will have to say *adiós* to Jamie, won't we?"

"Yes, I fear so. And you and Hugh will find a place to work and I will teach English grammar to spoiled little girls who couldn't skin rabbits if their lives depended on it. Oh, botheration, let us return to the gentlemen."

Hugh and Jamie had borrowed armfuls of cut timothy grass from the nearby field and arranged it around the fire. The soldier spread out the heavy sheet from his rucksack over one pile and motioned toward it as Omega and Angela came into the clearing again. Angela sank down in the soft hay at once, patting it until the lumps were distributed to her liking.

Omega sat down beside her, her ears tuned to the pleasant rustle of the hay. I must store all this in my memory, she thought as she poked and prodded the hay. I must remember the River By and the porridge in the cattle byre and the good feeling of rough sheet on bare skin. Most of all, when I am lonely this winter, I must remember these people. Tears came to her eyes unexpectedly and she brushed them away.

Angela leaned closer. "Did you hurt yourself?"

"Gracious no," said Omega. "I must have . . . must have gotten some grass in my eye. It's gone now."

She lay down and Angela cuddled next to her. After a moment's hesitation, Omega slid her arm under Angela's neck. Angela sighed and nestled in the hollow of Omega's arm.

"Omega, tell me a story about a handsome prince."

"I don't know any stories like that," she replied, looking up at the stars that winked through the leafing branches overhead like random sequins on a dark gown. "There really aren't any handsome princes."

"I saw one once," said Angela. Her voice was drowsy. "He was William, Prince of Orange. The soldiers called him Little Frog, but I thought he was handsome."

"I'll tell you a story about a prince," Omega said suddenly. "A prince with red hair and—"

"Princes don't have red hair," Angela interrupted. Her voice was faraway.

"This one did," said Omega firmly. "Dark, dark red." She sighed. "And it was gloriously straight, *unlike* my own. And he had brown eyes and absolutely no freckles."

"Was he wealthy?"

"Oh, yes." She giggled. "Rich as Croesus."

"Was there a princess?" asked Angela, long after Omega thought she was asleep.

"Well, no, not really. There was a lady who loved him fiercely."

"Such a strange word," murmured Hugh Owen.

Omega looked over at him, aware for the first time that someone else was listening besides Angela.

She didn't look at Hugh. She hadn't the courage. She stared straight up at the stars overhead. "It is the correct word," she said softly. "Fiercely. Not jealously, not even protectively, for he could take care of himself. Fiercely."

"Like a fox with kits?"

"Yes, I suppose." Omega considered. She would gladly have died for Matthew Bering without a whimper.

She was silent then, until Angela jostled her in the ribs. "What became of the prince?"

"I do not know. One day he disappeared—"

"Was he a soldier?"

"No, no. He was what I suppose you could call a country gentleman."

"And the lady?"

Omega pulled her arm out from under Angela's head and sat up. Angela rested her head on Omega's lap and the woman stroked Angela's black hair. "He left her at the altar. Just standing there holding her little Bible and bunch of flowers."

"Good God," said Hugh in a low voice.

"And that's *all*?" asked Angela in disbelief.

"I'm afraid so. That's the ending."

"Well, it isn't much of a story," said the girl. "I can tell you a better one. Prince William came into our encampment one night in Brussels and I sewed a button on his shirt."

Angela's words recalled Omega to the present. "Imagine!" she exclaimed.

"Yes. It was so cold he did not take off the shirt. I just stood right next to him and sewed on the button."

Hugh laughed. "And blushed the whole time, I own!"

"I did not!"

"She did. And when she finished, Prince William bowed and kissed her hand and she swore a mighty oath never to wash the spot again," teased Hugh.

Omega hugged Angela to her. "That's a much better story than mine. From now on, you are appointed to tell the bedtime tales."

"But not now," said Hugh. "Why don't you follow Jamie's lead and go to sleep? We still have a march before us tomorrow."

Angela was silent. Omega feared she was sulking, but soon she heard the even, deep breathing of the girl. Gently Omega lowered her head back to the timothy-grass bedding and covered her with a small corner of the blanket.

Hugh was quiet then too. Omega thought he had drifted off, but then he spoke. "You see why I could not leave her in a Brussels orphanage."

"I envy you," she said simply.

When Hugh spoke again, he sounded much closer, as if he had raised himself up on one elbow and was leaning toward her. "Come with me down to the river."

She rose and followed him. They sat at the edge of the water. Omega took off her stockings and shoes and put her feet in the water. Minnows darted about and tickled at her feet.

"He just left you at the altar?"

Omega managed a laugh, but it was devoid of any humor. "That was for dramatic purposes. I suppose I must be accurate. I was standing in the back of the church, waiting for Matthew and his best man to walk out by the altar so my father and I could proceed down the aisle. We waited there an hour, until Papa and Alpha escorted me out of the church."

"Did you . . . did you know him very well?" Hugh cleared his throat. "There probably isn't a way to ask such things nicely, I suppose, and see here, probably you would prefer that I get my nose out of your business."

"No, no." Omega paused. There really wasn't any way to tell Hugh that she was relieved for the opportunity to talk. She sensed, somehow, that he understood that fact without having to be told. "Matthew was—or is . . . I don't know—from one of England's finest families. All of Papa's connections told him how lucky I was." The word stuck in her throat. "How lucky . . ."

Hugh touched her hand. "I cannot imagine a worse thing to befall a lady."

Omega laughed again. "Oh, that was nothing; a mere diversion, Hugh. Two weeks later I found my father hanged by the neck in his dressing room." She paused to let that sink in. "It seems there had been serious reverses on the Exchange that Alpha and I were blissfully ignorant of. Papa killed himself."

Her voice broke then and she was silent, waiting for the tears to form so she could brush them away and get on with it. Hugh said nothing.

"Alpha was finishing his third year at Oxford—thank the Lord for that—and he always had a scholarly mind. As soon as everything we owned was sold at auction, he was able to secure a position as a lecturer of English and composition."

No need to tell Hugh of her own solitary ride to Plymouth in answer to an advertisement in the *Times* for a teacher in one of the shabby-genteel schools for the daughters of ship's captains. And the fear that even in that less-exalted hall of learning someone would mention Deardon Chartley and his suicide and the scandal at St. Alphonse's that was the continuing gossip of that London Season.

"But that was eight years ago," she said, "and we have done well enough since then. Alpha married the perfectly lovely daughter of a vicar at Banbury, and he is now head of English at St. Andrew's, near Amphney St. Peter." She smiled to herself in the dark. "And there are three little Chartleys, each as smart as their papa."

"And their aunt, I vow."

"I have managed," she said simply.

Hugh took her hand and held it this time. "And you never heard from Matthew . . . Bering, is it?"

"No. Not ever. Not a word. Alpha and I speculated at length. All we could come up with was that somehow he had gotten wind of Papa's financial misery before we knew of it, and cried off in time to save himself from marriage to a penniless girl without a sixpence to scratch with. . . . Oh, do excuse my language."

Hugh chuckled. "Nor a feather to fly with?"

She could smile at that. "Not a single one." And then her voice was serious again. "I've certainly gotten over whatever silly *tendre* I may have had for that man. I don't expect to see him again. But I do wish . . . I just wish I knew what it was that so disgusted him about me that he could not bring himself to face me again. I would like to know that."

Hugh let go of her hand. "I imagine you would. What does he look like? If I ever see him, I promise you I'll draw his cork for you."

"You wouldn't!" she exclaimed, hugging her arms around her knees. "He's tall. I come up to his shoulder, but barely. And I already told you he has wonderful red hair. He's a serious man, but he could be so diverting. There's something marvelously original about his mind." She sighed. "But that was so long ago. And he's older than I am by eight years. I suppose he would be thirty-four now. Goodness."

"He is probably bald and fat now and loosens his pants at the dinner table."

She laughed, and this time her humor was heartfelt. "I hope so!" She dried off her feet and put on her shoes.

They walked back to the clearing. "I have a question for you, Hugh, and it's quite impertinent."

"Fire away."

"How is it that your English is so good? We had a Welsh gardener once, and he was so singsongy . . . oh, and his grammar!"

"My mama was English, and she had been raised in the home of an earl." He shook his head at the memory. "She would wallop me good if I ever talked like one of the colliery boys. 'How can you amount to much if you sound like a Welshman?' " he mimicked.

"I've never met anyone quite like you," Omega said, "but now, good night, sir."

"Good night, Omega Chartley," Hugh said. "You're a charming lady and certainly deserving of a swift change of fortune."

"The same to you," she said obligingly. "I own that we deserve some good fortune."

When Omega waked in the morning, Hugh Owen was already busy at the fire. One-handed, he had managed to start a fire, and was kneeling in front of it, blowing on the flames. He next went to the river and returned with a canister of water, into which he dumped last night's rabbit bones and set it on the flames.

As the rabbit water turned to broth, Omega marveled

again at their good luck in falling in with such artists. She said her morning prayers, and woke Angela and Jamie.

They breakfasted on rabbit soup livened with a scraping of salt, and turned their attention to Byford.

"We should be there soon enough," said Hugh. "I have an idea. Jamie, you walk with me, and, Angela, you stay close to Omega. If Mr. Timothy Platter is about, he'll be concentrating on a woman with a boy and a soldier with a girl. It isn't much, but it might allow us an avenue of escape." He grinned. "My captain, God rest his soul, would call that a master stroke."

"And so would I," agreed Omega. "I shall force my curls under a cap, so Mr. Platter will not call me a wildwoman."

"And do try to stand taller," said Hugh. "Add three or four inches, if you can. Add a stone or two to your weight, and you'll escape all notice."

A morning's walk, and then Byford spread before them, cupped in a small valley. The remnants of a wall around the town indicated the age of Byford, as did the squat-looking Romanesque church set stolidly in the middle of the village.

"Well, let us march," said Hugh. He put his arm around Jamie. "You and I will go in first to reconnoiter. Omega, you follow in five minutes with Angela."

The man and boy walked ahead. Angela sat down, while Omega continued to look over the fields and houses of Byford. The village was tidy to a fault, with a preciseness that appealed to her sense of order, that sense so badly scattered in the past few days. To the south, a mile or more beyond the village, was a large stone house, far larger than anything in the adjacent neighborhood, shaded well with tall trees that had probably been mere seedlings when Ceasar's Roman legionnaires encountered the blue-faced folk of early Britain. To say that the house was large did not quite put it in the category of an estate. It was stone and two-storied, with white shutters and ivy twining up the walls.

I suppose that is the residence of the Viscount Byford, she said to herself. Jamie should have a nice home there.

She hoped again that the viscount was a good man, and that his wife would not object to a rather quiet, solemn boy who, every now and then, showed flashes of huge enthusiasm. All he needs is a chance, please, she thought.

"Yes?"

She must have spoken out loud. Omega shook her head and touched Angela's shoulder. And you too, my dear, she thought.

"Let's go, Angela."

They strolled into Byford, crossing the bridge over the River By that looked as old as the church, walking past trim houses close together, and into the town itself. It was not hard to blend with the crowds; an agricultural fair was in progress. Omega walked slowly, keeping Hugh and Jamie in her sight.

Hugh paused to talk to one of the shepherds standing, as well-groomed as his long-nosed sheep, close by the horses. The shepherd leaned on his crook and listened to Hugh, and then pointed in the general direction of the large house Omega had noticed earlier. Hugh nodded to the man and looked behind him. He motioned with his head, and Omega and Angela followed.

A walk of some ten minutes took them across a stream and then beyond the broken wall that had once protected Byford. The way was easy. The cobblestones were as evenly spaced and tidy as the houses, with no weeds sneaking up between the paving.

"I've never seen a better-regulated town," said Omega as they walked along. "It speaks well for the viscount."

Hugh and Jamie were waiting for them at the gates to the viscount's manor. The gates were open, as if someone was preparing to ride through. The gatekeeper was nowhere in sight, so the four of them walked up the curving lane with beeches on either side to the front entrance.

There was nothing pretentious about the house; in point of fact, it was smaller than the former Chartley country house in Lincolnshire. But it was splendid in a kind of magnificence unequaled before in Omega's admiring eyes. It was tidy, with no hint of crumbling mortar between the stones, no buckling of paint on the windowsills, no thin patches in the gravel of the front carriage drive where the ground showed through. The windows were so clean she had to look twice to make sure there was glass in the frames. Each bit of ivy scaling the walls appeared to have been dusted and arranged by hand. It was too clean.

The splendor had affected Angela too. She leaned against Omega. "Do you think people really live here?" she whispered.

Hugh shrugged his shoulders. "I almost hate to touch that knocker," he confessed to Omega as he rapped twice.

Immediately the door swung open on perfectly noiseless hinges. The man who stood before them was as precise as the house, ineffable in his splendor. Angela sucked in her breath but said nothing. Jamie stared in wide-eyed amazement, but he found his voice before the others.

"Are *you* the viscount?" he asked.

The man at the door did not bother to reply. Jamie stepped back and hung his head. Omega squared her shoulders. How dare that man be so insulting, she thought as she looked at the resplendent figure before her. She cleared her throat and pretended that he was one of her pupils, and a particularly ill-favored one, at that.

"Sir, we are looking for the Viscount Byford."

She thought for a moment that he would not speak to her either. She tried to stand a little taller and stare him down. "Are you the butler?" she asked at last.

"Dios mío," whispered Angela behind her back. "He looks like the Duke of Wellington! And you call him a butler?"

"Please tell the viscount that James Clevenden is here to see him," she persisted, placing her hands on Jamie's shoulders and keeping him in front of her.

"I cannot fathom what interest my employer would have in seeing this young person," said the butler, and stepped back to shut the door.

Before he could close the door, Hugh Owen bounded up the steps and stuck his maimed arm in the way. The butler showed surprise for the first time, gasping and stepping back. Hugh spoke over his shoulder to Omega. "I knew that would stop him."

The butler stayed on his side of the door, eyeing warily the place where Hugh's hand used to be. His coloring had gone from sanguine to pasty in a remarkably short time.

"See here, sir," said Hugh as he took another step into the hall. "Is your employer a justice of the peace?"

With a visible effort the butler regained his composure and pulled it about his shoulders like a tattered cloak. "Indeed he is, but he is otherwise engaged this afternoon."

"Is he in residence?" asked Hugh point-blank.

"That, I am *relieved* to say, is none of your concern," said the butler.

Hugh went farther into the hall, and motioned Jamie in after him. "We have a serious matter to discuss with the justice of the peace." He raised his voice, his fine Welsh voice. "And is it not the right of all Englishmen to demand the presence of the justice?" He thumped the door frame with his good hand. "Didn't men and women die at Runnymede for this privilege?"

"Follow me," said the butler, and turned on his heel.

Omega ushered Angela in front of her and caught up with Hugh. "That's the biggest particle of nonsense I've ever heard," she whispered. "Who taught you history?"

"Yes, it was a real hum, wasn't it?" Hugh agreed. "I, my dear, am entirely self-taught."

Omega smothered a laugh as she hurried to keep up with the butler. She looked about her with real delight. The house was magnificent, all warm woods and gently blowing white curtains. An elegant Persian rug traveled the length of the hall, and felt so soft under her shoes.

Adding to the total picture of understated elegance was a pleasant fragrance, one she could not identify immediately, but which nagged at her. The scent, quietly insistent, competed with the smell of furniture polish and fresh-scrubbed carpets. She frowned as she hurried along. The fragrance was sharp and faint at the same time, and the memory of it clanged somewhere in the back of her brain.

Omega hurried Angela along, though the girl wanted to stop at every open door for a glimpse of splendors within. The butler paused at last and opened a door. He peered in and started to open the door wider, but glanced back at the ragged party following him and evidently reconsidered.

"This will never do," he said severely. "Remain here in the hall. Mind you, don't touch anything!" He glared at Angela, who put her hands behind her back.

With a sigh that emanated from a great depth, the butler swept back to the staircase they had just passed on their march down the hall. Omega heard a door close upstairs, and footsteps in the upper hall overhead. They were measured and slow, as if their owner was pausing every now and then to make last-minute adjustments to his person.

"That will be the viscount," declared Omega triumphantly.

The steps came closer. The butler went to the foot of the stairs just as an aproned lady came in another door. Her face was red and she was breathing hard, as if she had just hurried up a flight of steps. With only the smallest glance in Omega's direction, she approached the stairs too.

"I'm first, Mrs. Wells," said the butler, sounding amazingly to Omega like her grammar girls queuing up for treats.

"But, Mr. Twinings," the woman protested, wiping her forehead, "this is truly important. I simply cannot locate a hare for tonight's game course. And I particularly wanted one."

"I, Mrs. Wells, am representing the law in this instance," said the butler. He looked up the stairs. "My lord, there are some . . ." He stopped, wondering how to classify the soldier, two ragtag children, and the woman who was obviously a lady fallen on hard times. ". . . some people below. They seem to require your presence as justice of the peace."

If the viscount made a reply, Omega could not hear it.

"My lord, they insisted. Perhaps if you hurry down, you can clear up this matter at once and be on your way to the judging."

"Very well, Twinings," said my lord, and he began to descend the stairs. He stopped. "The bookroom?"

"No, my lord," replied the butler, and he made no attempt to spare the feelings of the people in the hall. "They did not look precisely . . . tidy, and I feared for the upholstery on the chairs. You can deal with them in the hall, I am sure."

"And, my lord," said Mrs. Wells, wringing her hands together, "your gamekeeper has failed us. There is not a hare to be seen for tonight's dinner."

"Tell Antoine to fix up something or other in one of his sauces. No one will know."

Omega listened to the high drama being enacted right over their heads. Something else about the tone of that conversation set off another bell clanging in her head.

"My lord!" exclaimed Mrs. Wells. "Antoine will have palpitations!"

"Oh, surely not, Mrs. Wells," said Twinings, intruding in the conversation jealously. "This is a trifling matter."

Mrs. Wells fired her final salvo. "Not to your French cook, it isn't," she declared in round tones, addressing herself to the viscount. "And didn't I hear Lord Cabot inquiring after his services last week?"

"Drat! I'll talk to him, Mrs. Wells."

The viscount did not hurry. "Drat!" he said again.

"Heads up, Jamie," whispered Omega. "You're drooping." She smiled at him. She took a deep breath by way of improving example, and the smile froze on her face.

His lordship continued down the stairs. Omega could see his booted legs. She stood where she was and took another tentative whiff, and then another. It was the same odor she had noticed in the front entrance, the sharp citrus tang of lemon cologne.

"Has something gone cock-a-hoops?" Hugh watched her. "You're quite pale, Omega," he whispered.

She opened her mouth, but nothing came out. She knew she looked like a fish hooked and tossed up on the bank. Omega could only stare at Hugh, not daring to turn around.

She looked down at Jamie, who was watching her in that intense way of his, his head angled to one side. As she stared at him, she knew suddenly where she had seen the boy before. Or one very like him.

"Come, come," said the butler. "The viscount hasn't all day, and you insisted upon his presence. State your business."

"Yes, do," said the viscount, "but turn around, please. See here, I don't bite."

Omega closed her mouth, grasped Jamie firmly by the shoulders, and turned around. "Matthew, may I introduce you to your nephew, Jamie Clevenden?"

The viscount paused in the act of raising a quizzing glass to his eye. The glass slipped through his fingers and swung from the end of the ribbon.

It was the viscount's turn to open his mouth and stare. He blinked his eyes and looked from Omega to Jamie and back to Omega, where his eyes remained fixed to her face.

"Omega Chartley," he managed finally.

"The same, Matthew Bering," she said.

Omega was going to say something else—what, she wasn't sure. Every thought, every polite remark that had ever crossed her lips (growing whiter by the second), rushed out of her brain and left it completely bare. The only urge she felt was the instinct, entirely primitive, to pluck up her skirts and run.

Before she could move, she heard a sound behind her. Omega looked back and could only watch in wide-eyed, stupefied silence as Hugh Owen shouldered his way past her. Before she could even speak, Hugh pulled back and smashed his fist into Lord Byford's elegant face.

The viscount's eyes rolled back in his head. Angela scrambled to get out of the way as Matthew Bering, the Viscount of Byford, thudded to his knees and fell forward, sprawling on the carpet.

Hugh stepped back in quiet triumph. "I told you I'd draw his cork, Omega. Who'd have thought it would be so soon?"

"Who, indeed?" said Omega Chartley. "Oh, Hugh, we are in a real broth now."

6

The butler reeled back as if Hugh had struck him too. He lost his footing and stumbled into a small table, upsetting a Chinese vase. The fragile porcelain keepsake teetered back and forth and then fell to the floor, shattering into a pile of antique rubble and scattering roses and water.

With a low moan the housekeeper sat down hard and toppled over in perfect imitation of the vase. She lay in the middle of the roses and gave herself up to a good faint.

"Do you think she was more concerned about the vase or the viscount?" murmured Hugh as he watched the carnage in the hall.

"Oh, Hugh! Do behave!" exclaimed Omega, not knowing where to turn.

Twinings recovered himself sufficiently to run to the door and shout, "Help! Murder! Murder!" at the top of his lungs. His intentions were earnest, but fear had raised his voice one octave and his cry of desperation was scarcely audible.

Omega looked about her. To her mind, the housekeeper was better left alone. And as long as Twinings gathered no more breath, they were in no immediate danger from the constable. Omega threw herself to her knees and grasped Matthew by the shoulders. She turned him over so he was lying faceup, his head in her lap.

"*Dios mio*," exclaimed Angela, "is he dead?"

"No, and more's the pity," said Omega through gritted teeth, amazed at the sudden anger that washed through her whole body. She regarded him with some satisfaction. Blood dripped steadily from Matthew Bering's nose and deckled his snowy waistcoat and the intricate stock he had obviously taken great pains to tie. His nose was pushed slightly to one side, and his eye was already beginning to blacken.

Omega untied the stock about his neck, wiped the blood around his nose, and pinched the nostrils between her thumb and forefinger. "Open your mouth, Matthew, if you have any intention of breathing," she commanded.

He did as she bade him, and opened his eyes too, or at least the eye he could still open. "*Who* is making that unholy racket?" he managed to ask.

"Your butler."

Matthew rose slightly in her lap. "Twinings," he croaked, "stop that infernal noise!"

The butler looked at the viscount and shuddered. "I can have the constable here in an instant, my lord! We have been set upon by thieves!"

"Oh, stow it somewhere!" said the viscount, and flopped his head back. He touched his swelling eye, wincing and muttering something perfectly awful.

The butler remained where he was by the door until Hugh started toward him, a purposeful glint in his eye.

"Oh, Angela, this is famous!" whispered Jamie.

With a shriek, the butler backed up to the housekeeper, stepping over her with a nimbleness Omega would not have thought possible. His eyes never leaving Hugh Owen's face, Twinings grabbed the housekeeper under the arms and towed her toward the open door that led belowstairs. She was soon out of sight; only the flop-flop of her feet on the stairs could be heard as Twinings dragged her to safety in the servants' hall.

Jamie shook his head. He knelt on the floor beside Omega and regarded his uncle. "I don't think this is quite the impression we wanted, Omega," he stated. "But only think how helpful Hugh has been up to now."

Omega didn't know whether to laugh or to cry. "Oh, Jamie," she said as she hung on to the viscount's nose. "This is your uncle and his name is Matthew Bering. You bear somewhat of a resemblance to him."

"Happy to see you, sir," said Jamie, and held out his hand.

Matthew Bering groaned and took his nephew's hand. "Pleased to see you again, James. It has been years . . .

Good God, what *am* I saying? Oh, the deuce take it, Omega, let go of my nose!"

With a little twist that made him yelp, Omega released his nose, wiping around his nostrils to make sure the bleeding had truly stopped. She touched the rising bump on his nose.

"Matthew, you have been reorganized," she said.

Other than the unexpected calamity to his face, Matthew Bering looked much the same to Omega. His hair, the rich chestnut hair she had always thought so handsome, was the same glorious color. He was a little fuller through the chest, but she had previously thought him too lean anyway. Eight years had scarcely altered him. She almost touched the little mole by his eye before she remembered herself.

"How is it that you are the Viscount Byford?" she asked.

"And how is it that you are here?" he challenged in turn. "What the devil is going on?" He turned his head slowly and regarded his nephew, bewilderment at war with indignation in his brown eyes. "And you, James Clevenden, why are you not at your Uncle Edwin's estate?"

Jamie raised his chin and returned the same brown-eyed stare to his uncle. "I ran away, sir. I have come to live with you."

The viscount groaned and closed his eyes again.

Omega watched him for a considerable moment. "Matthew?" she asked finally.

"I'm not going to open my eyes until you all disappear," was his reply, from the depths of the bloody cravat he held to his nose.

"Oh, I like that!" declared Omega as she grabbed his nose again and held it. "I've lost my luggage and my money, ruined my reputation very likely—*if* there was any of it left to ruin—and now I'm hunted by the law, just because I snatched your nephew from a Bow Street Runner."

"Omega," said Hugh, giving her shoulder a little shake.

"Not now. Let Jamie and me help the viscount to his chambers and—"

Matthew Bering struggled upright, waving away Omega's hand. "I am supposed to be judging a horse show in . . ." He pulled out a watch from his waistcoat. "Good God, fifteen minutes. If you will be so kind as to help me to my feet, I will be on my way."

Hugh helped him up. "My lord, you're in no condition to go anywhere. I ought to know, because I'm the one that hit you."

But the viscount wasn't attending to Hugh Owen. He whirled around to stare at Omega. "Did you say the Bow Street Runners? What curious business is this?" he asked no one in particular.

"It is a rather long story, Uncle," ventured Jamie.

Again Matthew was not paying attention. He lurched over to the hall mirror and looked into it, aghast. He touched his nose in disbelief, and turned around to stare at the people who watched him. "I am supposed to meet two gentlemen whose influence will weigh heavily on the future of this little village." His voice was rising. "And I look like some Johnny Raw just come foxed from a cockfight!" He turned to Omega. "If this is your idea of retribution, Miss Chartley," he shouted, "you are wonderfully revenged!"

Omega gasped, and tears sprang to her eyes. Before she knew what she was doing, she grabbed the front of his shirt. "This doesn't even begin to touch what you did to me!" she hissed. "How dare you!"

As soon as the moment came, it passed. Omega burst into tears and sat herself down on the stairs, as far away from the viscount as she could manage.

Omega's tears seemed to recall the viscount to himself. He sat down beside her, not looking at her, not touching her, his hand still clutching the stock to his bleeding nose. "That was a terrible thing for me to say," he began, his voice much subdued. "Miss Chartley, I have no idea what is going on, not a single clue. I do know that I have to be at a horse judging." He spread his hand out in front of him. "What am I to do?"

"Sir, if I may suggest . . ." began Hugh in his quiet voice.

"Oh, anything, anything," declared the viscount.

"Give me a suit of your clothes. We are much the same size. I will judge that horse show."

"We look nothing alike," said the viscount dryly.

"Oh, I do not attempt a masquerade. Send me with a letter of introduction . . ."

". . . stating that he is a friend of yours, recently returned from the Battle of Waterloo . . ." continued Angela, her eyes lighting up.

"Yes, Uncle, you had a . . . a trifling accident . . . something to do with . . ."

". . . an open door," contributed Omega, blowing her nose in the one remaining handkerchief in her reticule. "Oh, Hugh, do you know anything about horses?"

"No," he admitted. "But I will politely defer to the other judges and admire their taste. When I bring them back here for dinner, if that was your intention . . ."

"It was," said Matthew. "Which reminds me. I have a disgruntled cook belowstairs." He sighed. "And my servants have probably all fled by the back door." He looked about him in disbelief. "This room was so tidy only a moment ago."

"Oh, it was, wasn't it?" said Angela. "I have never seen such a home. Not even in Spain," she added generously.

"It looks like Bedlam now," said Matthew. He looked down with great distaste at his bloody shirt front. "Or perhaps a slaughtering pen."

"Sir, time is passing," Hugh reminded him.

"So it is." The viscount rose to his feet, touching Omega's shoulder for an instant to regain his balance. "Leonard!" he shouted. "Come down here at once!"

In another moment a man appeared at the top of the stairs. He made strange gargling sounds in his throat as he surveyed the scene below.

"Not a word, Leonard, not a word," warned the viscount. "I'll explain everything to you as soon as I know what is going on. Now, help me upstairs and find a suit of clothes for . . . Sir, who are you?"

Hugh pulled himslf together smartly. "Hugh Owen, my lord, former sergeant in His Majesty's Fifty-first Rifles, Picton's Brigade, God rest his soul."

Matthew allowed a tiny smile to come to his lips. "No, not now. You are Major Hugh Owen of His Majesty's et cetera, et cetera. We were classmates at Oxford."

"Indeed," said Hugh, "and I gave it up for King and Country."

"Exactly. And, Leonard," continued the viscount, "find a black silk scarf of mine to use as a sling for Hugh's arm. It will make him appear more romantic."

"Indeed," echoed Omega.

"Miss Chartley, you are to go belowstairs and promise my cook the sun, moon, and stars, or, failing that, a hare for the game course. When this . . . this charade is over, we will discuss the matter of my nephew. And . . . and anything else that comes to mind."

Without a word, Omega went to the open door, motioning Angela and Jamie to follow.

The servants' hall was deathly quiet, for all that the servants were seated around the dining table. Nine pairs of eyes stared at Omega as she came to the head of the table and clasped her hands tightly together so they would not shake.

"There has been a most unfortunate row upstairs," she began calmly, "and I know that you heard it. Your master is well. No great damage has been done, but I know you are all disturbed."

The eyes didn't move from her face. She looked at them all in turn. "Mrs. Wells? Mrs. Wells, there will be a hare for the game course." She put her hand upon Angela's shoulder. "Angela and Jamie will trap one for you." She put her hand on Jamie's shoulder. "This is James Clevenden, the viscount's nephew. He will be staying here." She paused, and for the first time in eight years felt strangely young as the servants continued to stare at her. "As for the rest, you will simply have to trust me."

Still no one moved. Omega's heart began to drift in the direction of her shoes. She held her chin high and looked into each face again. "I am Omega Chartley. Some of you may know who . . . who I am, but it really is of no importance. I will not be here long. Now, please, help your master."

The silence deepened. Finally Mrs. Wells rose to her feet.

"I wouldn't stay another moment in this deranged household," she began, her face red. She opened her mouth to say more, but Omega spoke up.

"Then leave it, Mrs. Wells," she said quietly. "I have managed a household before, and I am certain I can do justice to this one for the short time I will be here."

Mrs. Wells's eyes seemed to start out of her head. After a long second of floundering about for the correct word to express her sentiment, she turned on her heel and stalked from the room.

Omega glanced at Twinings and was quick to catch the gleam of appreciation in his eyes. "You, sir," she said. "Can you delegate the parlormaid and footman to perform a miracle in that front hall?"

"I can," he said. "Come, Tildy, Michael, you have work to do. And bring a broom and dustpan."

The cook rose next. If Omega had had any doubt that it was the cook, he began to speak in rapid French, gesturing wildly, grandly, pouring out his woes to the ceiling. When he stopped for a breath, Angela plunged into the conversation, her French as rapid-fire as his. Omega's eyes opened wide. Angela turned to her at last, a note of undisguised triumph in her voice.

"He will stay for two rabbits and a trout."

"A trout? Oh, Angela, however will you produce a trout?"

"Omega, she probably has a line and hook in her bag," Jamie said.

"You peeked!" accused Angela.

Jamie just grinned and started for the stairs. Angela hurried after him. She said a few more hurried words to the cook, who smiled and kissed his hand at her. Humming to himself, the cook pulled the scullery maid and the potboy to their feet and headed in the direction of the kitchen.

"Omega, we need you upstairs," Jamie called.

Omega hurried upstairs. Hugh stood before her, immaculate in Matthew Bering's clothes. She walked around him. "Well, the coat is large," she said, "but have you not been in hospital for over a month?"

"I did lose weight in hospital, Omega," Hugh agreed.

Matthew had removed his bloody shirt and was wrapped in his dressing gown. He straightened the sling of black silk. "You'll do," he said, handing Hugh a letter. "This should give you the introduction you need. Bring them back here after the judging, and we'll see if my Banbury tale is convincing enough."

Hugh saluted smartly and took the hat from Leonard and left. Matthew shook his head. "This is very odd," he said to no one in particular. His eyes lighted on Omega next; he appeared to be seriously regarding her for the first time.

"Tildy," he called over his shoulder. "I want you."

The maid handed the broom to Michael, the footman, and curtsied in front of the viscount.

"Take Miss Chartley upstairs and find her a dress." Without another word, he went up the stairs, shaking off Leonard, who tried to help him.

"Follow me, Miss Chartley," said Tildy, and started up the stairs. Omega stayed where she was until she heard the door upstairs close, and then she followed the maid.

"Is Lord Byford married?" she asked finally.

"Oh, no, ma'am," said the maid.

They were passing the viscount's room. "Then how is it that he has dresses?" Omega whispered.

"That I do not understand, ma'am," whispered Tildy in turn as she opened a door beyond and stood back for Omega to enter.

Omega went to the window immediately, opened the draperies, and let in the sunlight. The room was stuffy; she opened the window, flinging it wide, and then leaned out to appreciate the gracious flower garden below the window.

"I do recall that my lord specifically required flowers to be planted there. My brother did it," said Tildy. " 'Just broadcast the seed,' his lordship told my brother. 'Let it be like a meadow.' It *is* beautiful, isn't it, Miss Chartley?"

"And so is the room, Tildy," said Omega. The ceiling was low, but this troubled her not at all. There was a coziness that made Omega smile for the first time since she had crossed the threshold of Matthew Bering's house. What a pleasant room this would be in the winter. When the day was gray and rainy outside, this place would be a sanctuary, a place to sew, and read, and just think about things. Omega thought briefly of her damp room in Plymouth that looked over the sound, and then dismissed it forever from her memory.

Again there was that persistent smell of lemon cologne, even in this closed room. How singular.

"Well, Tildy, what have you here?" she said at last.

Tildy appeared not to be attending. "Begging your pardon, miss," she said. "I sometimes wish I had leave to come up here and just sit. Sometimes Lord Byford asks me to dust in here, and then I do sit for a moment, but only for a moment."

Omega smiled again. "I can understand."

"But here is why we have come," said the maid. She passed into the little dressing room. Omega followed, and her mouth dropped open in surprise.

The room was lined with dresses, dresses of all colors and fabrics, walking dresses, morning dresses, sleeping gowns, simple muslin frocks, more elaborate afternoon dresses, cloaks and capes, dominoes. Rows of shoes peeped out from under the dresses, and there were hatboxes on the shelf overhead.

"Oh, Tildy, whatever *is* all this?" she exclaimed.

"I do not know, Miss Chartley." The maid touched one of the dresses. "They're a trifle outmoded, but not by too many years. They were here when I took up my position in this house four years ago." She paused a moment, as if wondering if she should pursue this conversational thread. "It is a subject of some interest belowstairs, ma'am. We have—oh, you'll laugh—we have created our own mythology."

"I would have done the same thing, I am sure."

Omega took one of the frocks, a basic muslin dress, and held it up to her. The hem just brushed the tips of her shoes. It would likely be a perfect fit.

Tildy clapped her hands. "How lucky we are! Oh, Miss Chartley, you can take your pick!"

"It will be something simple," said Omega, "if I am to become the housekeeper for the day."

"As to that, I cannot say that I am sad," confided Tildy as she searched through the dresses. "Mrs. Wells was ever so difficult belowstairs. And none of us could bring ourselves to tell his lordship about the quantities of port she put away when she thought none of us were watching."

"Well, I will not do that. Oh, look, that one, that blue dress. That will be quite the thing, don't you agree? Now, where can I find an apron?"

"I have an extra down in the servants' hall. Now, Miss Chartley, let me see to a bath for you."

"I would like that," Omega murmured. Her last ablutions had been hastily performed in the River By with a sliver of soap that had seen much duty in Spain, France, and Belgium. "And if there is any shampoo . . ."

"I'll find what you need." Tildy handed her the dress. "There are linens and things in the drawers. Do we ask too much . . . do you think the shoes will fit?"

"It's possible."

After Tildy left the room, Omega sat down on the bed. She had no doubt that the shoes would fit. So would the chemise and camisoles. Matthew must have prepared this wardrobe for her eight years ago.

Omega took off her shoes and tucked her feet up under her. She hadn't thought of it in years, but she remembered showing off some of her trousseau to him only days before the wedding, letting her excitement at the beautiful clothes spill over probably where it should not have. Her companion had told her later how improper she was, but she had not cared overmuch. She had been deeply in love with Matthew Bering. She wanted him to see what the Chartleys considered fine enough for such a wonderful marriage.

The trousseau was long gone, sold at auction with everything else. She smiled to herself for no good reason. None of her pretties would have mattered. She could have come to Matthew Bering in her shift, and there would have been this magnificent wardrobe waiting for her.

And there was a time I would have come to you in my shift, Matthew, she thought, if only . . . if only you had told me why.

Such melancholy reflections were not improving the tenor of her mind. When Tildy, Michael, the scullery girl, and the potboy returned with tin tub and buckets of warm water, she was only too grateful to hurry their preparations and close the door on them. The thought of a bath was almost enough to make her mouth water.

Even though she had not time for the luxury of a long soak in the tub, Omega washed her hair, scrubbed herself briskly, and took an idle moment to sit in the warm water, her chin resting on her drawn-up knees, contemplating the strange workings of fate.

She made idle circles in the water. How was it that Matthew was the Viscount Byford? It was a title unknown to her. She looked across her knees to the dressing room and the rows of beautiful clothes. Why would he do such a thing? She sighed and splashed the circles. How little I really know of him. How strange is the human mind.

"Now, if I were a Roman," she said, "I would put it down to the capricious humor of Jupiter. As it is, I must blame dreadful coincidence and awful fate."

It was a simple matter to dress quickly, not dwelling overmuch on the dainty underthings and other personal items in the drawers. She gave her hair a vigorous brushing and wished for the millionth time that it did not curl in such an exasperating fashion. "This is not the hair of an educationist," she told the mirror.

Exasperation always led eventually to resignation. With a sigh that came all the way from her shoes, she found a pretty lace cap and planted it firmly on her curls, resolving to indulge in no more peeks in the mirror. There was work to be done.

Angela and Jamie had not yet returned when she entered

the main hall again. The gardener had brought in an armful of flowers. She followed him downstairs and located a large crystal vase.

"Mrs. Wells was going to place this epergne on the table," said Tildy. "I took the liberty of sending my brother for flowers instead."

"That was a much wiser choice," replied Omega, eyeing the monstrous silver centerpiece. "Rather quelling, isn't it?"

"Yes, and it does not fit our dining room."

Our dining room. Omega liked that. Obviously the servants of Byford's house had taken the place to their hearts. It spoke well of Matthew Bering.

"Beg pardon, Miss Chartley?"

Had she spoken out loud? "Oh, nothing, nothing. Here, Tildy, would you like me to arrange these flowers?"

"Oh, yes, if you would. I'm all thumbs with flowers, and Twinings asked me to hurry with the front hall so I can polish the silver. It has been a long time since we had any company, and some of his lordship's best pieces are quite tarnished." She paused a moment and took a good look at Omega. "And, Miss Chartley, how well that dress fits you! Blue is surely your color."

"Oh, my, thank you," said Omega in some confusion. She had not heard a compliment in years. "Hadn't you . . . hadn't you better hurry with the upstairs front hall?"

Omega arranged the flowers in the vase, wondering how Angela and Jamie were faring, wondering if Hugh could carry off his charade, wondering if Matthew should see a doctor. Matthew Bering. If people had told her at the start of her holiday that she would be arranging flowers in his house, she would have thought them all about in their heads. It remained only to see Jamie safely settled here. And surely there might be a place for Hugh in Byford, and Angela too. Omega kept thinking of Angela's eyes as the girl had looked about the house. Surely there must be a place for Angela.

The chef came to admire the flowers, speaking in his rapid French and gesturing grandly to her. Omega's schoolroom French had been mutinously learned and quickly forgotten. She could only smile and nod as the cook went on and on, and wish Angela were here to interpret.

He paused and looked at her inquiringly. Omega nodded and smiled again, and then squeaked in alarm as the Frenchman grabbed her around the waist, pulled her close, and planted a kiss on her lips.

She looked around wildly for assistance, but she should not have worried. As suddenly as he had grabbed her, the cook released her, kissed his fingers to her, and pinched her as he strutted back to his kitchen.

Omega could only stare after him, resolving then and there to improve her French instead of relying on smiles and nods. She looked about her. No one else had seen the Frenchman's demonstration of affection. Twinings was wiping glasses in the pantry, and Tildy was only now returning to the servants' hall from abovestairs. Omega picked up the vase and beat a hasty retreat up the stairs.

The flowers looked particularly well on the table. Someone—it must have been Tildy—had placed a lace runner the length of the table. The wood contrasted darkly with it and created a dramatic effect. She centered the vase and stepped back from the table to survey her handiwork, moving forward to touch a rose here, a fern there.

She sighed and stepped back again. "Oh, I simply must be on my way to Durham," she said.

"Durham?"

She hadn't heard Matthew enter the room. He was dressed quite casually in trousers and open shirt. And he was fuller in the chest. She hadn't imagined it, after all. Maybe his chest had even dropped a little. She surveyed him as critically as she had looked at the roses, and decided that a little added weight suited his mature years.

"Durham," she repeated. "St. Elizabeth's Academy for Young Ladies. I will be paid a small salary, plus room and board. And there is always extra for private tutoring. Thank heaven English is so mysterious."

Matthew's eye was swollen shut. His nose no longer looked pushed to one side, but there was a bump in it that hadn't been there before.

"Oh, Matthew, your face," was all she could say.

He came no closer, but leaned against the doorframe. "I don't think my guests will fall for any cock-and-bull story about a suddenly opened door."

"I think not," she agreed. "You must tell them that you bent over and caught yourself on an open drawer. Alpha did that once."

"Omega! That's even worse than the door story!" he declared.

"Yes, I suppose it is. Perhaps Hugh has told them something entirely different by now. It only remains for him to return and enlighten you. If you will excuse me . . ."

She wanted to get out of the room. Even after all these years, it was hard to stand there and make polite conversation with the man she had wanted beyond all bounds of propriety and who had left her at the church door.

He made no comment, only stepped aside.

She got no farther than the front hall. Angela and Jamie came in the door, Jamie bearing two hares, their ears threaded through a long cord and draped over his shoulder. Angela carried a trout that threatened to slide from the brown paper wrapped about its middle. Both children dripped water on the carpet.

"Oh, Jamie, Angela!" Omega exclaimed as she hurried to them. "The chef will be so pleased! But how wet you are!"

Jamie looked at his uncle and smiled broadly. "Uncle, I hope you don't mind my saying so, but your hares are remarkably stupid hereabouts. I don't know that there is anything you can do about it," he added generously, to soften the blow, "but it ain't much sport."

Matthew's lips twitched and he laughed in spite of himself. "This is not the best hunting country, lad, for rabbits or otherwise. I go to Northamptonshire in the season. Or rather, I used to."

"My papa was a hunter."

"I remember, lad, I remember." The viscount clapped his hands together. "But see now, Angela is struggling with that leviathan of a trout. Wherever did you find this, child?"

Omega noted with approval that when he addressed Angela, he got down on his knees so as to look into her face. How does he know children particularly like that in adults? she thought.

Angela struggled with the limp fish, which slid out of her grasp and plopped onto the hall runner. She tried to wrestle it back into the brown paper, but the paper was soggy and disintegrated in her hands. Omega thought for a moment she was going to cry.

Matthew must have thought so too. He took a handkerchief from his pocket and wrapped it around the fish. "There, now. My dear, did you purchase this beast?"

Angela nodded, too shy to speak.

Jamie took up the story. "I almost thought we had one for you, Uncle, but it moved before Angela could grab it." He looked at Omega. "And do you know what Angela did then?"

"I have no idea, Jamie, but I want to hear."

"She went to the fishmonger and traded Napoleon's prayerbook for the biggest trout he had!"

"Good God, wherever did you get Napoleon's prayerbook?" exclaimed Matthew in amazement, and then spoke over his shoulder in Omega's general direction. "I wouldn't have thought the Anti-Christ to possess one."

"Perhaps I was not entirely truthful," said Angela scrupulously. "But I did pick it up on the Waterloo battlefield near Hougoumont, and I think it was in French." She lowered her voice. "I do not read. Maybe it was Latin."

Matthew got to his feet and handed the trout to Angela. "Then who is to dispute you? A genuine battlefield souvenir ought to be worth a trout."

"That's what I thought, sir. Come along, Jamie. The cook will be wanting these."

Lugging her trout, she started for the stairs. Matthew touched her shoulder. "And you gave up your souvenir for my dinner?" he asked gently.

She smiled at him, and Omega watched with delight as

the dimple came out in her cheek. "It wasn't hard, sir. We—Hugh and I—we owe you something. I hope you aren't too mad at all of us."

His hand went to her hair. "Perhaps I am not so angry anymore. Now, hurry up, you two. That horse show will be over soon, and my guests will be wanting their dinner, provided they are still speaking to me."

"Yes, hurry, my dears," echoed Omega. "I'll be down in a moment. There's much to be done yet."

Matthew held the door for the children. Omega couldn't see his face, but his shoulders shook slightly, and she knew he was chuckling to himself. He looked back at her and then at the sopping, smelly carpet.

"Come, Omega, let us roll this up. It smells fishy."

She nodded and began at her end of the runner. Matthew began at the other end, but in a moment he waved his hand and sat down on the stairs. "I can't," he said. "Every time I bend over, my face feels as though it is going to fall out on the floor. What did he hit me with?"

"The only fist he has left, sir."

"Am I such an ogre?" he murmured. "What on earth did you tell him?"

Her confusion returned. Omega lowered her head so he could not see her face, and continued rolling up the carpet. "Very little, sir. Truly I am not in the habit of idle chat."

"Then I think he is very protective of you, Miss Chartley. You, uh, you have a way of bringing that out in people, obviously."

"Some people, sir. Shall I leave this here?"

He nodded. "Michael will take it belowstairs."

"I will tell him." The dearest wish of her heart was to leave the hall by the fastest possible route. "I must go help Tildy with the silver."

"Very well. And I will seek my bed again. I am sure Jamie will think I am a granny goose, but my head is still ringing. By the way, Omega, thank you for saving my cook."

"You can thank Angela and her wild game," Omega replied crisply. "Your wretched cook took advantage of my lamentable French and kissed me and pinched me!"

"Oh, did he?" Matthew began, a little light coming into his eye again.

"Yes, and I'll very likely have a black-and-blue mark." She hadn't meant to tell him that.

Matthew rose to his feet. "Well, I shall speak to him later. But you must own, Miss Chartley, that you're much less an antidote than Mrs. Wells, and after all, he *is* French."

"Sir," she burst out, "I am twenty-six and much too old for that sort of thing!"

"I know precisely to the day how old you are, Omega Chartley, and I don't scruple to tell you that you've rarely uttered a bigger prevarication. And if you think that lace cap adds years and wrinkles, you'd better continue to keep an eye out . . . for my cook. Good day, Omega. I am returning to my hunk of sirloin, which Leonard is convinced will help my black eye. Do excuse me."

She watched him go up the stairs and heartily wished him to the devil.

7

Omega remained belowstairs, prudently out of reach of the chef's hands. Tildy had already divested the children of their wet clothing. They sat wrapped in blankets by the fire as the maid spread their clothes in the warmest part of the kitchen.

Before much time had passed, Angela was seated on a stool by the cook, who was speaking to her in French as he cleaned the fish. Omega was pleased to note how eager he was to converse in his own language. Feeling more charitable as she watched him work and talk to Angela, Omega put his impropriety down to loneliness.

She could understand loneliness, she thought as she polished Matthew Bering's silver. No other instructor at Miss Haversham's school in Plymouth had her background; for whatever reason of class or boundary, no one had chosen to pursue her acquaintance, and she was too shy to force herself on others. She had no friends at the school, only colleagues. And probably that is why I have become so used to talking to myself, she told herself. Gracious, it only lacks for me to start collecting cats and knitting useless tea cozies to complete my spinsterhood.

Perhaps that was why she found the company of Hugh Owen so pleasant. How nice it was to talk to someone again, someone besides distant fellow-faculty and fubsy-faced children, pasty from long winters of inactivity and too much heavy pudding. Her admiration did not end with Hugh, but included Angela and Jamie. How much there is to learn from children, she thought. And how quickly they have become indispensable to me.

She finished polishing the salt cellar and filled it, resolving to leave the moment this matter of Jamie was resolved. She stacked a tray with china for the table upstairs and started up the steps, careful to keep a firm grasp on her skirts. How *did* servants manage on stairs?

Omega lugged the tray into the dining room, admiring the effect of the flowers in the crystal vase. Oh, if this were my house, I would place a small table under that window and there would be flowers all summer. And chrysanthemums when the air turned cool, and holly during the cold days of winter.

She arranged the plates quickly, the ticking of the clock on the sideboard reminding her that horse shows don't last forever. She was placing cutlery about when she had a lowering thought: I have absolutely no money. How on earth am I going to get to Durham?

She sank down into the chair at the head of the table and rested her elbows on the arms. If she wrote to Alpha for a loan, he would send her one. He was scarcely a day's drive away in Amphney St. Peter. This thought was followed by a more chilling one. He would do no such thing. Alpha Chartley, beloved Alpha, would demand her direction and insist on meeting her in person to find out what kind of scrape she had got herself into. And if he saw Matthew Bering, Alpha would surely call him out.

Omega closed her eyes and put her hands over her face. Dear, dear Alpha, gentleman, scholar, father, who had never fired a pistol in his life. He must never find out where she was.

She tried to think what to do. The only other recourse was to apply to Matthew Bering, Vicount Byford, for a loan. "Oh, God, I cannot," she said.

"Cannot what, my dear?"

Omega jerked her hands away from her face and opened her eyes. Matthew was standing quietly in the doorway. He was dressed carefully in the elegance of a country gentleman again, stock neatly tied, coat smoothed across his shoulders without a wrinkle. He walked slowly to the other end of the table and sat down. "Cannot what?" he asked again when she did not seem disposed to reply.

There are moments when only the truth will do. "I cannot ask you for a loan to quit this place, Matthew," she answered. "And I dare not tell Alpha my whereabouts, for he would surely challenge you to a duel. I hardly need scruple to describe the outcome of that to you, sir."

Matthew considered her predicament. "If you cannot apply to me to bring you up to scratch, and you don't want to risk Alpha's health, whatever will you do?"

He was teasing her. There was a twinkle in his eye as he leaned back in the chair and regarded her. He was playing with her emotions like a musician with an instrument. How dare he? She rose to her feet slowly, horrified by the intensity of her rage. Had there been a pistol within easy reach, she would have shot him.

He saw the anger in her face. The twinkle left his eye and he sat up straight again. "That was unthinkable of me," he said. "I have no business being unkind to you." He waited a moment. "Oh, say something, Omega!"

She could think of nothing that would do justice to her feelings. There weren't enough words in the language. She could only shake her head and hurry to the door, desperate to get belowstairs again.

There was another look in Matthew Bering's eye that she couldn't identify. A chill settled around her heart. She got to the door first and stepped into the hall in time to narrowly avoid Twinings, who was hurrying to the front door.

Hugh had returned. Thank God. That would be sufficient diversion to allow an escape. Besides, there was much to do belowstairs. Omega Chartley chose discretion over valor, and fled to the safety of the servants' hall.

The dinner was a total success, from soup to fruit. Tildy, Michael, and Twinings had no time to comment as they hurried up and down the stairs, but the look of triumph in the maid's eyes told Omega that all was going well.

Omega continued where she was belowstairs, and Angela and Jamie too, shuttling dishes from the kitchen to the table in the servants' hall, where Tildy and Michael bore them upstairs. Angela's eyes grew wider with each course that passed before her.

"How many people are up there?"

"Four, I believe," said Omega.

"Jamie, there is enough food here to feed a Spanish village," she said to her companion, who had been assigned the task of wiping up any spills on bowls or platters. "And look how much they bring down that is only partly eaten."

Jamie shrugged. It was nothing new to him.

"Jamie, only think how well you will eat here!"

"I haven't heard my Uncle Byford say anything about my staying," was his reply. He looked at Omega for reassurance, but she could give him none beyond a smile and a touch on the head. Omega was past attempting to divine what Matthew Bering would do. She had no expectations. If Omega had had the remotest knowledge of whose estate she had so blithely led Jamie to, she would have kept walking and put him in Alpha Chartley's capable hands, hang the consequences.

I may have done the lad a dreadful disservice, was her thought as she carried empty bowls from Tildy's hands into the washroom, where the scullery maid was already elbow-deep in suds. Her instinct for flight grew by the minute. The only thing that kept her working was a certain determination to see a task through, no matter how distasteful.

Hours passed. "Dear God, will they never go?" she said to Tildy at one point.

Tildy had taken advantage of a rare moment and was seated at the servants' table. "Surely that is a good sign, Miss Chartley," she said. "You know how people always hurry off when they are not happy."

I can well appreciate that, Omega thought.

"This means the business is a success. I can't wait for Hugh Owen to tell us about it," the maid continued. "Think what it will mean for our village!"

"What *will* it mean?" asked Omega. In all the bustle and the anxiety, she had no idea what the issue was.

"Lord Nickle and Sir Martin Dorking are the silent backers of a carting firm out of London," explained Tildy as she scraped plates into a pan. "It's between Byford and Regis as to which of our towns becomes a stop on the route."

"And if it is Byford . . ."

"Goods will travel that much quicker to the markets in Oxford and London. My papa says it is the best thing to happen to us since the old viscount died."

Omega blinked. "Whatever do you mean?"

"He was a dreadful man, always drinking and wenching. Papa would never let me work here if the old viscount hadn't cocked up his toes. Matthew Bering is such an improvement." Tildy eyed Omega. "I . . . we are all so pleased to serve him, Miss Chartley. I must admit . . . I do not understand why you seem to get a little white about the mouth when you have to talk to him."

"Oh, it is . . ." How could she possibly explain what she didn't understand herself?

She was saved from wallowing about for the right words by a step on the stairs. Hugh Owens came down into the servants' hall. Angela ran to him and he gave her a quick hug.

"You look magnificent," she said. "Much better than usual!"

"Oh, I like that!" said Hugh, and smiled over Angela's head at Omega. "There is much to be said for being a gentleman—the best sherry, a truly masterful cigar, clothes that tolerate sitting hour after hour. Angela, I think I will become a gentleman."

Angela laughed and pushed him into a chair. "Have they gone?"

"Almost. Lord Byford is even now walking them to their curricle. No one seems in any hurry." He looked back over his shoulder at Omega. "I think the issue is won, Omega. I impressed them—and me—with my knowledge of horseflesh, our chef here bowled them over—thanks to our wily hunters —and everyone remarked on the sophisticated yet simple arrangement of flowers."

Omega sat down across from Hugh and rested her elbows on the table. "Whatever did you come up with to explain Matthew . . . Lord Byford's eye?"

"I told the truth."

"The truth," Omega gasped. "And they *stayed*?"

The door opened and Matthew Bering descended the stairs, followed by the butler. From the look Twinings gave the other servants as he followed his master, Omega could tell that such condescension was not an everyday occurrence. The servants began to rise.

"No, no. Stay where you are. You, too, Miss Chartley. Sit, sit."

The servants looked at each other. Twinings pulled out a chair for his master. Matthew sank into it with a sigh. He glanced at Michael, who was leaning against the dry sink. "Michael, could I trouble you for a rag dipped in cold water and wrung out? My eye feels like the Cyclops' orb." Michael did as he was bidden. "That, lad, is *much* better. Yes, Hugh told them the truth. But it's your story, Owen."

Hugh nodded graciously. "I told 'em I had struck my best friend Matthew a mighty blow when he attempted to wake me from a sound sleep. Forgot myself. I thought I was on the battlefield at Waterloo." He grinned. "Not that anyone was sleeping at Waterloo, but sudden shocks, you know . . . So we have been refighting the battle for the last two hours, Angela. Who would have thought Waterloo would become a dinner-table diversion so soon?"

Matthew shrugged. "It must have sounded plausible to Lord Nickle and Sir Martin. Of course, my good friend Major Owen had already made serious inroads on their affections at the horse judging. Again, Hugh, it is your story."

Hugh smiled modestly around the table. "That was the easiest part, my lord . . . and lady," he said with a nod in Omega's direction. "It was a mere matter of follow-the-leader. I hung back from the lord and the sir, nodding when they nodded, patting where they patted. Oh, Angela, I could read those two like Señora Muñoz read her tarot cards!"

His words were boastful, but accompanied by such a grin that everyone at the table smiled. "I was so agreeable. Happens we made some good choices. There are some devilish fine horses in this country, my lord."

"There are. 'Happens' I own some of them." Matthew took the cloth from his eye. "And thank you, Miss Chartley, for your role in this evening's events. And you too, Angela and Jamie. Angela, what's this? Are you drooping?"

Angela rested her head on her arms. Matthew reached across and touched her head, shaking it slowly from side to side. "And thank you again, child, for surrendering your battlefield souvenir for the good of Byford—and the viscount."

Angela mumbled something but did not open her eyes.

"Tildy, find a bed for Angela . . . and for Jamie and Hugh too. It appears I have houseguests." He pushed his chair back from the table and crossed his legs, giving himself over to an enormous yawn that stopped almost before it started.

"The devil, my face hurts," he said. "Friend Owen, please tell me that I'll feel better in the morning."

"You might, my lord," replied Hugh. He rose to his feet and prodded Angela. "Come along, *muñequita.* Let us follow where Tildy leads. You too, Jamie." He followed the maid up the stairs, pausing at the top step, his face suddenly serious, the smile gone. "I don't really have any regrets about drawing your cork, my lord. Good night, Omega. Don't stay up too late. Tomorrow may be even more trying than today."

"He is a quixotic combination of parts," murmured Matthew. His face was red with embarrassment, and he made no attempt to look her in the eye. "You have obviously found yourself a champion, Omega."

"It is of no consequence," she replied, taking off her apron and draping it over the chair. "And, Matthew, I will apply to you for that loan. I need only enough to get me to Durham. I'll repay you after the first quarter. I just wanted to see Jamie situated."

Matthew reached out suddenly and took her by the hand, compelling her to sit down again. "Omega, you know I can't keep him here."

She jerked her hand away, but she did not rise. She leaned toward him across the table. "I know no such thing, Matthew Bering! He's been beaten by that . . . that man who is his guardian. Surely you do not countenance such things!"

He shook his head, and she could see, despite her own impulsive fury, how very tired he was. And there was something more, something she could not explain, but which sent shivers down her spine.

"I do not look with favor on such things, Omega, but there is the matter of the law. Lord Rotherford is James Clevenden's legal guardian."

"Can't you fight for him? Defend him? God, does your nephew have no friends?"

His voice was level, rising a little to compete with hers. "I cannot keep him. And I cannot tell you why."

"I suppose you cannot tell me why you left me at the altar, either, can you, Lord Byford?" she lashed out.

"No, I cannot." His voice was barely a whisper now.

"Damn you, Matthew Bering," she said, her voice as low as his.

He raised his eyes to hers then. "That's already been done, Omega, rest assured. Good night."

Without another glance at him, she ran up the servants' stairs, and resisted the urge to slam the door behind her.

Twinings had put out the lights and the hall was dark except for two candles on the table under the mirror. Jamie stood beside the table, waiting for her.

"Jamie," she exclaimed, "I thought you were in bed."

He shook his head. Omega touched his shoulder and felt him tremble. "I came back down for a glass of water," he whispered. "Omega, he's not going to let me stay here? Is that what I heard him say? Oh, I didn't mean to eavesdrop, but I couldn't help it."

She put her hands on his shoulders and drew him close. "Oh, Jamie, I wish I knew what was wrong here. But please, please, don't worry. Go to bed now, and sleep, and in the morning Hugh and I will think of something." She paused and thought of her brother. "There may be someone who will help us."

"But it's not going to be my Uncle Matthew." His voice was the voice she had prayed never to hear again, flat and devoid of hope.

She sighed and hugged Jamie. "We'll . . . we'll think of something. Things always look better in the morning."

Jamie let go of her and stepped back, looking into her eyes. "Do you *really* believe that, Omega?"

There was nothing she could say. She steered him up the stairs and into his room. She sat beside his bed a moment, but when he would say nothing else, but only stared at the ceiling, his lips tight together, she rose and quietly closed the door.

Tildy met her in the hall. "Here, Miss Chartley, you forgot your candle."

She took it. "Where am I to sleep, Tildy?"

The maid looked surprised. "Why, in the room with all the beautiful clothes."

Omega shook her head. "I wouldn't sleep in there for anything. Just . . . just let me get a nightgown and show me where Angela is sleeping. Surely there is room with her."

Omega darted into the room. A fire glowed in the hearth and the chair had been pulled up close to it. The bed had already been turned down and a nightgown lay across it. She snatched up the gown and followed Tildy to Angela's room. Angela was already asleep. Omega blew out the candle and undressed in the dark, crawling in beside the little girl, who sighed and tucked herself close. Gradually Omega felt herself relax. She closed her eyes and slept.

Rain was falling when she woke. The room was still dark, and she feared she had overslept. Angela was already gone. Omega threw back the covers and then hugged them to her again. The room was chilly. She wiggled her toes under the blanket and sank down deeper in the feather bed.

She was drifting back to sleep again when she heard Angela crying in the hall. Omega sat bolt upright, listening. She leapt out of bed and threw open the door.

Angela stood in the hall with Matthew Bering. His hand was on her shoulder, and he was talking earnestly to her, but she was not listening. She raised her face to Omega's wide eyes.

"Jamie's gone," she sobbed. She ran to Omega, who grabbed her and hugged her. "Hugh went to look for him. I wanted to go too, but *he* wouldn't let me!" She raised stormy eyes to Matthew's face and then looked away from him.

"It's too rainy outside, and besides, the river rises when it's like this."

"Angela's not afraid of rain, Matthew," Omega chided, "and she probably swims better than you do. Come, child, let me get dressed and we'll go look for him too."

"No, Omega."

Matthew grasped her shoulder, but she shook him off. "If there ever was a time you could tell me what to do, Matthew, it's gone." Her eyes clouded over. "I can't believe you are so unfeeling. Maybe I never really knew you."

She went back into the room with Angela and locked the door behind her, dressing quickly, dragging a comb through her hair. She thought of the warm cloaks in the pretty bedroom next to the viscount's room, and then dismissed them. It was only an August rain. She wouldn't melt.

Matthew had left the hall. Omega took Angela by the

hand and walked toward the stairs. "Do you have any idea where Jamie might be?" she whispered as they tiptoed past the viscount's room.

Angela shook her head. The door to Matthew Bering's room opened and she jumped. Omega took a firmer grasp on her hand and started down the stairs.

"Omega, wait!"

She turned around to look at Matthew, who was coming down the stairs right behind her. Omega let go of Angela. "Go ahead. I'll find you in a moment." Angela ran out the front door, leaving it wide open for the rain to blow in.

"Omega, you don't need to go look too," Matthew said. His voice was conversational. He came closer on the stairs. "I wish you would be reasonable about this whole matter."

She could match him calm for calm. "I'm not going to abandon someone who needs my help. I have a peculiar habit, Lord Byford. I like to see something through to its conclusion."

He winced at that, but did not stop. "Even if aiding a fugitive is against the law?"

"Yes, if it comes down to that." Little sparks of anger flicked about in her brain. "And I feel responsible. I'm the one who helped him find this place, which has only multiplied his troubles! Excuse me now, Matthew."

She turned to follow Angela, forgetting there were two more steps to go on the stairway. When she hit the first step, she fumbled for the banister. Matthew made a grab for her and missed, and she tripped down the next step and sprawled on the floor, slippery with rain.

Omega cried out as pain laced through her ankle. She felt sick to her stomach and thought for a moment she would disgrace herself entirely in front of Matthew and the servants, who had heard her shriek and were running up from the servants' hall.

Matthew knelt by her and touched her face. "Omega, are you all right?"

She nodded, not sure enough of herself to speak. Tears of frustration and pain came into her eyes and she tried to brush them away. She grabbed the banister and hauled herself to her feet. The pain in her right ankle made her gasp.

Matthew scooped her into his arms. "Omega, you're . . . you're . . ."

She burst into tears.

His voice was more gentle then. Matthew held her closer to his chest. "You're getting my coat all wet." He sighed and spoke into her ear. "Now, how am I going to go look for Jamie if I'm soaked through before I even leave the house?"

She sobbed louder.

"Michael, go get the doctor. Tildy, come with me."

Despite Omega's protests, he deposited her on the bed in the little room next to his. "Tildy, get her into a nightgown. I'm going downstairs to wait for the doctor."

"But you said you were going to look for Jamie!" Omega wailed.

"My tiresome runaway of a nephew can damned well wait until the doctor has seen you, Omega. Lord, but you're stubborn!" He put his handkerchief over her nose and made her blow. "Now, hush a minute and do what Tildy says. And if you don't cooperate, I'll help her."

She grabbed his handkerchief from him and wiped her nose, giving him a speaking look.

He stared right back. "And don't say 'You wouldn't dare,' because I would."

By the time Tildy had helped her into a nightgown, Omega's ankle was swollen to twice its normal size. "Oh, Tildy, what am I going to do?" she said in vexation. The pain was still turning her stomach.

"You're going to let me prop this pillow under your foot and you're going to lie down, Miss Chartley," said Tildy in a firm voice. "And if you feel like you're going to chuck last night's dinner, you'd better let me run for a pan."

"Hurry, Tildy!"

The maid darted for the door, only to be met by Matthew, who had a pan in his hand. He hurried to Omega's side just in time to shove the pan on her lap and hold her hair back while she vomited.

Omega clutched the sides of the pan and retched and gagged until her stomach was empty. She shuddered a few times but didn't relinquish her grip until Matthew pried off her fingers and set the pan outside the door. He came back to the bed.

"Move over, Omega." He sat down beside her and wiped her face with a damp cloth. She lay back in exhaustion on the pillow. Tears welled in her eyes again.

"I'm so embarrassed," she said, and tried to push him away.

The viscount wouldn't be pushed. "Don't be a goose, Omega. Let me raise your head and give you a sip of water."

She did as he said, and he sat down on the chair by the bed. Omega closed her eyes and did not open them again until Tildy knocked on the door and ushered in the doctor.

The doctor poked and prodded her ankle while she hung on to Matthew's hand.

"Young lady, I don't believe it's broken." The doctor shook his head. "Likely you'd feel better if it were." He looked at Matthew. "My lord, I will instruct the maid to keep Miss Chartley's foot elevated, and to apply cold cloths. Two days of that should be sufficient, and then I'll look at it again and we'll see where to go from there."

"Two days!" said Omega. She released Matthew's hand. "But I plan to be out of here this afternoon at the latest!"

The doctor laughed. "You're a funny one, Miss Chartley. Tildy has a sleeping powder here for you. Take it like a good girl."

"I won't."

"She will."

She did. After the doctor left, Matthew watched her a moment longer. Her eyelids began to droop and he appeared to grow larger and smaller, and then to disappear altogether. But he hadn't vanished; he was kneeling by her bed.

"Omega, can you hear me?"

She nodded.

"I'm going after Jamie now."

She nodded again. Her lips felt dry, and his voice was so far away.

"And when I bring him back, Omega, we'll talk."

She nodded again. She thought he kissed her on the forehead, but the room was dark, the rain thundered down, and she was so tired she couldn't be sure.

8

The rain continued throughout the day. After the sleeping powders took effect, Omega dozed and wakened, only to have the sound of the rain drumming on the windowpanes pull her back to sleep. She was conscious of a dull throb in her ankle, but she was too sleepy to care.

She woke finally in the afternoon. Tildy had pulled back the end of the coverlets and was applying another cold cloth to her foot. The pain was intense and she cried out.

Tildy nearly dropped the pan of water. Her eyes filled with tears. "Oh, I so hate to cause you pain," she said.

Omega struggled into a sitting position and pulled back the covers entirely. Her ankle was swollen beyond twice its size now. She touched it. Despite the cold compresses, her flesh was hot and red.

"Oh, Tildy, what a mull I have made of things," she said as she lay back down and the maid tucked the blankets around her again. "Has anyone returned yet?"

"The master returned several hours ago for his horse, and I have not seen the others. I sent my brother off to look too. They'll find him, Miss Chartley." She brushed back the hair from Omega's eyes. "But then what?"

"I wish I knew," replied Omega, closing her eyes again.

The rain stopped as night fell. Omega awoke to the silence of the house, and then to the welcome sound of Angela's voice.

"Omega! Omega!"

"Hush, Angela, you'll disturb Miss Chartley."

The voices were right outside her door. "Angela?" she called. "Oh, do come in."

The girl came into the room, followed by Tildy. She was soaked through, and shivering in her light dress and shawl, but a smile covered her face.

"Omega, we have him! Or rather, Lord Byford has him!"

"Thank God," said Omega. "Is he all right?"

"Just angry. And he's not speaking to anyone. You know how he is. Lord Byford rained a regular peal over his head. It was a royal scolding." Angela came closer to the bed, but was careful not to drip on Omega. "I think he's secretly relieved that we rescued him. I shall ask Jamie tomorrow, when he is not so angry."

"And now, my dear," said Tildy, "you will follow me. There is a hot bath in your room for you. Miss Chartley, you'll pardon me, but I took the liberty of taking one of the nightgowns from this room. It's for a small lady, and almost fits Angela."

"Anything for that little scapegrace," said Omega. "It's not mine, so I can be generous," she joked.

Angela came closer again. "I like it when you tease me, Omega. Are you feeling better?"

"Oh, yes, wonderfully," lied Miss Chartley. "Now, where is Jamie?"

"The master is bringing him."

"I want to see him."

"You're sure, Miss Chartley?"

"Positive. Now, help me sit up, please."

A few minutes later, Omega heard footsteps at the door, familiar footsteps, and then a knock. "Come in, please."

Matthew entered the room, followed by Jamie Clevenden, who was soaked to the skin and shivering like Angela. Omega shook her head at the boy. "Jamie, you have caused us no end of trouble."

Jamie hung his head and said nothing. Matthew came closer to the bed, carefully removing his cape, which dripped water on the floor. "I've already delivered a blistering lecture, Omega," he said.

Omega raised her eyes to him, secretly delighted with Matthew. It was only a small defense, but he was taking Jamie's side. Good for you, she thought.

Omega reached out her hand for Jamie. He looked at her then, his eyes twin pools of misery. Without a word, she held out her arms and Jamie hurled himself into them, sobbing. She stroked his wet hair and rocked him in her arms until he was silent.

"Jamie, all I ask is this: please do what Matthew says. We're simply going to have to sit down together and figure out what is to be done. Running away won't help."

Jamie wiped his nose on his soggy sleeve. "But, Omega, I've been seen!"

The words chilled her heart. "Mr. Platter?"

Jamie nodded. "It was at the Regis and Byford crossing, I think." He looked at Matthew, who nodded. "Uncle Matthew swooped me away, but I know Mr. Platter saw me. How soon before he figures out where I am?"

She kissed the top of his head. "All the more reason for you to do exactly as your Uncle Matthew bids. You must promise me, word of honor, that you will not run away again. I have no power to keep you here. I cannot chase after you. You must give me the word of a gentleman, Jamie Clevenden."

"I shall not run away again, Omega," he said finally.

"And that will do for now, lad," said Matthew. "You've soaked Miss Chartley's gown. Come, lad. Did I heard Tildy say something about a bath? And then to bed with you. Run along, now."

Omega gave Jamie another hug and touched his cheek. "Come see me in the morning, dear," she said.

Jamie hurried from the room. Matthew sat down wearily in the chair. "I found him at the crossing, waiting for a carter, I suppose, or a farmer going to market. Platter must have been watching from the inn." He leaned back in the chair. "Omega, I started to give Jamie the scold of his life, and he put his hands up to his face as if to shield himself from a blow. Omega, I would no more strike him than I would strike you!"

"But he doesn't know that," Omega said slowly. The implications of Matthew's words sent tendrils of cold down her spine.

"How true. I think I begin to understand how his other uncle has been treating him. Well. It was a revelation to me."

The air was heavy with unspoken words. "Where . . . where is Hugh?" Omega asked at last.

"He is here too. He did not wish to disturb you." Matthew ran his hand through his wet hair. "No more do I." He raised the coverlets off the foot of the bed and looked for a long minute at her ankle.

"Not a pretty sight, is it?" she said.

He shook his head, and tucked the covers in again. "Perhaps I should summon the doctor in the morning." He patted her other foot. "Between us, we have three eyes and three feet. Is this what my late father used to refer to as 'damned old age'? A lowering thought."

"Lowering indeed," agreed Omega.

"Well, I must change. Twinings said something about dinner. May I bring my plate up here and eat with you?"

"Oh, no, please, Matthew. I'm not up to dinner yet. I'm afraid even the smell of food would make me long for that pan again."

"Very well, then, I'll be back in a little while." He stopped, and she could see the indecision on his face. "Omega, I know you're in pain, and I know you're tired, but I simply must talk to you before I lose whatever nerve remains. Please."

She nodded, her eyes on his face. And soon you'll know, Omega Chartley, she thought as she watched him, her eyes touring for a brief moment the face she knew so well, and, before yesterday, had thought never to see again. The swelling on his nose was going down; his eye was black and blue, but he was Matthew Bering. She realized with a wrench that nothing had changed: she loved him as much as she had ever loved him, even as he exasperated and unnerved her.

He tried to smile, but it went nowhere. "Well, Omega, now that you have memorized my face, I'll go . . . and return before you chance to forget what I look like."

She closed her eyes when he left. That short interview with Jamie had exhausted her. How wearing pain is, she thought. I will only rest my eyes this minute before Matthew returns. The pain is so great I surely will not sleep.

Omega woke hours later. The house was still, her room dark, except for the light that glowed from the fireplace, and the lamp dimly flickering beside the bed. She thought for a moment she was alone in the room, but she heard Matthew's steady breathing. As her eyes became used to the gloom, she saw him in the chair by the window, the draperies pulled open and his feet propped on the sill. The rain had begun again and the room was chill.

She regarded him from her bed, bemused all over again how little, really, he had changed in eight years. How is it possible for him to be handsomer? she asked herself. I only wish that I had fared as well.

And then his breathing changed, and she knew he was awake.

"Matthew?"

"Yes." He yawned and put his feet on the floor. "Don't breathe a word of this to Angela or Jamie, but I swear I am too old for adventuring." He laughed softly. "My chief delight in the world is to sit in a dressing gown by my fire with the London *Times*. That is slow work indeed to you mettlesome folk who seem to have attached yourselves to my household like barnacles."

He was silent another minute, and then he turned the chair around to face her. "But this is idle chat, my dear." He spread his hands out in front of him. "Where am I to begin, Omega?"

"You can prop me up and put another pillow behind my head."

He did as she said, plumping the pillow behind her head and adding another one. "Now where do we go?"

Omega closed her eyes. It was easier somehow not to look at him. "First you must tell me how it is that you are

Viscount Byford. I never knew there was a title due to you."

"I seldom thought about it, and it was almost a surprise to me, Omega," he said, pulling his chair closer. "My mother had a cousin, Rufus Laws, who was the Viscount Byford. He died without issue, and indeed, without anyone really to mourn him. You may have heard the servants mention him. No young girl was safe here during his tenure." He laughed dryly. "Things have changed with a vengeance," he added in almost an undervoice. "Well, I succeeded to his title and land. This was . . . five years? . . . six years ago, almost." His voice was lighter as he continued, and she could sense the affection in it, even as his words were deprecating. "Believe me, it is no great honor. I find myself justice of the peace and called upon to settle the pettiest of differences and to participate in hurried-up weddings. It is a curious fact, Omega, my dear, but when you have a title and money, people seem to think you know everything. I do not understand the correlation. I am called upon to be wise, impartial, and above reproach, rather like the Archbishop of Canterbury." He sighed. "And now?"

She opened her eyes. "What I want to know is probably a very small thing to you. I suppose it doesn't really matter, after eight years, and maybe it is just my female vanity. Please don't think me foolish . . . but I must know: did you . . . did you feel some . . . some great disgust for me all of a sudden?" Her voice faltered. "If you did . . . if you do . . . just say so, and I'll not plague you further."

Her words sounded silly to her own ears, and stilted, and altogether nonsensical, rather like the whining of a child. A look of great sorrow came into Matthew's eyes, and she almost wished she hadn't said anything. She could have gone to her grave gladly without seeing that look of pain cross his face.

He reached for her hand. "Omega, I loved you almost from the first moment I saw you." The look of anguish left for a moment, and he seemed almost young again. "I would wager you don't even remember when that was, do you?"

She shook her head. He took her hand and rested it on his knee. "I remember so well. You and Alpha were at the Kensington Hall Gallery, both of you poring over a guidebook and looking genuinely interested."

"But we . . . we *were* interested!" she protested, and took her hand from his knee.

"Exactly so. You two and no one else. Didn't anyone ever tell you two country children that one goes to the gallery only to see and be seen? And there you were, both of you enjoying yourselves so immensely. I was struck by your . . . your integrity, I suppose, for want of a better word. I think that if one of us Bond Street Beaux had strolled over and said that such enthusiasm was not at all the thing, it wouldn't have mattered a straw to you. You were there for the paintings." He touched her hand again. "You had on a dress of the palest pink muslin and carried the most useless-looking parasol. And your hair was everywhere at the same time." He laughed, and again the years melted away. "I wanted to sneak up and tweak one of your marvelous curls, just to see if it was real. You probably would have slapped me."

"I would have."

"I found out who you were, and discovered immediately that you had far too few years in your dish for me. But somehow, I couldn't stay away from you."

She remembered. Scarcely a day had passed without a little note, a handful of violets, or a funny drawing from Matthew Bering. She remembered his visits to Alpha, when they discussed Oxford and laughed over dons who were ancient when Matthew was there, and were still lecturing on. Almost before Omega had realized what was happening, she was in love with him. Not all the long walks in the garden, or quiet afternoons sitting in contemplation in one gallery or another had sufficiently convinced her that at eighteen she was too young for this man who had been on the town for years. He had never seemed too old for her then. He did not seem too old now.

"I told myself over and over it was foolish beyond reason to be struck dumb by a chit barely out of the schoolroom." He shook his head, the wonder still in his voice. "I don't understand how such things happen, but I felt comfortable around you, at peace, completely free to be myself. You had not an ounce of pretense in your whole body. I've never met anyone so utterly without guile. Or a woman so intelligent. You were the kind of person so utterly suited for me . . . and for children."

"Then why, in heaven's name, did all this happen?" She couldn't look at him, even in the dark, and turned her head away. "If I know, then I won't trouble you further."

It was the question she had asked almost daily for eight years, even when she wasn't consciously dwelling on the matter, as she had not in recent years. During the oddest moments—when she was grading papers, or listening to her pupils recite—her mind would take a leap back to that morning's work in the church, and then move forward again, almost as if memory had parted for an instant and let her glimpse inside.

"There are two reasons," Matthew said slowly, "two reasons that have given me cause to regret every day of my life since then." He rose suddenly and went to the window, opening it a crack and letting in the cooler breezes. "One is terrible and the other no better. I shall begin with the terrible one first."

He wouldn't look at her. "I was the guest of honor at a bachelor party that night before our . . . that night. Do you remember?"

She did. They had dined together, her father and Alpha, with Matthew, making last-minute plans, laughing about one thing and another. "You left early. It must have been before ten." She regarded him thoughtfully, pulling the memories up from eight years. "I seem to recall that Alpha was to accompany you, but he begged off."

"Thank God that he did," said Matthew fervently. "It was the worst night of my life." He laughed, and there was no mirth. "Or perhaps just the first night of eight years of worst nights."

He took a deep breath and plunged in. "My brother-in-law's brother had arranged a party. That was Rotherford."

"Rotherford? You mean the one who is hounding Jamie?"

"The very one. Edwin Clevenden, Lord Rotherford. You never met him. He was older than I by a few years, and scarcely ever in from the country. Indeed, I was surprised and a little flattered that he would plan this party. I did not know him well. Jamie's father was there—at least he was for a little while. I do not perfectly remember. There were three others of my closest friends there."

"Where was this party?"

"Oh, I do not know. Rotherford had rented rooms near St. James Square. I probably could find them again if I looked hard enough, but I never had the heart to do so."

Matthew was silent then. He left the window and paced in front of the fireplace, hunkering down for a moment to stir at the coals. Omega said nothing, only watched him.

He paced again, and then stood still. "This is devilish hard, Omega. I've never discussed this with anyone, and most assuredly not with a woman. You will think so ill of me." He laughed his mirthless laugh again. "Well, what am I saying? I'm not precisely in your best books, am I?"

"Oh, Matthew, don't."

He took another deep breath. "I was the main attraction at the party, and destined to become the entertainment. We drank ourselves practically into a state of catatonia, and then Rotherford fetched in the *pièce de résistance*. Oh, God."

It was as if he were seeing the whole event again. He sank down into the chair as if his legs would not hold him. "She couldn't have been more than fourteen. Just a prostitute from Covent Garden. Someone scarcely older than Angela."

He looked at her. "I am glad it is dark, Omega. It was always so easy to tell precisely what you were thinking, only by looking at your face."

She held out her hand to him. "Pull your chair closer, Matthew," she said. When he did not move, or reach for her hand, she folded her hands in her lap again.

"Rotherford invited me to remove my clothes and

partake of some Covent Garden honey. I was so foxed I don't know how I got my clothes off, but there I was, ready to take on that poor little whore, surrounded by my best friends, everyone cheering me on."

Omega took a deep breath. There was a sour taste in her mouth, a churning of her stomach again. She gritted her teeth against it.

"So while you were sleeping the sleep of the innocent, and perhaps dreaming about your loving husband-to-be, I was trying to lay a London drab."

"Matthew," she began, but couldn't speak.

"We're not a very good lot, Omega, we *bon ton*." Matthew got to his feet again and crossed the room. "But remember, dear, I haven't gotten to the terrible part yet. And there is worse beyond that. I'm not a performing bear, Omega. I vaguely remember everyone cheering and clapping and encouraging me, but I was totally unable to satisfy either that whore or my friends. It was mortifying, all the more so because I really didn't want to be there."

"What . . . happened then?"

"She laughed at me and I struck her so hard I bloodied her mouth. Then I remember someone putting me to bed. When it was—earlier? later?—I'm unsure. I heard her screaming and crying, pleading with someone, and then I didn't remember anything else until morning."

Matthew shuddered and the chill seemed to pass into Omega's body too. He went to the window and flung it open wide, leaning out, breathing in the cold and the rain. He remained that way, elbows on the sill, until Omega wanted to cry. She made no sound, only wished she was able to cross the room to him. What he was telling her was abhorrent and evil, and alien to every code of conduct she knew, but Omega Chartley knew what it was to hurt, and to see Matthew hurting was the worst thing of all.

He turned around and sat on the window ledge, distancing himself from her. "When I woke in the morning, I was not alone in bed. Oh, God, that girl lay beside me, and she was dead."

"Dear God," Omega said, and swallowed.

"Her face was practically transparent, drained of all

blood, but everywhere else was covered with blood. The sheets, the floor. We were both awash in it. The room stank of blood. It was the worst nightmare you could imagine, except I was not dreaming."

"What of . . . the others?" Omega's voice sounded far away to her own ears. Her heart was pounding so loud she put her hand to her chest to quiet it.

"There was only Rotherford. He told me the others had fled. He alone remained. He assured me that he would get me out of the mess. Promised that no one would ever hear of it. My secret was safe with him."

Matthew closed the window and pulled two blankets from the chest at the foot of the bed. He covered her with one of them and wrapped the other around himself and sat down in the chair again. "I had time to bathe and dress and show up at St. Alphonse."

"Oh, Matthew." Omega reached for him again, but he would not let her touch him.

"I rode past St. Alphonse in a rented hack. Everyone was already inside, waiting for you to walk down the aisle. I tried to go in, but I fled. I kept going until I was home in Shropshire."

A heavy silence seeped between them. I must say something, thought Omega. I must continue this until it is done.

"Why did you not write to me later, or communicate somehow? Couldn't you imagine my distress?"

He winced at that and settled the blanket high on his shoulders. "I was so ashamed, so utterly devastated. Someone had died because of me. Someone no one would ever miss, someone so expendable. Someone my name would never be connected to. Her life was . . . so cheap, and I was afraid I had ended it."

"Your friends?" she asked in the stillness. "What of your friends?"

"One of them wrote to me. I did not answer. Another came to Shropshire. I refused to see him. The third rejoined his troops immediately. The only one I ever saw again was my brother-in-law. Even he seemed happy enough not to mention the workings of that evening."

"But that poor child!"

He laughed but there was no mirth, and the sound drilled into her brain like an awl. "You have said it, Omega. She was poor, and she was a child." He clapped his hands together in frustration, and she jumped. "Did you never look about you in London? In Plymouth? It is not we wealthy men who ever suffer. No, Omega, we were all of us glad enough to overlook the doings of that night. God damn us."

The rain stopped. Somewhere far below in the house a door opened and then closed. Morning was coming. Soon the servants would be about. Omega's ankle throbbed but she said nothing, unable to bring herself to interfere with his train of thought. She dreaded what he was saying, but she had to hear it, and he had to tell it.

"I thought later of writing to you, I really did. Then I began to reason that you would be better off with someone else. Surely there could be no lack of suitors. Your life would go on." He sighed. "Imagine my further dismay when I learned that your father had killed himself over his reverses on the Exchange. I knew then that you would not have a pleasant time of it, after all. But it was too late for me to make any amends. Not only had I ruined two lives; I had ruined yours too, and that was unforgivable."

Dawn was lighting the sky outside now, and she could see his face. He looked old and tired, the fine lines around his mouth and eyes more deeply etched, his eyes as hopeless as Jamie's. He would not allow her to touch him.

"I'm not done yet, Omega," he said, his mouth twisting into a caricature of a smile. "I told you it gets worse. I thought long and hard about seeing you, but I did something unforgivably stupid instead. I procured myself another whore and tried again. And failed again. And again. After that, I tried no more. The next two years were spent deep in my father's wine cellar. I have been through some very good years, Omega, down-cellar in Shropshire."

He leaned forward suddenly and wiped her face with his fingers. She hadn't realized that she was crying. His fingers were so cold.

"So you see, my dear, even if we had found a way to overcome the simple matter of a brutal murder—excuse my sarcasm . . . I can only almost bear it when I am sarcastic—we still could not have made much of a marriage, considering my inability."

He stood up and went back to the window, the blanket tight around him. "And that was what I wanted to tell you. Have you ever known a greater sinner?"

She couldn't help herself. The tears streamed down her face. She tried to stifle her sobs, but it was useless. She sank lower on the pillow and cried into the blanket.

Matthew stood with bowed head by the window. He opened it again and breathed deeply of the fragrance that the breeze of morning was bringing up from the flower garden below. He closed the window again and stumbled like an old man to the door, the blanket still tight around his shoulders.

"I'll leave now, my dear." He looked at her. "I suppose you have been frightfully compromised by my presence in your room all night. I might add that you have probably never been in less danger from any man."

He opened the door. "Good night, Omega, or good morning. There's more to tell you, and it touches on Jamie. Perhaps if we ever feel up to it . . ."

He closed the door quietly behind him, not looking back.

9

Omega cried in earnest until her pillow was soggy, and then she turned it over and tried to sleep. It was day now, the air cool and smelling fresh after the long rain. The birds that had been silent yesterday made up for the lack, and right under her window, too, singing, quarreling, and shrieking at each other until she wanted to throw something.

Her ankle ached amazingly. It hurt so badly that no amount of discipline that Miss Chartley possessed could convince her to fling back the covers and have a look at it. If my leg is turning black, with shooting red streaks, she told herself grimly, there is not a single reason in the world for me to watch it happen.

Her mind could dwell on nothing but the pain, and the anguish of Matthew Bering's disclosure. Somehow she knew that when all this was over, as everything must end eventually, she would always associate the two.

Omega wished he would come back into the room, wished that he felt like talking more, and she like listening. That he had made a shocking mull of a terrible situation was not lost on her. And what would I have done in a similar circumstance? she asked herself as she gritted her teeth and tried to find a comfortable position. Had I been Matthew Bering, could I have faced me?

She concluded that she could not. How could anyone have dropped such a disclosure into an eighteen-year-old's lap? The thought brought the only comfort available to her.

There was a scratching at the door. Two heads peeked in.

"Oh, come in," Omega said gratefully.

Angela and Jamie entered the room, Jamie edging along the wall, half-dreading another scold from her, and Angela eyeing her with worry of another kind. She came close to the bed.

"Lord Byford said we were under no circumstances to bother you. But . . . but he doesn't understand!" Angela's eyes filled with tears.

In her surprise, Omega forgot her own hurt for a moment. She put out her hand and drew the little girl closer. "Why, Angela, what is the matter?"

Angela knelt down and rested her head on the bed, her voice muffled. "He doesn't know what it's like to wait outside a hospital and wait and wait and then be told it's too late or told to run along and not bother the wounded."

Without a word, Omega rested her hand on Angela's hair, smoothing it back from her face. "No, he doesn't understand, my dear. I'm glad you came to see for yourself." She managed a smile for Angela's benefit. "I'll be fine in a few days." She put her fingers to her lips, kissed them, and touched Angela on the cheek. "And that's all you needed to know, wasn't it?"

Angela nodded.

It was Jamie's turn. "Omega, I'm sorry for the trouble I caused. It's my fault, isn't it?"

She held out her hand and he came closer, standing beside Angela. "It's no one's fault but my own that I was clumsy. Don't be a goose, Jamie. Come here, you scamp, and give me a kiss." He laughed and did as she said. "Now, my dears, I would recommend that you hurry belowstairs and see how very helpful you can be today. Lord Byford is not precisely . . ."

Angela's eyes opened wide. "Oh, miss. I've never seen anyone with such a case of the megrims! And all because Jamie was such a *fulano*!"

Omega considered. Perhaps there would be no harm in prevarication. No good would be served for the children to have even an inkling of Matthew's agony. "Jamie, Angela. Lord Byford is not used to having children in his house. I am sure he will come around. Now, run belowstairs before you find yourself in trouble."

"It is already too late," came a voice from the doorway. "Omega, you know you should not encourage these graceless beggars."

His voice was light, but there was nothing light about Matthew's demeanor. Omega had to admit that he looked better today than yesterday; his blacked eye was open now, and the bump on his nose scarcely noticeable. It was the lack of expression in his face that was so disconcerting. Upon hearing Matthew's voice, Jamie shrank back against the wall again, watching his uncle's every move.

Matthew noticed Jamie's fright. He knelt by him with that wonderful instinct of his that Omega so delighted in. Jamie drew away, closer to Omega.

Matthew put out his hand slowly, as if he were trying to

touch a skittish colt. "Jamie, Jamie, if we are to rub along together in this household, there is something you must know. It is something that will never change."

Jamie was too terrified to raise his eyes to his uncle. He continued his minute examination of the grain in the wooden floor until Matthew slowly reached out his hand, raised the boy's chin, and forced him to look in his uncle's eyes.

"Jamie Clevenden, I will never strike you. I do not hold with beating children, no matter what the provocation. I mean what I say. It is more than a promise, Jamie; it is a covenant." He rested the back of his hand against Jamie's cheek for a second. "Now, run along. Tildy is waiting downstairs to take your measurements. Yours too, Angela. I can't have such ragged children in my household. How on earth am I to puff up my consequence in Byford if you look like workhouse brats?"

Jamie smiled then, and took Angela's hand. "Let us hurry! Do you think the cook will teach me some French words? Papa used to say some, and Mama would scold him."

"Jamie, let me warn you, I have no objection whatsoever to soap applied to the mouth," said Lord Byford.

Jamie laughed and tugged Angela out of the room with him.

Matthew waited until the children were gone. "I was afraid they would be bothering you, Omega." He came to the foot of the bed. "But see here, you look hagged."

Without a word, he took the blanket off her foot and stood another long minute looking at it. "I've already summoned the doctor, Omega. I'll be gone with Angela on our errand as soon as he arrives. There is a fair nearby in Templeton, and Tildy informs me I can find secondhand clothing for children."

He left her alone then. Omega lay back and stared at the ceiling, biting her lip to keep the tears back. He hadn't once looked her in the eye.

The minutes shuffled by like hours. Omega was ready to gnaw her knuckles against the pain when Matthew returned with the doctor. He ushered the man in, but did not leave the doorway. "I'll be off now, Omega."

Omega pulled herself upright. "Matthew, don't you dare leave me!" she cried, and then looked at the doctor in embarrassment. "Can't you just . . . can't you just hold my hand again?"

The doctor looked from one to the other, and then discovered a fascination with the beech tree outside the bedroom window, strolling over to it and gazing at each leaf in turn. When the doctor's back was turned, Matthew knelt by the bed. "You . . . you truly want me here? After everything I have told you?"

"Oh, shut up!" she whispered back fiercely, clutching for his hand. "You cannot fathom how doctors terrify me! How am I to bear it if you are not here?"

The doctor did not turn around, but he seemed to have taken his mind from things arboreal. "May I be so bold as to suggest, my lord, that you do as the lady wishes? I, for one, never argue with women."

Without a word to either of them, Matthew pulled the chair nearer and laced his fingers through hers.

The doctor bade her bend her leg at the knee, commanded her to wiggle her toes, and then turned her ankle this way and that, as Omega drew her lips into a thin line and clung like death to Matthew. The doctor desisted finally, looked at her over the tops of his spectacles. "I am finished. Miss Chartley, I recommend that you turn loose of the viscount before you quite curtail all circulation in his fingers."

Matthew covered her fingers with his other hand too. "She's all right. But tell us, please."

The doctor shook his head. "I still cannot see that you have broken your ankle, Miss Chartley. I believe the application of cold cloths will eventually do the trick. I hold that sprains are worse than fractures." He cleared his throat. "I trust you have changed your plans about quitting this place immediately?"

"She has," replied Matthew for her. "I'll make sure that she does not exert herself in any way."

"You will be doing her a great favor, my lord. Miss Chartley, I will place this wire frame over your ankle. It will keep the blankets from weighing too heavily on it. I can do little else until the swelling goes down. I expect you will see a change in the next day."

He shook some powders into the glass of water beside the bed. "Drink this like a good girl. That's capital, my dear. I will bid you both good day."

The doctor took up his bag, pausing only to peer at Matthew's face. "My lord, your eye . . ."

Matthew managed the smallest of smiles. "It was a mere accident."

"I heard how it happened. News gets about fast in Byford." The doctor allowed himself a chuckle. "Lord protect us from our friends, eh?"

"Indeed, sir. Good day to you."

"I can communicate with a London surgeon, if you wish," said Matthew after the doctor had gone. His fingers were still laced through hers.

"No. No." Omega scooted herself down lower in the bed, but she did not release her hold on him. The medicine was already making her drowsy. "No. I think all that I need is time."

Gently Matthew let go of her hand. "Omega, I did not think that after last night you would ever want me about."

She sighed. The bed was warm and soft, and Matthew smelled wonderfully of lemon cologne. The pain in her ankle felt farther and farther away, as if someone were stretching her out to a great length. "I think . . . I think I am tired of groping my way through muddles alone," she said, and then shook her head. "I suppose I am not making a great deal of sense right now, but, Matthew, can we not be friends?"

He was silent so long that she feared she had said the wrong thing. He chose his words carefully. "Of course we can be friends. And when you're feeling more the thing, we have a matter to discuss that has given me considerable food for thought since last night's conversation. I want to try it out on you."

She could not understand what he was saying, but little was making sense to her. Her eyes were closing when the children came into the room again.

"Ah, Jamie," said Matthew, getting to his feet. "I particularly wish you to remain right here with Omega until I return. If she needs someone to hold her hand, you have been appointed, nephew."

"Yes, sir," said Jamie. He leaned toward Matthew. "Is she . . . is she. . . ?"

"Half-dead?" Matthew chuckled. "No, just medicinally foxed, a little bit to let. Angela and I are leaving now to visit the fair. It probably would be best if you did not show yourself about Byford just yet. We must discover if Mr. Platter is lurking about."

Jamie nodded. "I will not leave the room. Only, sir, there is one thing."

"Yes, Jamie?"

"Could you get a bottle of lavender scent?"

Matthew stared at him. "Jamie, I don't perfectly understand. Are you partial to lavender scent?"

"Oh, Uncle, it is not for me, but Omega!" His expression was earnest. "She smelled of lavender when I first met her, and do you know, it reminds me of my mother."

Matthew looked down at Omega. "Yes, I seem to remember Diantha and her lavender." He touched Jamie's shoulder, his eyes remembering. "And Omega and hers." He recalled himself. "Nephew, Angela and I will find the biggest bottle to be had and Miss Chartley can dribble it all over herself if she chooses."

"Matthew, don't be nonsensical," Omega said. She wanted to say something else, but her words were slurred.

Matthew leaned closer. "My dear Miss Chartley, you are the one making absolutely no sense. Do be quiet and go to sleep. In less than a month you will have an entire class of eager pupils looking to you for guidance and syntax. Now, just hush, hurry up and heal. Come, Angela."

Angela skipped out of the room and the door closed quietly behind them. Omega made a great effort and turned her head toward Jamie. "Hugh?" she asked, reduced to one-syllable sentences.

"Oh, it is famous, Omega!" declared Jamie as he settled himself into the chair. "He is out in my uncle's stables, just sitting in one of the stalls, memorizing a horse! I cannot imagine what he is about, but he told me that perhaps he ought to learn something about horses. Do you think he expects to continue his masquerade?"

Omega thought of a number of things in reply, but none of them reached as far as her mouth. She closed her eyes and abandoned herself to the doctor's sleeping powder.

When she woke, the shadows had changed places in the room, but Jamie was still sitting beside her. Hugh was there too, sitting on the blanket chest at the foot of the bed. She looked about her with a feeling of deep comfort, and less pain. She wagged her ankle experimentally. The sharp pain seemed more dull; it was still there in abundance, but the edge was gone.

"Are you feeling in better spirits?" Hugh asked.

She nodded. "A little." She looked at him. "Did Jamie tell me something about horses? Something about memorizing horses?"

Hugh laughed. "You have hit on it. Lord Byford told me that as long as I am about Byford, I should continue my masquerade. And he seems to think I will not quit the place until you are gone." He paused to reflect. "He could be right."

He stood up. "I think he is a bit smitten with Angela too, if you want the truth. And even your guardian angel here. Come, Jamie, Tildy told us to scatter when Omega woke up."

Tildy entered the bedroom with sheets draped over her arm and summoned Hugh back. "Please, miss, could Hugh pick you up while I change your sheets?"

Omega nodded and held up her arms for Hugh, who picked her up carefully, wincing when she winced, and sat with her in the chair. Tildy was just tucking in the blankets again when Angela bounded up the stairs, followed by Matthew.

Why she felt shy as she rested against Hugh's chest, Omega couldn't have said. Something in Matthew's face made her blush. Whatever it was she saw there was quickly gone. Matthew motioned to Angela, and when she came close, whispered in her ear. The girl glanced at Omega, covered her mouth with her hand to stop the laughter that bubbled in her, and darted down the hall.

"What is it all about?" Omega asked Matthew when he seemed not disposed to offer any information outright.

He shrugged. "You will have to wait until she returns. Jamie, we have purchased a large bottle of scent which will probably keep Miss Chartley reeking of lavender until she is in her dotage."

"Matthew!" declared Omega in her best teacher's voice. "You are an outrage at times, you know."

His returning smile was genuine. "You used to say that. My dear, it is nice to hear it again. And now, Hugh, if your arm is tired, I will relieve you of Miss Chartley."

Hugh shook his head. "I carried far heavier burdens over the Pyrenees Mountains, my lord."

"That strikes me as a dubious compliment," said Omega. "But really, Hugh, I do not wish to tax you."

He shook his head. "It is a small matter, and look, Tildy is finished."

He set her carefully down in bed again. Tildy straightened the covers as Angela pranced into the room again.

"Angela!" exclaimed Omega, and clapped her hands. "How magnificent you look!"

Angela stepped forward, her hands on her hips like a Gypsy dancer, and twirled around at the side of the bed. Her dress was deep blue Egyptian cotton, with a row of bone-white buttons that marched in file down the front from neck to ankle. It was simple and serviceable. The light that shone in Angela's eyes told Omega that it was much more.

The girl executed one more twirl and flopped against the bed. "Oh, think, Omega, this one is almost new! I was going to ask the woman at the booth if it belonged to someone who had died, but Lord Byford told me that would be rag-mannered. See, it has not been cut down." She leaned closer and Omega took her hands. "And do you know, Lord Byford bought me another one, a green one! And that is not all. I have two petticoats on, Omega. And other things . . ."

Angela flashed her magnificent smile at Matthew, who had pulled up a stool next to the chair Hugh sat in. "Lord Byford, I've never had *those* other things before."

"Angela, spare my blushes," he murmured. When Angela stood up again, he winked at Omega.

"Angela, you are a lucky girl," Hugh said.

She was serious then, touching the folds of the dress, gathering them to her, stroking the fabric as if it were a living thing. "The lady said the dresses were taken apart at the seams, washed, and sewn together again. I did not have to check for lice! *Mira*, Hugh, I never suspected England would be like this."

"Nor did I," the ex-soldier said softly, the same wonder in his voice as in Angela's.

"Miss Chartley, there is a cloak too, and a bonnet, and even shoes, which *no one* has ever worn before. But I will save those," Angela added. "The shoes are too beautiful to wear."

"Don't be a goose, Angela," said Matthew. "If you save the shoes, you will outgrow them and they will never fit you."

Tears stood in Angela's eyes then, as if suddenly the excitement was too much. She burst into noisy sobs. Jamie snorted and made a face, muttering something about Angela not being any more fun now that she had dresses.

Omega yearned to pull Angela close to her, but before she could act, Matthew gathered Angela to him and set her on his lap. She sobbed into his jacket while she rested her head on his chest and he toyed with her black curls.

"Angela, between you and Omega, I'll not have a single coat without watermarks. Hush, child." He looked over her head to Hugh. "Every soldier deserves some reward, and this is yours, Angela. I only wish they were new clothes." He winked at Omega. "However do parents manage without a seamstress on permanent duty? This abominable brat will grow too fast."

Angela cried a moment more, and then her tears vanished as quickly as they had come. She pulled herself away from Matthew, looked at him for a tiny moment, and then kissed his cheek before hopping off his lap and hurrying from the room.

It was Matthew's turn to struggle within himself for a moment. Omega had the good grace to look away and invite Jamie to open his parcel, which he did, sitting cross-legged at the foot of her bed.

"Omega, this is famous!" he exclaimed. "I have never had clothes like these! A person could really *do* something in these clothes!" He pulled out ordinary working clothes from the brown paper, shaking out the shirt of heavy cotton and pants of nankeen. "I could climb trees in these," he declared, and spoke to Omega confidentially. "Lord Rotherford used to tell me that I must always set a good example for the lower orders."

"There is scarcely anything more tiring than being a paragon," said Matthew, his voice controlled again. "I expect to see you in a tree before nightfall. Only please, I beg, do not break your arm. I am certain the doctor already thinks we are raving lunatics."

Omega noted with some gratification his use of the word "we." Almost as if he were a part of this, she thought, noting how happy he seemed at that moment and how young it made him look, how like the man she'd fallen in love with years ago.

"And what, pray, are you smiling at, Miss Chartley?" Matthew asked.

She said nothing, but succeeded in annoying herself by blushing fiery red. Hugh laughed and got to his feet. "I always leave the room when women blush like that," he said as he went to the door, motioning Jamie to follow.

Matthew had the diplomacy not to say anything else right away. In her confusion, Omega wished he would follow Hugh, but he moved from the stool to the chair and pushed the door closed with his foot.

"I saw Timothy Platter again." He shook his head. "We both took each other's measure, nodded, and walked on. How strange."

Omega forgot her embarrassment. "Matthew, what are we to do?"

Lord Byford spread his hands out in front of him. "I have no legal power to keep Jamie . . . Now, don't interrupt me, Omega! Don't rip up at me! How can I think when you nag? I shall have to think of something. I am tired of being such a coward."

He left the room before she could say anything else. She watched him go, mentally kicking herself, wondering at what point in the last eight years she had ceased being a young lady of gentle manner and had become a nag and scold. She berated herself until she was thoroughly out of sorts, and until there was nothing to do but sleep, and resolve to do better at their next meeting.

As dinnertime approached, she woke and began to feel frightfully ill-used. She also discovered how hungry she was. Delightful odors were drifting up from the dining room. She imagined everyone sitting around the table laughing and joking, and she longed to be part of it.

How many years have I sat wallowing in my own company? she thought. How many meals have I eaten, book in hand, moving food from fork to mouth, finding no pleasure beyond the thought that it was one less meal to contend with? She stirred restlessly. It would never do to think of such things, those things she had so resolutely put out of her mind, but she lay there and remembered evenings around the table with Alpha and her father, and later Matthew, talking and laughing until they were all a little silly.

Omega stretched out her foot tentatively. It throbbed, but some of the pain was gone. "It will be different in Durham," she said out loud. "I will seek out the other teachers." Her former teacher would be there for advice and company, too. And surely there would be pupils about Angela's age who would care to spend an evening discussing good books and great ideas. "And if they should chance to ask about me," she said softly, "I will tell them, and not hide within myself anymore, wasting my time wondering what they are thinking. So much time I have wasted."

She heard Matthew's step in the hall then, and put her hand to her hair, patting the odd curls under her cap. He opened the door without knocking, and brought in her dinner tray, which he set on her lap.

"Antoine told me to hurry up with this."

She looked at him in surprise. "Your chef orders you about?"

He nodded. "Of course. And I pay him outrageously. But the results, madam, the results."

She was hungrier than she thought, eating quickly as Matthew watched. He made only one comment as she worked her way through the delicious dinner. "Antoine told me to pay close attention to what you did not eat, and he would try to remedy your paltry appetite tomorrow. I have the happy task to inform him that the only thing you did not eat was the gold border around the plate. I am sure he will try to correct that oversight."

Omega laughed and waved him away. He sat back with a smile on his face and closed his eyes, his hands folded across his stomach. When she finished, he took the tray from her and set it outside in the hall.

She expected him to leave then, but he did not. "Let me tell you something curious about this whole nasty business, Omega. I haven't ever really considered it before, mainly because I did not want to—as you can well imagine. But now that Jamie is here . . . well, I must speak of it."

"Are you sure you want to talk about it?"

He nodded. "Positive. Omega, I have never spoken to anyone about this matter before. It seems easier, now that you know. Do you recall that I told you four of my best friends were present at that . . . that party?"

"Yes." Omega's eyes were on his face.

"Three of them are dead now, and one I have not heard from in years. I fear that he is dead too. Don't you see, there's no one alive to relate any of the events of that night. I have only Rotherford's word for what happened."

He leaned forward and looked her straight in the eyes.

"I am beginning to wonder if I am part of a huge blackmail, Omega." He paused to let that disclosure sink in.

"But . . . but, Matthew, why would Rotherford do this to you? Did he dislike you? Did he want to destroy my happiness too? I don't even know him."

Matthew sighed. "He doesn't hate me and he didn't know you. But the thing I have not considered before—before you and your entourage barged in on me—is Jamie . . . Jamie and his fortune."

"I don't understand," said Omega.

"Then I shall tell you. Play devil's advocate, my dear." He took off his shoes and propped his feet on the bed. "My friend Colonel Merrill Watt-Lyon, Lord Mansfield, was at the party, and he died in Spain during the Peninsular campaign."

"Matthew, that is war," she said.

"Ah, but he did not die in battle. His troops found him and his horse at the bottom of a ravine outside Ronda. Word got about that he had been drinking, but Merrill seldom drank. Liquor made him sick. I remember how sick he was that night."

"Friend number one," murmured Omega.

"Friend number two was David Larchstone. I believe you remember him?"

She nodded. "He was the first person I ever danced with at Almack's."

"And let me tell you, that was only because he got in front of me and had no scruples about loping across the ballroom floor!" said Matthew with a smile. "I had a certain reputation to maintain then. Dashed if I can remember why, now."

"And is he dead?"

Matthew nodded. "About six months after Merrill. He was a bruising rider after hounds. He went to take a fence that his horse could not jump. It didn't yield when he struck it, and he died after a day and night of the most acute agony."

"Dear God," said Omega. "But it was a hunting accident, was it not?"

"The top rail on the fence—a fence he had jumped many times—had been raised and nailed quite firmly into place. There was no way he could have avoided what happened. I learned these particulars from the solicitor whom our families share." Matthew started to reach for her hand, and then thought better of it. "I remember wondering at the time who could have had a grudge against that charming scapegrace. And then there is my brother-in-law, Marchant Clevenden, Lord Rotherford's younger brother and husband to my sister Diantha."

"I knew so little of him," said Omega. "Was he not in business with the East India Company?"

"He was. What you probably did not know—because goodness knows, such things never seemed to interest you—March was a very wealthy man. He took to Indian trade and intrigue like a duck to water. He amassed a magnificent fortune." Matthew chuckled. "It makes mine look like I'm only a stagger away from the workhouse. Lord, but that man had a talent for raking in the ready! It used to send Diantha into whoops when she considered how Rotherford sneered at his little brother's 'smell of the shop.' "

Omega sighed and rubbed her arms.

"I am tiring you," Matthew said.

Omega shook her head. "I am cold."

Matthew got up and pulled the blanket up from the foot of the bed until it was arranged comfortably around her. He sat down again and put his feet under the edge of the blanket. "I am cold too. I am also frightened. Omega, March and Di were visiting the Clevenden estate in Somerset about five years ago when their carriage tipped them into the ocean. They drowned."

Omega opened her eyes wide. "I never knew. And what of Jamie?"

"He was supposed to have been with them, but at the last moment Di left him behind at the house because he was napping. The fortune is his." Matthew looked away from her. "And the guardianship fell to Rotherford, as somehow I think he had known it would. Do you see what has happened?"

He was looking at her so earnestly then, his eyes searching deep into hers, almost pleading with her to understand.

"Is Rotherford an improvident man?" she asked slowly, feeling her way through this puzzle.

"Yes, or that is the rumor. Again, my source is my solicitor, who keeps me well-informed." Matthew clapped his hands together in frustration. "I would give my whole stable right now to find out if Rotherford has been dipping into Jamie's trust. But I was never included in any dealings regarding Jamie's guardianship."

And then Omega understood clearly. "And he knew you would never contest his guardianship. Oh, God, Matthew, you owed him his neat little wrapping-up of that dreadful evening's work!"

"Exactly, or so I am beginning to believe. And to think I was so grateful to him for protecting me in that mess!" he said bitterly.

"Don't berate yourself, my dear," Omega said.

He looked at her quickly then, but made no remark on her address. "For all that I have behaved stupidly, I am no fool, Omega. All the witnesses to whatever happened that night are dead, or at least far away. If I were to make any motion to challenge his guardianship—Clevenden left no will—Rotherford would have trussed me like a Christmas goose and delivered me to the hangman. He *knew* I would say nothing."

"But, Matthew, that would mean he has been planning this for . . . for years!"

Matthew took her by the hand. "Yes, it does, doesn't it?" He shook his head. "Rotherford has one virtue that I used to admire. He is a patient man. You should see him with his horses, how he trains them carefully and slowly. He would think nothing of patiently weaving a web of this kind."

"Is it possible?"

"Yes, indeed, my dear. Time was on his side. He knew I would do nothing. At some point in this dirty business he examined my faulty character and *planned* it that way."

Omega shook her head. "It is hard to imagine that

someone would be so cold-blooded. I cannot take it in."

"Well, my dear. I can understand how you would feel that way. You have no guile. You never in your deepest nightmares could have imagined that anyone would leave you standing in the church, exposed to the ridicule of the world, did you? So how are you to believe this?"

He was silent then. Omega scooted herself to the edge of her bed and leaned against his arm. He started, and then looked at her in surprise. "Omega, my dear, I obviously do not understand women. I tell you this terrible story, and you only seek to give me comfort."

He did not touch her, but he did not move away either. Omega put her arm through his. "Matthew, don't you think you have berated yourself enough in the past eight years? I know that I have scolded and railed against fate and excoriated myself until I am sick of it."

Matthew stirred himself and put his hand over hers again for a brief moment before he moved farther away from her. "One thing remains for us to do, my dear. I had better locate Timothy Platter. Do you think . . . could we possibly ask him to help us?"

10

Matthew did not bring her breakfast in the morning. It came direct from the kitchen in the hands of Antoine, who was followed by his interpreter, Angela. After Angela tucked a napkin in the top of Omega's gown, Antoine set down the tray with a flourish, exposing several ladylike slivers of Yorkshire ham, crepes nestled in raspberry sauce and topped with a spoonful of clotted cream. There was tea in the pot, and a small basket of pastries.

"Antoine, *magnifique*!" she exclaimed, exhausting her French.

Antoine beamed and dabbed at the corners of his eyes.

He spoke rapidly to Angela and then folded his arms.

"I am to tell you that if there is any little morsel that he can create for you, he will be so grateful," Angela said. "He begs to tell you that he will prepare a small restorative to be eaten around ten o'clock."

"Oh, tell him that will not be necessary," Omega replied, her eyes on the crepes.

"I cannot do that!" Angela protested. "It will wound his feelings. He is so dreadfully sensitive, and besides, Jamie and I will eat the goodies at ten o'clock."

"Very well then, dear," Omega said, "although I do not believe for a moment that you are being a martyr."

After staying long enough to watch Omega eat one of his crepes, Antoine dabbed at his eyes again and left the room, overcome with strong feeling.

"You have made him the happiest Frenchman in England," said Angela.

The dignified Miss Chartley snorted and poured herself some tea. "That is a whisker, Angela! Only wait until I cross him on some issue about dinner or luncheon. Then he will rain rapid French down on my head until we are all quite weary."

She finished the crepes. "Tell me, what of Lord Byford? Is he about yet?"

"Oh, long since. He took Hugh with him into the garden and they walked about for some time and talked. And then Lord Byford walked into Byford by himself. I do not know what it is about. I teased and teased Hugh, but he would not tell me."

Omega sipped her tea. So now Hugh Owen is acquainted with the whole sad story. She sighed. It is better so, she thought, even as she colored faintly with embarrassment for Matthew.

Jamie came into her room dressed in his new clothes. He said hello politely and paused only long enough to claim Angela. "She has promised to teach me to trap rabbits, Omega. Besides," he added, looking darts at Angela, "didn't Uncle Matthew make us both take an oath not to disturb Miss Chartley?"

"I was merely telling her the news," answered Angela

with great dignity. She collected Omega's tray and suffered Jamie to tow her toward the door. "Boys have no sense about anything."

When they were gone, Omega pulled back the bedcovers and swung her legs over the edge of the bed. Her ankle was still puffy and angry-looking, but she could tell that much of the swelling had subsided. I wonder if I could stand on it? she thought, even as she grabbed the bedstead and pulled herself to her feet. She was reaching for the chair, with her eyes on the dressing table across the room, when Tildy came in, shrieked, and hurried to her side.

"Miss Chartley! Oh, should you be doing this?"

"Yes," said Miss Chartley through gritted teeth. "Help me to the dressing table. Be a good girl, Tildy."

Tildy shook her head in vast disapproval, but took Omega by the elbow and steered her to the dressing table. Omega surveyed herself in the mirror. "Do you know," she said in shocked surprise, "I really *do* look green when I am pale."

Her hair was wild about her head, reminding her of Medusa, but it was nothing compared to her pallor. "Tildy, Miss Haversham, the headmistress at my last school, used to tell the pupils that fragile women were 'interesting.' That is a great hum. It's hard to believe that I could go downhill so rapidly."

"Now, Miss Chartley," said Tildy, "let me brush your hair for a minute. A bath would do you wonders too. And then, when you are done, you can sit in the chair by the window and look 'interesting.' " Tildy giggled and reached for the hairbrush.

Tildy's recommendations were all accomplished by noon. Her hair neatly composed under another lace cap, and wearing a fresh nightgown and robe, Omega sat by the window, her foot propped on a stool. She seldom sat without something to do, but it was pleasant to feel the warmth of the noonday sun on her face, with no thought of a task that needed to be done. I could grow used to such indolence, she thought. Tildy had turned down the covers on the bed and fluffed the pillows, "for when you feel like a nap, Miss Chartley."

Miss Chartley felt like looking out the window, listening to the birds and the faint sounds of cow bells in distant fields. Until she was surrounded by the peace of Byford, she hadn't been aware of Plymouth's noise. For eight years she had accepted the racket of the busy seaport, listening with resignation to the sounds from the docks, the screechings of the fishmongers as they exhorted their customers block by block, the gruff talk of sailors, and over all, the deep sounds of harbor bells.

There was none of that here in Byford, only a blissful sort of quiet that was more restful than a hundred naps. She hoped that Durham would prove like this, even as her heart told her that it could never be as special as Byford, and her head reminded her that she was leaving as soon as she could.

Omega was dozing in the chair when she heard voices in the hall. Tildy was talking to Matthew. Omega answered, "Come in, Matthew," to the firm knock on the door.

He stuck his head in. "Ha! I told you she would see me!"

Tildy pursed her lips and stepped aside. "My lord, she needs her rest."

Omega started to rise from the chair. Matthew hurried across the room and picked her up, depositing her on the bed. She put her hands on his chest. "Matthew, I think I would rather be downstairs."

"In a moment," he said. "Tildy, I'll carry her down to the parlor in a moment, if you will arrange the pillows on the sofa."

Matthew turned back to Omega, looking at her ankle carefully, comparing it with the other one, and then nodding. "The doctor was right, Omega," he said as he spread the blanket over her. "It looks better." He leaned close to her hair and sniffed. "And you smell of lavender. As Jamie would probably say, 'This is famous!' "

She smiled and looked at him in turn. "Your eye, Matthew. My goodness."

He bowed. "Yes, I have reached that dreadful green-and-yellow stage. Whereas you, my dear, may languish and appear mysterious, I look as though I keep low company." He grinned. "Come to think of it, perhaps I do."

But that was not what he had come to say. "Setting all this aside, I must tell you that I have searched for Mr. Timothy Platter and he is nowhere to be seen."

"This is vexing," she said. "Do you suppose . . . could he have returned to Lord Rotherford's estate with his intellligence?"

"He could have."

"Where is his estate?"

"Somerset, near Taunton. I believe that Platter is still about, but don't ask me why. I just don't think he would have left the area, especially as we are closer to London, where Mr. Platter will surely be repairing soon."

"You don't think he would spirit Jamie away, do you?"

"There is that possibility. I will set a strong watch about the house. Still, I expect we will hear from Mr. Platter when he feels the time is right." Matthew rubbed his hands together. "Let us hope it is soon."

He carried her down to the parlor, admonishing her to hold tight to his neck. "For if I should stumble on the stairs, my dear, neither of us will be fit for a midden. I am already convinced that Jamie and Angela consider us two of the most decrepit people of their acquaintance."

The sofa was ready for her, with pillows to prop her back and a basin of cool water and epsom salt for her foot. Tildy was there with her mending; Twinings came to bring up roses for the vase at her side and to assure her that her time was his, should she need any assistance. Jamie raced through with another snared rabbit ("Omega! This is famous! *I* snared it!"), and Angela followed more sedately, pausing to ask Omega how she did. Soon Antoine ascended from the kitchen bearing a pot of tea and yet another French pastry for Omega's weakened constitution. Hugh wandered by with several drawings of horses and a distracted look on his face.

Matthew watched the stream of people through his parlor with a combination of exasperation and amusement. "Before your precipitate arrival, I could have sat here all day and never seen another living soul," he said. "Now, Omega, if I want a private word with you, I will have to fill out a card and wait my turn, just like an Assembly Room ball!"

His tone was censorious enough, but the effect was mitigated when he grabbed Angela around the middle as she drifted about and set her on his lap.

"I am too old to sit on your lap, my lord," she said gravely.

"I think not. I will release you on one condition: that you go upstairs and see what is on your bed."

She leapt off his lap and ran up the stairs. The next sound was a scream of delight, and then loud crying.

"My God," said Omega, "what have you done?"

"Do you suppose that Spanish females carry on in such fashion whenever they are overcome with emotion?" he murmured. "It's a wonder Beau Wellington did not wash his hands of the whole Peninsula."

"And what have you done, Matthew?" she asked again.

"A small thing. I also bought some muslin at the Templeton fair yesterday, and promised one of our local seamstresses a ridiculous stipend if she would make a dress from it by this morning. You know, a church dress, a fancy dress." He looked at her for a reaction. "Do you know, Omega, I like the way your dimple shows, even when you are trying to be stern with me. Ah, there it is!"

"You are so good to Angela."

"It is purely selfish, Miss Chartley." He took her hand and raised it to his lips. "You resist taking a loan from me so you can get on your way to Durham. I shall spoil Angela out of spite . . . and also because I have become fond of both children." He rose and went to the window. "Almost as if they were my own."

She could think of nothing to say, and was spared comment when Hugh came through again, and Angela, red-eyed and smiling, came downstairs and threw herself into the viscount's arms. He hugged her. "Just tell me one thing, Angela: are you happy?"

She nodded and burst into tears all over again. Matthew threw back his head and laughed. "Is she always this way, Hugh?"

Hugh grinned. "I wouldn't know, my lord. Up to now she has been content with one meal a day—on a good day—and a castoff dress. You've probably ruined her forever. How can we leave this place?"

Matthew rested his arm on Angela's shoulder. "Perhaps you will not have to, Hugh. When this . . . this issue is settled, perhaps there will be occasion for another discussion."

By the time Matthew carried her upstairs that evening, Omega Chartley was ready to go. How a healthy woman could become so tired from sitting in a comfortable parlor and doing nothing was a thing she did not understand. She wanted only to sleep now, to sleep and not worry about the disturbing past, her uneasy present, and her uncertain future. She would try to walk in the morning, try to be of some use in the household where she was treated with such kindness.

"Can I do something else for you?" Matthew asked after he blew out the candle by the bedside and arranged the blankets on her legs again.

You could love me, she thought. Even if you thought you could not, you could try.

"No. I am fine. Matthew, thank you again for all you are doing for us. I know I am such an imposition. As soon . . . as soon as I am able, I'll accept your offer of a loan and be on my way to Durham."

"Suppose I should withdraw my offer?" he teased, his eyes on her face in the dark.

"Then I will apply to Angela to instruct me in the art of snaring rabbits and catching fish, and I'll be on my way in any case," she said calmly, wishing that he did not look so good to her, even with his eye decorated in moldering shades of green and his nose slightly swollen. Did he have to wear that marvelous lemon cologne? Why did he not wear bay rum, like other men? What a nuisance he was. How much she would miss him.

He touched her face. "And will you think of me occasionally when you are grading papers and listening to recitations?"

"I will not, my lord," she said firmly. "I shall

concentrate fully on my duties, and have time to wool-gather only during vacations and holidays."

He smiled. "Well, spare me a thought, then. And now, good night. Call me if you need me."

Omega fell asleep promptly and slept soundly all night, paying no heed to the creakings of the old house as it settled itself, and ignoring the cats orchestrating by the back wall of the garden.

In that period of dawn just as the light was beginning to stream in the window, she opened her eyes, suddenly alert. Nothing discernible woke her; it was just a feeling, a feeling that she was sharing the room with someone else. Her heart leapt to her throat as she opened her eyes and slowly turned her head toward the window.

At first she could see nothing, but she waited and watched and her vision cleared. The curtains rustled. As she watched them, a man threw his leg over the windowsill. She opened her eyes wider and held her breath as the man straddled the windowsill and just sat there, as if wondering what to do.

That he had come recently from the flower garden was amply clear to her; his coat was sprinkled with pollen. A pair of morning glories from the climbing vine outside her window had caught on his pocket, a dapper, if somewhat unlikely, buttonhole flower.

Omega raised herself on her elbows, careful not to make a sound, and regarded the intruder with more amazement than fear. His face was still in shadow and she could not make out any features, but there was something deliciously funny about her unexpected guest. I should name him Floribunda, she thought, or perhaps Glory. She opened her mouth to scream, mainly because it seemed like the thing to do.

Before she could scream, the flowery man in the shadows reared back his head suddenly, "Ah . . . ah . . . choo!"

His sneeze was so powerful it seemed to circulate around the room, making the air vibrate. He sneezed again and again, even as he tried to brush the offending pollen off his coat.

This was a mistake. He lost his balance and fell out of the window, maintaining a tenuous grip on the sill even as he sneezed and cursed and beat with his feet against the side of the house.

Omega lay back and surrendered herself to laughter. "Matthew!" she gasped. "You'd better come in here. Matthew!"

Even before she had finished shouting, the door slammed open and Matthew stood there, clad in his nightshirt, pistol in hand. "Good God, what is that caterwauling?" he asked, and then stared at her as she sat up and clutched at her ankle.

"Oh, it hurts when I laugh! Matthew, you must help that . . . that man at the window!"

Openmouthed, Matthew dropped the pistol on the bed and ran to the window, leaning out. "Oh, hold on." He peered closer. "I do believe you are Timothy Platter, are you not? Pleased to meet you, sir. Perhaps we should shake!"

Omega's laughter gave way to occasional hiccups as Matthew grabbed the Bow Street Runner by the pants and the back of his coat and hoisted him in the window. The morning glories were wrapped around Mr. Platter's ear by now, and Omega decided that he looked quite lovely.

He sat down with a thump inside the window, gazing about him with a dazed expression. Matthew held his hand out in front of him. "Don't move. Don't even think about moving. I'm going to get my pants on. Omega, point this pistol at him if—and only if—you think you can collect yourself enough to be useful."

She took the pistol from him, trying not to smile, and failing miserably. Matthew glanced down at his exposed legs and snatched the blanket off the end of the bed. "I'll have you know that in some circles these are considered quite shapely," he snapped. "You need only ask Gentleman Jackson or any number of my fellow inmates at Oxford!"

He exited with as much dignity as he could muster, returning moments later stuffing his shirt into his pants. He leveled a withering glance at her that did nothing to foster her sobriety, and pointedly turned his back to her as he hauled Timothy Platter to his feet.

"And now, you will explain yourself!" he said as he pushed Mr. Platter into a chair.

Mr. Platter removed the flowery vines from about his ear and muttered something about "bleeding roses." Matthew winced. "Sir, remember yourself," he ordered, looking with no sympathy on Platter.

"You see, Lord Byford, if that is who you claim to be, I thought I was in your room. I climbed the trellis."

The viscount sat down on Omega's bed. "I have a front door, Mr. Platter. At least I did the last time I checked."

"Happens you do, sir, but I am no flat. Timothy Platter's mam raised no half-wits."

"Words do not express how relieved I am to hear that. Pray continue," said the viscount. "It is early, and I fail to see the connection between your mother and my front door."

"Do you know that your place is devilish well-guarded?"

Matthew nodded, a trace of a smile on his face.

"I thought I would try the window."

"I am incredulous. Is this something new in law enforcement?"

Platter took exception to Matthew's tone. "Sir, when a gentry mort searches the pubs and scatters about messages that he wishes my presence, I get leery."

"So you thought the window would be best."

"I did. I thought this was your room."

"As you can see, it is not." Matthew glanced at Omega, who had regained her composure. "If this room were occupied by anyone less . . . shall we say . . . lively of mind than Miss Chartley, you would probably be pitched on your head by now."

"I like that," said the lively Miss Chartley.

"I thought it was your room," the Runner insisted. "I stayed in the flowers until the guard went away, and then I climbed up, and there *you* were, sitting in this very chair! It was dark, but I could see your face."

Omega stirred. "Matthew, what are you up to?"

"That's what I'd like to know," declared Timothy Platter virtuously.

"I come in here every night to make sure you are well," he said softly.

"But you sat and sat!" said Platter in triumph. "And so I thought this was your room. An honest mistake, gov'nor."

"I must have fallen asleep," Matthew suggested, more for Omega's benefit than the Runner's.

"Your peepers was wide open, my lord. I watched you. I couldn't make a move in the window however, because that guard came back." Platter attempted a diversion. "Your guards would have been the first to drop at Waterloo, sir."

The tactic failed because Matthew ignored it. "In future dealings, Mr. Platter, if we are so blessed, be assured that you may approach my front door with temerity."

The men eyed each other. "And now I am here, my lord. Where is your nephew?"

The men eyed each other for a moment in a room filled with silence. "It must be the early hour that troubles me again, Mr. Platter," said Matthew slowly. "I cannot understand the connection between my nephew and your ante-dawn climb. Is there one?"

Platter said nothing for a moment. Omega watched his face grow redder and redder. When she thought that he would burst, he pointed a finger at Matthew. "Don't bait me! Don't be calm and well-bred!" When Matthew said nothing, he turned his attention to Omega. "And you! It was you who nabbed Jamie out from under my reach, right when I had him. Don't give me that wide-eyed missish look," he shouted. "You know where he is, and it's my commission to find him and restore him to his uncle."

"You'll have to do better than that!" snapped Omega. "If you think I would willingly turn over a child to an ogre who beats him, then you've got windmills in your head!"

"Speaking of my head," Platter snapped back, "I'd give more than a shilling to know what you spiked me with."

"A paperweight," she hissed, "and I'd do it again in a minute."

"I could ruin you," he said, his voice quieter. "You gentry morts may not think we Runners are much, but I could ruin you."

"I have already been ruined, sir," she replied, her voice matching his. "I haven't a thing to lose by defending James Clevenden."

"Here, here, now," interjected Matthew. "You don't need to mill each other down." He looked at Omega first. "My dear, pull your claws in. The boy is in no immediate danger." He turned to Timothy Platter. "Yes, my nephew is here, and here he will remain until I am absolutely satisfied about his welfare. If this disturbs Lord Rotherford, he can come and tell me himself."

"He'll likely do that, my lord. I have already sent for him."

Omega sucked in her breath. She knew it was unreasonable to hope that Platter would not fulfill his commission, but she had hoped that he would wait a bit.

There was silence in the room again, broken at last by Matthew. "Would you believe me if I told you that you have made a terrible mistake?" he said quietly.

Platter passed a hand in front of his face. "I might believe anything, my lord. You can't imagine what a summer this has been. My boss, he told me, 'Tim,' he says, 'this will be a regular holiday for you. A chance to breathe the air of the country again.' " Platter sighed and shook his head. "Like a gull, a real flat, I believed him. And what have I done except get sacked by an ostler's yard boy, clobbered by a paperweight and nearly drowned, and . . . and generally just been discommoded."

"At least you still have your clothes," Omega began.

"Omega, please!" said Matthew.

She allowed him to wave her into silence, but sat, arms folded, lips tight, in grumpy silence.

Matthew regarded her a moment, as if to assure himself that she would behave. "Setting all this aside, Mr. Platter, I would like to accompany you to London. I have a matter of business that might interest you. I hope that it will explain some of our reluctance to release Jamie to his other uncle."

"Anyone can travel on the common stage," said Platter, not about to be placated by Matthew's gentler tone. He looked pointedly at Omega. "I *had* a horse, but it departed my company when I found myself floating downstream."

Omega opened her mouth, but Matthew glared at her. She closed it.

"You have my word—and Miss Chartley's word—Oh, yes, Miss Chartley—that Jamie will remain here," said Matthew. "I will happily provide you with one of the mounts from my own stable, and we—"

"I can't be bought," interrupted Platter.

"I'm not buying," said Matthew evenly. "When we get to London, I expect my horse back. I need to acquaint you with a story that might arouse your interest, particularly if you denizens of Bow Street have a file of unsolved murders. I must engage your services, Mr. Platter."

"I'll consider it," said Platter. "But no promises, do you hear?"

Matthew clapped his hands together. "Excellent. That means that I will likely not be required to engage in a bit of real unpleasantness and have the constable incarcerate you for breaking and entering, coupled with possible attempt to do bodily harm to a female invalid."

Omega sputtered and Platter fumed.

Matthew smiled at the Runner. "Our constabulary here is so efficient. I could have an officer of the law here in—could it be?—five or ten minutes."

The silence was heavy in the room again. Platter thoughtfully brushed the rest of the pollen off his coat. He sneezed several more times, and then slapped his knee. "Let's go. I've had all the peace and quiet of the country that I can stomach, my lord."

"I knew that you would understand, Mr. Platter," said Matthew, his voice filled with cordiality. "Let me show you to my stables." He winked at Omega before he left the room, his hand on the shoulder of the Bow Street Runner.

Matthew Bering and Timothy Platter did not even wait

until breakfast to leave. Two horses were saddled and ready to ride even before the children woke.

"It's better this way," said Matthew as he pulled on his gloves. While the impatient Mr. Platter waited in the hall below, Matthew had requested Hugh's presence in Omega's room. "Hugh, I would ask that you resume the role of Major Owen." He buttoned his glove. "Rotherford may be here before I get back from London. He's more likely to be intimidated by a major. My dear Omega, you must continue your role as housekeeper, I fear, and that means a return to the company belowstairs. Keep Jamie close by you."

"By all means." Omega held out her hand to him, and he took it. "But, Matthew, what are you going to do in London?"

"Something I have avoided for eight years," he replied grimly. "I am going to see what I can learn about what happened that night. It could be that I am innocent of all that Rotherford has led me to believe. It could also be that I am quite guilty." He sighed and sat down on Omega's bed. "And if that is the case, we'll have to devise another course of action for Jamie. Or, rather, I will," he amended. "At any rate, Omega, after you see this little masquerade out, you should be on your way to Durham soon enough, whatever the outcome."

"Yes," she agreed, keeping her voice steady. "I don't have much time left, do I?"

"Neither do I, likely," said Matthew. "Hugh, could you go below and see if there is anything Mr. Platter needs? I'll be right along."

When Hugh left the room, Matthew went to the window and stood there looking out at the flower garden, hands in pockets, rocking back and forth on his heels. "I have so enjoyed it here," he said at last. He turned around to face Omega. "Do they, as a rule, hang murderers who happen to be members of the peerage, or merely transport them?"

"Matthew, please!" she said, and held out her arms to him.

Without a word, he knelt by the bed and wrapped his arms around her. She hesitated only a moment, and then hugged him to her, resting her hand on the back of his neck, running her fingers against the nap of his hair. With an ache more immense than any pain she had felt in the last few days, Omega remembered that the last time she had fingered his hair was the night before her wedding, when she said good night to him.

He pulled himself away from her. "No one's done that for ever so long, Omega." His voice was strangely altered. "I can't tell you how good it feels."

She pulled him to her again, fiercely this time, as if she did not wish to let him go. "Matthew, be careful!" she whispered in his ear, and then kissed his cheek.

He sighed and gently disentangled himself from her embrace. "And even if I do win this one, my dear, dear Omega, it doesn't change anything between us. I wish that it could."

"Good-bye, Matthew," she whispered. "God watch you."

"And you, Omega."

11

The first few miles to London were covered in silence, neither man disposed to address the other. Matthew stole a glance at his traveling companion several times, the last time to find him staring back. Both men smiled. Matthew spoke first.

"I have become somewhat of a recluse in these past eight years, Mr. Platter," he apologized. "If I am silent, it is out of habit, and also because I am trying to work up my courage to acquaint you with this delicate subject. My dear sir, murder is hard to skate around."

Platter made a motion with his hand. "Murder, is it? Sir, I have probably heard all of these things before, so you may proceed whenever you feel like it. And by the way, this is a fine horse. What a pity that I cannot be bought."

Matthew laughed. "Yes, isn't it?" He sobered quickly. "Well, sir, lend an ear now. I seem to be making a habit out of telling my story in these past few days, but you are the first person who has the power to have me hanged because of it."

Riding along past the haying fields and the August harvest of the Cotswolds' bounty, Matthew Bering described the events of eight years ago, including every detail that would show him at his worst. He tried to keep his voice calm, but it was difficult. Many times he struggled and looked away, aware all over again of the magnitude of the crime committed, and acutely aware that he was confessing to an officer of the law. Matthew knew the road to London well, but he concentrated on keeping his eyes straight ahead on the highway before him, preferring not to see his crimes reflected in the face of the Bow Street Runner.

His hands shook and he tightened his grip on the reins as he told of that morning of his wedding when he woke up with the pale dead woman beside him. Matthew could not resist; he glanced quickly at Timothy Platter, and then found himself even more deeply disturbed. The Runner was struggling with emotions of his own. Platter was gnawing on his lower lip, even as he frowned. The very attitude of his body was tense. In response, his horse danced along, skittish and upset too.

The moment quickly passed, and Platter brought the horse to rights again. The Runner managed a tight smile. "My lord, for all that there is nothing new under the sun, this is interesting."

"That would not have been my choice of words, sir. You are kind," was Matthew's reply.

"No, I am not, sir," said Platter firmly, his own feelings submerged again. "Pray continue. I do not see the connection yet between you and Rotherford and the nephew you share in common. So far, your story does not fadge."

"I was sure it did not. Let us pause first, Mr. Platter," said Lord Byford with a sigh. "There is a tolerable inn ahead. They have a way of toasting cheese that is quite superior. My horses need a rest."

They dined in silence, Platter concentrating his thoughts upon the blank wall beyond his companion's shoulder, and Bering regarding his plate and wineglass as if he had never seen such utensils before. The viscount looked around occasionally at the others in the room, and couldn't help observing that the other diners were glancing his way in curiosity.

"We seem to be exciting some interest," he murmured finally to his fellow traveler.

"Runners seldom travel ordinary-like with toffs," said Mr. Platter as he reached for another slice of bread, which he tore in half and mortared together with apple butter. "I have a suggestion, my lord. If this village has a ready-made store, I would recommend that you visit it. We stand out like blackamoors in Glasgow."

The village, which boasted a large population of the farming society, indeed supported such a store. Nodding to his companion, Lord Byford visited it, returning to the innyard a short while later, his clothes in a bundle, clad now in shirt, trousers, and rough boots of a much-less-distinguished Englishman.

"I left my beaver hat with a somewhat mystified haywain driver. Will I do now, Mr. Platter?" he asked as he stuffed his other clothes into a saddlebag, and wondered what his tailor would think if he could see him.

"Decidedly," commented the Runner. "I should not be ashamed to travel with you now. My reputation, Lord Byford, my reputation."

Matthew looked at him sharply, and then caught the gleam in the Runner's eye. He bowed and managed a smile of his own. "Then, sir, pray let us continue. My horses have no more patience than their owner."

Matthew continued his story immediately they had left the village behind, wondering to himself for the thousandth time if the whole thing sounded false. Maybe it *was* foolish above half to suppose that Rotherford would have planned such an event with patience. Perhaps Omega was right; surely no one was so careful, so willing to wait.

He only wanted to believe it, only wanted to assure himself that he never could have killed someone.

Matthew finished and was silent, looking straight ahead again, not trusting even a glance at his companion, who sat in silence of his own.

"These friends of yours . . . all dead?" asked Platter finally. His question was spoken deliberately, as if he asked it in a court of law.

"For sure, only the three that I mentioned. The fourth one, Sir Horace Billings, I have not heard from since . . . since . . . I don't know . . . 1810 or 1811. I have written to him several times. The letters were neither returned nor answered."

"He could be alive."

"He could be. Horace never was one to take chances like the others. He was a bit of a priss and a dandy. He lives . . . or lived . . . in the wilds of Suffolk. 'A drafty castle, fit for Vikings,' or so he used to tell me."

The Runner considered this piece of intelligence, and sought another. "Was anyone else aware of the evening's events?"

Matthew shook his head, and then looked at Platter. "There was the landlord of the building. I remember him vaguely."

"Then we must find this set of rooms, Lord Byford, must we not?"

Matthew reined in his horse, turning it slightly to stop the Runner's also. "Then do you believe me?"

Platter would not look him in the eye. "Let us say that your story is intriguing, and I feel sorry for you, my lord."

The Runner raised his glance to Matthew for a second. Again there was that look in his eyes that had so disquieted the viscount earlier. Again it passed, leaving instead the calm and rather sour expression of a professional officer of the law.

"It's a discomfiting thought to be considered an object of pity," said Matthew finally.

"Go on, sir, finish your thought," said Platter, his voice rising slightly, and then lowering again to its professional tone. " 'An object of pity from one of my class.' " Platter sat straighter in the saddle. "But I do feel pity for you. More than your life alone has been affected. Other men may have died because of this. And there is a woman deeply hurt. And as a justice of the peace, you are aware of the laws of our land, my lord. It remains for you to prove yourself innocent. But I will say no more on that subject, my lord."

He was true to his word. Not another sentence was spoken during the rest of that long day. The silence greatly embarrassed Matthew at first, but then he grew used to it. He glanced occasionally at the Runner, and decided finally that the man was deep in thought. It would not have been polite to disturb him. Matthew's lively brain was fully occupied with his own predicament.

They reached the metropolis as the sun was setting. Neither man would admit fatigue to the other, but Matthew had watched Platter stand in his stirrups several times in the last few hours, as if weary of his seat.

The houses drew closer and closer together as the men rode in silence. Soon the houses were joined by stores and grog shops and the road grew even narrower. Smoke and fog of a most disagreeable consistency rolled down the street.

Platter took a deep breath and sighed. "It's good to be home," he said, breaking his great fast of silence. "London air."

Matthew took a whiff and wished himself immediately back in the country. "To each his own," he murmured.

Platter turned toward him with a faint look of surprise. "My lord, don't those early-morning birds ever drive you to Bedlam? Or the way it is so damned quiet the rest of the day? I wonder anyone can endure the country. Not this cove, any road."

Matthew smiled. "*This* lord's ways are mysterious, then, my good man. And perhaps since I am traveling incognito, it would be best if you were to call me Matthew."

"Certainly, my lord."

They continued deeper into the city down roads that

Matthew was unfamiliar with. It was a part of London he knew nothing of, for all that it teemed about him: people spilling into the noisome streets, beggars, maimed soldiers with begging bowls (he thought of Hugh Owen), and women, girls merely, standing on street corners leering at the men who passed, calling out to them. His face reddened and then he felt that familiar sickness in his stomach.

"Matthew?"

"Yes?"

"I was asking you, would you prefer to put up at your own establishment?"

"I have no house here. I sold it eight years ago." He looked down at his blue shirt, with the dark perspiration stains under the armpits. "And I do not think I would get past the doorman at Claridge's."

"Then come home with me, sir."

"Oh, I could not." Matthew noticed that look again in Platter's eyes. "And don't get your back up, man! I mean nothing other than it is not my wish to disturb your family. You need only recommend an inn."

"I'd like you to come to my lodgings, sir."

Matthew thought it over. "Very well, Timothy, I will." He paused, wondering how to frame his next question. "And . . . do you go to Bow Street first to make your report?"

Platter shook his head. "I do not. I think I have not finished this particular assignment. My master is a nitpicker. He likes everything tied in neat bundles. My report can wait a few days."

"Thank you."

They passed through another street and turned into an alley, which led into a warren of narrow houses, each more decrepit than the one before. They stopped at last before a building that Matthew knew he could never find again, even if he wrote down explicit directions. Platter dismounted stiffly and threw the reins to a young boy standing by. He bade Matthew to do the same.

Matthew did, but he looked at Platter with some

trepidation. "And will my horses still be here in the morning?" he asked in a low voice. "Not wishing to offer insult, but still, sir, I worry."

Timothy measured him with a long appraisal. "I would not have taken you for such a flat, my lord. Do you think the gulls in this alley will tinker with the mounts of a Bow Street Runner?"

"Of course they will not," agreed Matthew. "How foolish of me."

Stiff-legged, the men climbed the stairs, going past landing after landing, until they were near the top, lacking one. Matthew stood on the landing and clutched the banister, trying to regain some rhythm to his breathing. "Was there ever a truer indication of my rapid decline than the purgatory of that saddle, and now these stairs?"

Platter laughed. He went down the hallway and knocked on the door, listening as the bolt was thrown back. A woman not much older than Omega stuck her head out and broke into a smile. She took Timothy by the hand and pulled him into the room. She noticed Matthew then, and stepped back shyly.

"He can come in too, Maeve," said the Runner. "He won't bite."

"If you are sure." She opened the door wider. "But I must say, sir, that my Timothy has brought home all manner of strays in his career." Her voice had an Irish lilt that was altogether delightful.

Matthew wondered what Omega would say to such an address. He stepped inside. The room was small, but it was clean. A little boy, finger in mouth, stared at him and clutched at his mother's skirts. Over by the hearth, a baby lay in a cradle, contemplating, with the majesty of few months, the miracle of fingers.

Platter was watching him. "There are others of my calling who live much finer, Matthew. I believe I have already told you that I cannot be bought. We live well enough, and by God, my conscience allows me to sleep nights."

"I have come to expect nothing less of you, Mr. Platter," murmured the viscount. "My congratulations."

"And here are my wife, Maeve, and my children, Davey and Sarah," Platter said, his arm around his wife's waist. "Maeve, this is Matthew Bering. He will be staying with us a day or two."

She nodded, as if this were nothing new to her, and turned her attention back to the pot on the hook over the fire. Platter sniffed the air appreciatively. "Irish stew. Maeve, I am fair gut-foundered."

There were insufficient bowls for all of them to eat at once. Matthew and the lord of the house sat first at table, Davey on his father's knee, eating every other bite, as Maeve stood by the fireplace stirring the stew, holding the baby, and telling her husband in her pleasant brogue of the events of the neighborhood since his taking leave of it.

Platter nodded at the appropriate times and steadily ate his way through two bowls of stew. When Matthew finished, Maeve filled his bowl and stood by the fireplace eating out of it. Matthew took the baby from her and insisted that she sit down. He pulled the stool out for her, and she looked back in surprise.

Platter flashed him a warning look. "Not too fancy, Matthew, my friend. Think what attention Maeve will demand when you leave."

Matthew put the baby to his shoulder and let her rest her head in the curve of his neck. Her hair was brown and wild about her head. He sighed and thought of Omega as he fingered the curls.

When Maeve finished, she refilled the communal bowl with a little more stew for her son. Matthew watched as she helped him, and mentally resolved to order a whole set of crockery for the Platter household. His lips twitched. Wouldn't that be a surprise for Maeve? He wouldn't even tell her it was from Platter's latest "stray."

The baby fell asleep in his arms and he stood where he was, leaning against the wall, enjoying the pleasurable weight of the child, and the sudden knowledge that he would sleep well too, this night. He had told his tale; his fate was in the hands of this strange man. He could only surrender himself to the acceptance of the fact and enjoy the moment.

Bedtime came quickly, dictated by the sputtering of the tallow candle. "I could light another one," offered Maeve as she looked at her husband.

The Runner shook his head and put his arm around her, drawing her close. "No. Maeve, my dear, regard our guest there. He will fall on his face and black his other eye if he stays awake much longer."

"Am I that decrepit?" Matthew asked as he handed over the sleeping child to her mother. "Or do you merely want to look good, compared to me, Timothy?"

The Runner grinned. He pulled a pallet away from the wall and dragged it in front of the fireplace. "You'll find this soft as angel hair, my boy, and Davey will keep you excellent company."

Davy was too sleepy to object to his strange bedfellow. He allowed Matthew to help him into his nightshirt. After Maeve pinched out a candle, Matthew took off his pants and arranged himself on the pallet next to Davey, who hesitated only a moment before curling up next to him, sighing once or twice and surrendering to sleep. Matthew put his hands behind his head. The Runner and his wife retired to their bed on the other side of the room.

Breakfast was toast dipped in sweet hot tea and laced with cream. Maeve buttered each slice of thick-cut bread, humming to herself. The children were still asleep, so she sat with her hands folded in her lap, content to watch her husband as he ate.

"Mr. Bering, do you have a family?" It was the first question she had addressed to him.

He shook his head, touched by the look of real pity in her eyes. She gave him another piece of bread, and left more butter on it this time. Matthew took it with thanks and went to stand by the window, looking out on the dingy alley as Platter and his wife conversed in low tones. Gazing on the refuse-filled square far below, he reflected that it was a poor place to raise children, and wondered what he could do about it. He leaned against the windowsill. If he was unable to prove his innocence, he could always put a codicil in his will and provide Platter and his little ones with a place in the country. The thought was hardly comforting, even for a budding philanthropist.

At length Platter joined him at the window. "Well, sir, let us be off. We can reclaim our—your—horses and get a little closer to your part of London."

They rode carefully through streets already crowded with the commerce of a typical summer morning. Milkmaids and knife grinders competed with butchers and bakers as they shouted their wares to all about them, and screamed at the stingy.

The horses were left in a public stable off Piccadilly and the men continued on foot. The crowds were no less, but the quality of the people had changed. Instead of looking over his shoulder and staying closer to Platter, Matthew found the quality looking over their shoulders at him. Several women went out of their way to avoid him. He knew that he didn't smell good and that there was a day's beard on his face, but he smiled all the same. "Timothy, we do not precisely shine in the company of these men," he said.

The Runner snorted. "If you consider these fops and popinjays men, my lord."

"I did at one time," Matthew confessed. "I can't imagine why. I may even have looked like them."

Platter was silent a few more moments, and then he changed the subject. "Think, my lord. What do you recall of that evening?"

Matthew stopped in front of Eyestone's Bookstore and rested his back against the wall. He was hurried on his way by the proprietor, who stepped out of the door swinging a broom in front of him like a broadsword.

"I used to be his best customer," said Matthew. They walked a few paces. "I remember that we first went to Watier's, where I had another dinner—Omega had already fed me—and we played cards."

They reached the corner of Bolton and Piccadilly and stood in front of Watier's. Matthew looked about him. "We must have left after midnight. The air was cold and it hit me like a bucket of ice water. Ah, but you're not interested in that."

"Happens I am, my lord. Sometimes if you just walk backward in your mind, you think of things. What then?"

"We walked along to St. James Square," said Matthew, and turned in that direction, with the Runner following. "The house was on one of the streets off the square. Lord bless me if I can recall which one, but perhaps when we're standing in the square . . ."

They walked without conversation to the great square, where Matthew stood for a moment in silent contemplation. "Do you know, sir," he said at last, his voice soft, "I have not seen this square since that night. Sometimes in the years since, I have almost convinced myself that the whole thing was a bad dream." He looked at Platter. "Standing here again, I know it was not."

"Very well, sir, and what did you do then?"

Matthew shoved his hands in his pockets, a frown on his face. "It was the oddest thing . . . you will think this silly beyond measure, but my friend Merrill Watt-Lyon began to sing." He smiled. "What *was* it? Oh, I do remember! It was 'The British Grenadier,' only he had made up the most amazingly vulgar lyrics." Matthew glanced at the Runner again, and saw nothing but patience on that impatient man's face. "What made this something to remember was that he sang through four dreadful verses, and at the end of the fourth one, we were standing in front of the house."

The Runner nodded. "Then all we need to do is walk down this street humming the tune, and when we reach the end of the fourth verse, we will be there?"

"Something like that," agreed Matthew, "if I have not taken total leave of my senses. The trouble is, of course, that I am not sure which street. We shall have to try them all."

He looked about him and then pointed to Alistair Street. "That is as good a beginning as any other, Mr. Platter. Let us be off."

Humming to himself, Lord Byford strolled down the street, and came to a halt at the end of the second verse. The street was a dead end. Matthew stared before him at the stone wall covered with ivy that blocked his forward passage. "Obviously this is not the street. Come, my good man, let us do an about-face and try again."

They tried again and again, and nothing looked familiar, and nothing matched the song. "You're certain that it was St. James Square?" ventured Platter at last.

"Oh, yes, oh, yes," insisted Matthew, even as he felt the edge of doubt creep into his brain like a London fog.

"This is the last street then, my lord," said the Runner. His voice was matter-of-fact, but Matthew heard the beginnings of skepticism.

He shrugged off the gloom that threatened to settle over him and hummed his way down the street, looking about him intently, willing the house to appear, praying for some recognition, some lifting of that veil he had so deliberately drawn across the events of that night.

Nothing.

"Damn," he exclaimed when he came to the end of the fourth verse and no house materialized. They stood before a row of shops. Matthew couldn't bear to look at the Runner as they started back in silence toward the square again. Eyes to the pavement, he stepped off the curb and glanced idly down the alley, and stopped short.

He took hold of the Runner's arm. "I think I can do it now, sir," he said softly. "Let us return to the square and try this street again."

The Runner followed him without a word. Matthew hummed a little louder this time and stepped off the paces. When he reached the curb where the alley intersected, he turned instead of continuing straight ahead.

Matthew began the third verse. The alley was narrow, but well-tended, with a clean roadway. It was an ordinary shopkeepers' neighborhood.

The song ended. Matthew stopped and looked up. He had found the house. A shiver traveled down his back as if a cold wind had suddenly whipped through the alley. "This is not a place I wished ever to see again."

"You're certain this is it?"

"I'm certain."

They faced a long flight of stairs up to the front door. A

row of trash barrels, lids on straight, hugged the staircase wall. The shutters on the first floor were closed tight, but the windows higher up boasted window boxes filled to overflowing with petunias. The flowers formed the only bit of brightness on the building's facade. All else was dark stone, darkened further by the smoke of London's many fires. A curtain was drawn aside for a moment on one of the upper floors, and then brushed back again by an unseen hand.

The Runner looked inquiringly at Matthew. Matthew nodded. What he had not remembered, he remembered now: the many steps up to the door and the heavy brass knocker in the shape of a dolphin. He remembered with startling acuteness how Sir Horace Billings had picked up the dolphin's tail and knocked on the door, and then tittered about it.

And there it was again. He mounted the steps—wondering if this was how Louis XVI had felt when he climbed up to the guillotine—and knocked on the door. The Runner was close behind.

The door was opened a crack, and Matthew could just barely see into the long hall, dark with wainscoting. He saw two eyes, a nose, and a mouth, and little else against the darkness.

"I have no rooms to let."

"I am not here to rent a room, sir, but merely to ask for some information."

The door started to close in his face, except that Timothy Platter opened it wider and pushed his way into the hall. "See here!" sputtered the landlord, retreating to the stairwell.

Platter dug into his pocket for the small emblem all Runners carried. The man looked it over. "Close the door behind you," he said to Matthew, who obliged.

The man made no move to show them into a parlor. He stood there, his arms folded. "I have nothing to hide," he declared. "This is not a place where we are acquainted with the likes of you."

Platter bowed. "I'll not require much of your valuable

time, gov'nor," he said. "What I have in mind is a history lesson."

The landlord stared hard at the Runner, but added nothing to the conversation.

"Dredge your mind back to the early spring of 1808, sir," said Platter. "There was a party here on the night of . . ." The Runner looked at Matthew.

"April 9," said the viscount. "And it was in that set of rooms at the top of the stairs . . . the ones looking out onto the street."

The landlord laughed. "My, but that is a faradiddle! Me old mam has lived there these fifteen years and more! Laddie, you'd better take yourself off. You've got the wrong house."

"No, I have not," said Matthew quietly. He turned to Platter. "Sir, have you any jurisdiction to search those rooms?"

"Certainly I have," said the Runner. "And if Mr. Landlord here has other ideas, why, he'll soon be pissing in a bucket in Newgate."

"Well put, Timothy," said Matthew. "I do so admire your way with a phrase."

Platter smiled grimly and directed his attention at the landlord again. "Well? What's your pleasure, sir?"

The landlord removed a ring of keys from his pocket and climbed the stairs. He crammed the key in the lock and growled over his shoulder, "Me mam is visiting me sister in Kent. And it's a good thing for you!" he concluded, shaking the keys at the Runner.

"I'm all atremble," said Platter as he opened the door.

The room was as neat as a pin, with furniture carefully arranged and smelling faintly of roses. It was the room of an older woman, with one or two portraits badly in need of cleaning, and cheap landscape drawings here and there. The furniture was exactly as Matthew remembered it, right down to the doilies on the chair backs, and that lingering odor of roses. He felt the hairs rise on the back of his neck.

Matthew walked into the next room and stopped short in the doorway. It was the same; everything was the same. He recognized the brasswork on the bedstead that rose in a fanciful ogive in the center, with a smaller ornamentation echoed in the foot. He closed the door behind him over the protests of the landlord, preferring to be alone.

The viscount approached the bed and stood there staring down at it, almost hearing again his friends gathered around it, clapping and cheering him on, and then laughing. He shook off the fright that was settling around him and came closer, raising the coverlet until he exposed the mattress.

The bed rested on ropes. It was as tidy as the rest of the room. Matthew wiped off the sweat that had suddenly popped out on his hands and then picked up the corner of the mattress and looked under it. Faint rust stains speckled the edge of it. He raised the mattress higher and then dropped it. The rust stains merged into a larger pool of rust that covered the center of the mattress like a gigantic poppy. Someone had scrubbed and scrubbed at it, and then carefully turned the mattress over.

The room swam before his eyes. Matthew leaned against the bed, then ran to the window, slammed up the sash, and put his head out, gulping the cooler air, until he felt less light-headed.

He heard the door open, and he knew the Runner and the landlord were watching him, but he was powerless to do anything except stay where he was, taking deep breaths of air, and resting his arms on the ledge, filled with a fear greater than he had ever known before.

Finally he closed the window. "There was murder done here eight years ago," he said quietly to the landlord. "A drab was raped and killed. And you know nothing of this?"

The landlord's eyes never wavered from the viscount's face. He shook his head and smiled. "Laddie, I tell you, you're foxed. Maybe you're even crazy. Better get your keeper to take you back where you came from."

"There were six gentlemen in this set of rooms," continued Matthew inexorably, "here to celebrate the coming wedding of one with a last-night lay. And you remember nothing of this?'' He looked closely at the landlord. ''Or were you paid to remember nothing?''

The landlord returned him stare for stare. ''You'll have to leave. This is a respectable establishment. My mam has lived here fifteen years. Anyone in the neighborhood can tell you that.'' He laughed then, a peculiar laugh that sent chills down Matthew's arms. ''And she never had a party like the one you're describing. That's the kind of parties 'gentlemen' have.'' He spat the word out.

''Perhaps it is,'' said Matthew heavily. ''We're wasting our time here, Timothy. Let us go.''

''Yes, let us go,'' agreed the Runner. He took Matthew by the elbow and propelled him from the room. They hurried down the stairs and out into the sunlight. The landlord followed them downstairs and watched them. He slammed the door finally, and they could hear his laughter receding down the hall.

''There were bloodstains all over that mattress. Someone had turned it so they wouldn't show. God, Platter, is there no one who remembers anything? No one who will help me?''

''And I suppose the old lady will swear up and down and cry and carry on, and no judge will doubt her,'' said Platter. ''I've seen it in too many trials. The one who pays the most wins.'' He put his hand on Matthew's shoulder. ''And I think Rotherford must have paid a lot. How curious this is, to hush up a murder and yet use it to keep you forever in his debt.''

The front door opened again. Matthew looked back expectantly. The landlord stood there with a bundle in his hands. ''Ashman!'' he shouted. ''Ashman, come out!''

A small door opened by the ashcans and a little man ran out onto the walkway until he could see the landlord. He held his arms up and the landlord threw down the bundle and then slammed the door again.

The ashman staggered under the weight of the bundle and Matthew moved to steady him. The man looked at him, nodded his thanks, and then looked again. Instead of putting the garbage in the cans, he carried it in through the small door, looking over his shoulder one more time at Matthew.

Matthew shook his head. "Well, now what do we do?"

"I'm not entirely sure, my lord," replied Platter with more uncertainty in his voice than Matthew had ever heard before. "I need to think about this." He sighed. "And I need to go to Bow Street and check some records. Make a report. Dammit, but this is a difficult thing!"

"I think I can well imagine," said the viscount dryly. "I can't charge Rotherford with murder. I do not know all the circumstances. For all I know, I killed the girl. And if I make the slightest move to object to Rotherford's claim on my nephew, he will shout long and loud, and the landlord will have a miraculous recovery of his memory, and he will slip my neck through a noose."

The Runner took up the story. "And then in a year or so, when your nephew meets a mysterious end, there will be no one alive to even suspect. Rotherford will become one of the richest men in England, and there will be such a trail of dead bodies behind him that any respectable person would wonder how such a man sleeps nights."

"But people like that always sleep like babies," Matthew finished bitterly.

The Runner stopped walking. "We need someone who can tell us what happened. And, my lord, it appears there is no one."

Matthew nodded and pulled out his watch. "Mr. Platter, if you trust me, I would like to go to Hyde Park. It is almost time for the strut, and I have not seen it in years. Have no fear that I will elude you. All I want now is to get back to Byford and protect my nephew as long as I can. But I want to think. When you have finished at Bow Street, come for me."

"Very well, my lord," said Platter. "I am sorry about this."

"So am I. You can't imagine."

The men parted company at Piccadilly and Matthew walked to Hyde Park. He paid little attention to his surroundings, but hurried along, his long strides eating up the blocks until he came to Rotten Row. The horses, curricles, and high-perch phaetons were assembled there as he remembered them. Ladies and gentlemen were assembled there too, some walking back and forth, some riding around and around, seeing and being seen. It was the highlight of the day for many a young miss in her first Season or a lieutenant back from the wars. There would be balls and routs and drums and assemblies, and the opera, and dinners where people only toyed with their food and lived for the next *on-dit*.

All of a sudden it was the silliest society he had ever heard of. He longed to be back in Byford with Omega and her fidgets and scolds. Or, failing that, he yearned to retrace his steps to the Runner's house, where Maeve would butter him some bread and let him hold her baby or dandle Davey on his knee. Nothing else really mattered. He was shattered and filled with hope at the same time. After eight years of hiding, he wanted so much for himself and those he loved, even as he knew things were coming to an end.

He was desperate to get back to Byford, but there he remained, watching the men and women riding by and flirting, until the Runner came for him.

12

The Runner had both horses. Matthew took the reins the man handed him. "Where to now, sir? Bow Street for me, and then Newgate?"

With a look of surprise on his face, Platter shook his head vigorously. "Not a chance, my lord. I still don't have sufficient evidence either way."

"You are being kind," replied Matthew as he swung into the saddle. "Don't deny that you have arrested others on less evidence."

"I don't deny it," admitted Platter frankly. "You seem to forget, however, that I have only your word for the fact that a crime has even been committed. No one else has ever come forward. This is a singular case."

They rode in thoughtful silence, broken by only one remark from Platter. "I have forwarded Miss Chartley's trunk, valise, and box of books to Byford, sir."

"She'll be glad to see them. And was her money returned also?"

"Certainly, my lord. She's quite free to leave."

Dinner was a continuation of last night's stew, and it was no less welcome to Matthew. Maeve proudly set her bowl before him and he ate, thinking of his own table. Maeve would never believe me if I told her how much we waste in a single day, he thought as he carefully wiped out the inside of the bowl with a piece of bread as large as his plate.

He watched Maeve as she sat on the floor with Davey by her and the baby on her lap. How is it that I have reached the age of thirty-four and never been aware of these people before? England is full of them, and they might as well be invisible, for all that I have seen them.

He could not sleep that night. He lay on the floor staring at the ceiling, thinking of the landlord, wishing he could remember more of the events of that night.

Finally Matthew sat up. "Timothy, are you awake?" he whispered.

The mattress rustled. "Aye, sir."

"I'm going back to Quallen Lane. There must be something I have overlooked. At any rate, I cannot sleep."

"Mind you are careful, my lord. You may have noticed that this is not a savory neighborhood."

He reclaimed his horse with no trouble and saddled it himself, keeping his back to the wall, watching the men who watched him. He had few illusions about the fact that he was far from his fighting trim, and only hoped that his height and general bearing would keep them from getting any untoward ideas.

The streets were still populated, but it was a quieter crowd. Many slept in doorways, others wove down the streets in various stages of disrepair from grog and Blue

Ruin. The drabs unlucky enough not to find a bed for the night were still on the street. They eyed him with some hope and then shrieked at him when he rode on past, casting certain aspersions on his manhood that only made him chuckle. Oh, if you jades only knew, he thought as he navigated the streets and kept open the eye in the back of his head.

The horse he left in the stable again. The square of St. James was empty, except for a few peep-of-day boys. He avoided them, walking in the shadows of the great buildings. They looked to be students mostly, lads finishing the long holiday. He knew that they liked to shout out challenges and break the heads of those less worthy, so he made sure he was not seen.

Quallen Lane was empty and silent, the very model of propriety. Matthew looked up at the windows on the second floor. Doubts again assailed him. How could he have hoped to find the place again, and, even finding it, how could he be so naive as to think that anyone would help him?

Quietly he mounted the stairs and sat down halfway up them. The air was suddenly cool on his face as a little breeze picked up bits of trash and sent them sailing around the foot of the stairs.

A door opened. He sat, alert and silent, as the ashman tiptoed out of his room from somewhere under the steps and collected the paper. I have seen all this before, he thought; I have felt that rush of cold air, and it was right here on these stairs. He stirred and wished he could remember more.

The ashman glanced up, stepped back in surprise, and dropped his papers. To Matthew's surprise, he sank to his knees as if overcome. Matthew hurried down the steps. "See here, man," he whispered, "are you well?"

The ashman drew in a deep breath, and clutched at Matthew's arm, feeling up and down from wrist to shoulder, and then managing a weak chuckle. "You're not a haunt, laddie," he said at last. "Oh, my boy, if you had been a late-night devil, old Thomas Grissam wouldna be here now, and that's a fact!"

"I don't understand you, man," said Matthew. "Here, let us sit down."

The ashman looked over his shoulder at the house again. Satisfied, he settled himself on the bottom step. "I wouldna be doing this if the master were watching. He's devilish particular about the steps." The ashman peered down at Matthew more closely. "You gave me a fright, laddie, a real start. I remember another time when another cove sat right where you were sitting. I asked my master about him once, and what did he do but laugh in that way of his and say something about the man being 'snug as a fish in a bottle.' "

"Might that have been . . . about eight years ago?" asked Matthew finally, when the old man looked as though he would not bolt.

"It might have been entirely just then. My daughter was newly leg-shackled to a sailor and I was by meself again." He rubbed his chin, scratching at the days-old growth. "And now my daughter is a widow with a small boy to feed. And doesn't he eat a lot?"

Matthew sighed inwardly, but patiently pulled the thread of the story back. "And what happened here eight years ago?"

The ashman looked more closely at Matthew, taking him by the chin and turning his face this way and that. "You was here this afternoon, or someone like you. You look much like that man, that man on the stairs, but that man was a gentleman." He sniffed the air in Matthew's general vicinity. "Gentlemen smell better than you, laddie, and they look better too."

Matthew prepared to pull the conversation back again, but he stopped as the ashman continued.

"And we know about gentlemen here on Quallen Lane." He chuckled at some great private joke. "The joke's on my master's old lady, it is. She doesn't have a clue what happens in her flat when she goes to Kent to visit her daughter." He rocked back and forth in the clutch of silent laughter.

"What does happen here, Grissam?"

The ashman stared at him and tightened his lips as if he

had said too much. But his mirth caught up with him. He leaned close to Matthew, resting his head for a moment on the man's shoulder. "Oh, laddie, my master sows and reaps and never misses a penny." He put his hand over his mouth and chuckled. "He rents out that flat to gentlemen as want to have a sporting evening with no questions asked." He nudged Matthew. "And then by Sunday evening everything's all right and tight again, and nobody's wife or father is ever the wiser."

Matthew put his arm around the old man, his voice low, as if he were involved in the conspiracy too, even as his heart pounded loud in his chest. "And was the old lady gone that night . . . that night you saw the man on the steps?"

The ashman nodded. "She was, laddie, and it was a good thing. That was a wild evening, sir." He slapped his thigh, nearly carrying himself over backward. "I think it was even more than my master reckoned for." He sat up and shoved his face into Matthew's again. "We never had a murder before nor since, laddie."

"A murder?" echoed Matthew. His heart was thumping painfully loud now.

The ashman looked about him. "But I am not to say that, laddie, not to anyone, and not until it is in a court of law." He frowned. "And then I am to say only what my master tells me to say." He leaned closer again. "And that *wasn't* what happened."

The ashman was silent then. He leaned back against the steps, his elbows propping him up, and stared up at the stars as if they were a new experience to him.

"Ah, Grissam, you have my interest up now," said Matthew when he could stand the silence no longer. He tried to keep his voice casual, as if he were merely idling away his time. "What . . . what did happen?"

"You promise not to tell?"

Matthew nodded.

"Cross yourself, laddie."

Matthew crossed himself.

"That man on the steps. He sat there all evening. But I'm supposed to say that I found him in bed with a dead whore when I went in the room to clean up." He looked at Matthew, faintly puzzled, and then his eyes clouded over. "But it was not so!"

His anger subsided as quickly as it came. "But if I wants my rum, that's what I say." He nudged Matthew again. "And laddie, I wants my rum."

"The man on the stairs," started Matthew. "Was he very drunk?"

The ashman chuckled out loud this time, and then clapped his hand over his mouth and looked around. "Oh, laddie, I've never even seen a sailor any farther to the wind than that poor one. When the other toffs took their leave, he just grins at them like an inmate of Bedlam, bless my soul."

" 'The other toffs'? Was one of them tall and thin . . ."

"And with the silliest giggle?" finished the ashman. "Yes, laddie, and the other was a military man, leastwise he looked like one. Walked like he had a poker up his ass."

Matthew grinned in spite of himself. Never had he heard a better description of Merrill Watt-Lyon. Too bad his friend was not alive to enjoy it. "And the others? Was one of them a quiet man with a limp?"

The ashman stared at him. "The very him! And didn't he even look a bit like . . . like *that* man, the one inside. They could have been brothers. . . ." He stopped, and when he spoke again, his voice was shrewd. "And how would you know these things, laddie? You're too old to be the man on the steps, and besides, he was much trimmer."

Matthew shrugged. "I'm just guessing. Was there another man?"

"There was another cove, any road, and he didn't even look faintly pizzled. O' course, some men hold their liquor wondrous well. Happen *I'm* one of those. Well, that man, he patted the drunken laddie on the head and wished him happy. Said he would see him at the wedding in the morning, and reminded him about hunting in the fall."

There was no wedding in the morning, and there was no hunt in the fall. David Larchstone, that rascal in tight pantaloons, was dead before the hunting season was half begun. His dead friends, all of them accounted for except one, paraded before Matthew's eyes.

The ashman was speaking again. "There was one more. He paid me." Grissam stirred as if the step was suddenly uncomfortable. "He threw some money down the steps and told me to . . . to . . ."

He stopped, resting his hand on his chin, scratching himself and then staring at nothing in particular. "But I am not to say that, laddie."

Matthew stared ahead too. "I can buy you a bottle of rum, Mr. Thomas Grissam," he said softly. "As many bottles as you want. Your story . . . interests me."

Grissam said nothing, but held his hand out. Matthew put a coin in it. Without looking at him, the ashman bit the coin, grunted in satisfaction, and pocketed his wealth. "The man on the steps went to sleep, just right out there in the cold."

"Was he covered with . . . with blood?"

Grissam started in surprise. "No, no, laddie! He had on a frilly shirt and them short pants that gentlemen wear, and he wasn't tidy, but . . . bloody? No, not him. It was t'other one."

The same chill covered Matthew, the chill he had felt in the upstairs bedroom earlier that day. "Which man was it?"

"The cove who paid me. Lord, he came running out of the house, his mouth open, ready to scream. My master grabbed him from behind. And then . . . then they noticed the sleeping man, and just looked at each other. Lord, I thought I was dreaming. Without a word between them, they picked up that sleeping man and carried him into the house."

Matthew sat forward on the steps so the ashman could not see his face. He needn't have bothered. The ashman was so overcome with his own tale that he was paying no mind.

"Ah, laddie, it was such a night! Be glad you were not there. They carried that poor sod inside, stripped him, and arranged him nice-like next to the drab."

"You . . . you saw this?" Matthew asked. His voice didn't sound like his own.

The man nodded, and glanced back at the house again. "I followed them in and just stood there in the door of that bedroom like a Bermondsey boy. The man, the one with the bloody shirt, told me that if I ever breathed a word, even in my sleep, he would cut my throat from ear to ear." Grissam shuddered. "And don't doubt that he would. I went to sea once, laddie, and saw glimmers like that on a shark. Shark's eyes."

Carefully Matthew let out the breath he had been holding. It was no one but Rotherford.

"And so I should not tell anyone. And I will not, laddie," he said, filled with resolve that quickly melted away when Matthew pressed another coin in his hand.

"And then what?"

"The bloody man, the one with the shark eyes, he took off his cravat and shirt and threw them at me. Told me to burn them."

"And did you?"

The ashman smiled, showing a mouthful of gums and few teeth. "Lord love you, laddie, I can tell you're not an ashman!"

Matthew shook his head, faintly amused. I have called myself any number of things over the years, he thought, but not that.

"I took them bloody, reeking things, bowing and smiling me way out of the room. I even stoked up a good fire out back, but, laddie, I couldna do it. Do you know what a good shirt like that brings on the market?"

"I . . . I can't imagine," said Matthew faintly.

"I washed it and washed it, thinking I would sell it. But do you know, laddie, I couldna do it." He shook his head sorrowfully, as if chagrined at his own weakness. "I couldna bring myself to think that gentry mort's leavings would be on some other man's back. It didna set right with me. The shirt's belowstairs, laddie. Would you like to see it?"

On legs that had turned to rubber, Matthew followed the ashman down the stairs and into the little room under the front steps. Strange scurryings and rustlings heralded their entrance, but Matthew could see nothing for a moment. He lived in momentary dread that a rat would run across his foot, but followed his leader into the room, which was no more than a pathway through the discarded throwaways of years and years of tenants.

"Ah, laddie, I can't throw out a thing, as you can well see. Some of this is surely worth a ransom," cried the ashman, fondling a splintered chair leg as if it were a holy relic. "My precious jewels," he crooned as he worked his way back into the room to the cot where he slept.

With a grunt he threw himself down on his knees and reached under the bed, pulling out a wooden box. "Laddie, light that lamp over there."

Matthew did as he was told, scarcely able to take his eyes from the box, as the ashman tugged at the dirty string around his neck and produced a key. He fitted it into the box and clicked it open. Matthew leaned forward, holding the lamp high.

With a crow of delight Thomas Grissam took out the shirt, shaking out its folds and petting it. "Pretty, pretty linen, my laddie," he said, and his voice was soft and reverent. "Now, wouldna you like a shirt of this quality?" he asked. "And look at this cravat." He laughed. "I stood myself in front of that mirror scrap behind you and tried to tie one of them fancy bows." He gave a growl of disgust. "That's for them gentry morts as has time for folderols. Look at this, laddie."

He spread the shirt out on the cot. The material had faded to a pale yellow, and it was ringed here and there with the faintest outlines of rust spots. It was a large shirt, large and long, the shirt of a tall man. Matthew picked up the cravat. The stickpin was still in it, a gold fancy in the shape of a horseshoe. He thought of Rotherford's expensive stables and the horses he prized so highly. Anyone who saw the horseshoe pin would know it as Rotherford's.

"I wonder you did not sell this, Mr. Thomas Grissam," he said. "You could have bought lots of grog with it."

The ashman shook his head. "No, laddie. I took it to a

tavern once, and even plunked it down on the counter, but no, laddie. It's blood money I would have gotten for me troubles, and sure as the world, I would have choked to death on me rum that night. No. Better to leave it in this box."

Matthew traced the lines of the horseshoe with his finger. "I would buy this from you, and the shirt and stock too."

The ashman grimaced and grabbed them back. "You'd have nothing but bad luck, laddie."

This would be nothing new, thought Matthew. "You won't consider it?" he asked out loud. When the ashman only clutched his treasures tighter and shook his head, Matthew adopted a soothing tone. "Mr. Grissam, would you do something for me, since you won't sell me these things?"

The ashman quickly shoved his treasures into the box and locked it. "I might," he said grudgingly.

"Would you let me write down your story, and then would you sign it?"

"I can't write, laddie."

"Then would you make an X?" persisted Matthew.

"I might. I might. But you wouldna tell a soul, would you?"

"No," said Matthew. "There might even be another coin, sir."

"Then sit you down, laddie. What can it hurt if no one sees it? And you have an honest face, my boy."

"Thank you," said Matthew without a blink.

"I'm sure I have a pen and paper here somewhere."

"I'm sure that you do," agreed Matthew.

The room was becoming lighter when the ashman neared the end of his retelling of the story. "What became of the . . . the body?" Matthew asked, the pen poised over the ink bottle.

"Oh, laddie, that was my task." The ashman glanced slyly at him. "Remember how I told you I never throw anything away?"

"Good God!" exclaimed Matthew, looking about him wildly.

The ashman threw himself backward across his cot in a peal of silent mirth, his hands folded across his stomach as he laughed without making a sound beyond a gasp and wheeze for breath. When he could collect himself, he sat up and thumped Matthew on the knee, causing the ink bottle to rise in an arc and bounce against the bed. Matthew made a grab for it before the ink entirely spilled out.

"Just wanted to see if you were paying attention, laddie," said the ashman as he wheezed a bit more. "No. No. I dumped that little whore in a laundry bag and took her down to the river for a little swim. No one ever paid me any mind." He became serious again. "Just a little thing, she was, for all that she was a favorite of the men. I used to see her about the neighborhood. Name of Millie Platter."

The ink spilled again and Matthew made no move to right the bottle. His whole body went numb. He stood up and rested his forehead against the dirty pane of glass that served as the ashman's only window. The glass was cool. As he stood there, ignoring the ashman's loud questions, he understood Timothy Platter's look of anguish on that ride to London, when he had confessed everything. The look had struck Matthew then as unprofessional for a Bow Street Runner, but he understood now, and his purgatory was complete. His cup ran over and there were no words left.

When he was able, he sat down again, dipped his quill in what remained of the ink puddle on the floor, and finished the ashman's curious deputation. He dipped it one more time and wrote "Thomas Grissam" in large block letters. Once more, and he handed the quill to the ashman. "Make your mark, sir," he ordered.

There was command in his voice that he did not feel, but that communicated itself to Grissam, who took up the quill without a word and made his X.

"You'll not show this to anyone?" asked the ashman again.

Matthew shook his head. He reached in his pocket and spilled out a handful of gold coins. The ashman's eyes widened. "Coo, love," he breathed, "you're a bank robber."

"That's it," said Matthew. "You have hit upon it."

Grissam picked up one or two coins and pushed the rest back toward Matthew. "Oo, don't I seem to run with irregulars?" he said, more to himself than to his guest.

Matthew allowed himself a laugh. "Oh, I'm an irregular, sir, make no mistake. But what should I do with this money? It should be yours."

"No, laddie, not mine. If I start spending the ready—and I will, you know—my master will get wind of it, and I'll be in a vat of trouble. Send it to my daughter in Bristol, her what has the little boy. That'll do." He looked closely at Matthew. "And don't let on as it's bank money. My daughter is wondrous prune-faced about such as that."

"Not a word from me, sir," said Matthew. He wrote down the direction of Thomas Grissam's daughter as it was dictated, and rose to go. He held out his hand to the ashman, who stared at him.

"No one's ever shook my hand before, laddie." The ashman wiped his hand on his filthy pants. "Even if you are a thief and a bank robber, I'll shake with you."

Matthew folded the ashman's history and pocketed it. He threaded his way back through the maze that was Thomas Grissam's castle to the doorway. The sun was almost up, although the street still lay in shadow. He took a deep breath. Even London air smelled like Omega's lavender scent after his sojourn in the ashman's home.

"Good day to you," he told Thomas Grissam, and started up Quallen Lane.

He had gone no more than a pace or two when he heard, "Ashman!"

He looked up to see the landlord standing at the top of the stairs, a bag in his hands, watching him.

Matthew hurried on. Surely the street was still deep enough in shadow that the landlord would not know who he was. He touched the document in his pocket, turned the corner, and nearly ran into Timothy Platter.

The Runner had both horses with him. He leaned

against the building and snuffed out the cigar that Omega so despised. " 'Twas a long night, my lord," he commented.

"It was," agreed Matthew. "Timothy, he has told me everything."

The Runner's eyes opened wide. "Surely not the landlord!"

"The ashman. It is a long story, and I haven't time to tell it. Can I hire you on commission?"

"Perhaps."

"I want you to find my friend Sir Horace Billings. I'll give you his last direction in Suffolk. I want you to produce him in Byford, or have a statement from him, signed and notarized. Can you go right now?"

The Runner nodded. "If you'll trust me with this fine piece of horse again, my lord."

"Timothy, I'd trust you with my wife, if I had one." He took some coins from his pocket. "Take this too. And don't stare at me that way! You can't imagine the trouble I'm having getting rid of it. It's to speed your journey. Come to Byford as soon as you can." Platter took the coins without a word and swung into the saddle. "I'll see you soon, then, my lord."

Matthew put his hand on the horse's bridle. "One more thing, Mr. Platter. Do you . . . could you arrange a break-in for me?"

"Sir, we are the law," said Timothy in shocked tones.

"I know all too well," Matthew replied. He did not loosen his hold on the bridle. "If you had known of a, er, a free agent who could have been inclined to remove a box from under the bed of the ashman at 10 Quallen Lane, that would have been a good thing. But it is no matter, I suppose, particularly since you are the law." He released the bridle and stepped back. "Godspeed, Mr. Platter. Let me see your face soon."

Platter tipped his hat to Lord Byford. "You will, sir. And about that other matter: I'll see what I can do."

"I knew I could depend on you."

Matthew Bering, Lord Byford, shook the dust of London off his feet, but not without a visit to his solicitors, where he revised his will and signed it, and then directed a respectable sum of money to be sent to one Varinda Grissam Talbot of Chatting Crossroad, Bristol. He next ordained his solicitor to send a very junior clerk of respectable girth into the backwaters of Limehouse to deliver a set of crockery to the household of Timothy Platter.

"And mind that the lady of the flat has no notion of where it came from. You just make sure that it gets there, Mr. Pitney," ordered Matthew. "And now, sir, I am off to Byford. I think my presence will soon be greatly in demand in that spot."

His solicitor produced another document that had been requested. "And let me wish you happy, my lord," said Mr. Pitney. "Do I know the fortunate lady?"

"You did at one time, sir. She is an opinionated, fractious, meddlesome, irritating educationist who fights hammer and tongs if you happen to get her back up."

"My lord, I know of no one that meets such a description!" said the solicitor, disapproval written all over his face. "Whatever can you be thinking of?"

"Marriage, Mr. Pitney—at least, some sort of marriage."

"Sir you are bamming me!"

"I, sir, do not 'bam' solicitors. Good day."

13

After Matthew and the Bow Street Runner left so early that morning, Omega took herself back to bed. She toyed with the notion of taking another swallow of the good doctor's sleeping powders, but decided against it. With Matthew gone, the weight of the household fell on her shoulders, and the responsibility of Jamie. She needed to have her wits—or what was left of them—about her.

She spent another luxurious hour stretched out flat on

the comfortable bed, listening to the birds outside the window, her hands folded across her stomach, the picture of repose. Soon she would be back in the classroom, which meant early dawns and constant distractions. How pleasant it was to rest and not think much beyond the prospect of breakfast.

Angela's arrival in her room ended the peace and quiet. Without even knocking, the little girl hurled herself into the room and onto Omega's bed. "Oh, Miss Chartley, you'll never guess who is below!"

No, she could not. Her first thought was Rotherford, but she dismissed it. Surely even he could not arrive so quickly.

"It is those two gentlemen from the horse judging! They have come to take Hugh"—she giggled and put her hand to her mouth—"Major Owen to another horse judging in Claybrook, a town not far from here."

"Dear me," said Miss Chartley, and she threw back the covers. "Angela, help me find something to wear."

Clad in her blue housekeeper's dress again, and leaning against Angela, she hobbled down the hall to Hugh's room and knocked. The soldier came to the door, his cravat dangling from his neck. He sighed with relief when he saw it was Omega, and pulled her into the room.

"Here, you must do it," he commanded, extending the end of the cravat to her. "I cannot do this with one hand, and Matthew has sent his man Leonard off on holiday now that he is gone up to London."

She tied his cravat, grateful that Matthew was not there to laugh at her efforts. "Can you . . . can you judge another horse show, Hugh?" she asked.

"I had better," he said grimly as she helped him into Matthew's blue superfine coat and smoothed the wrinkles out across the back. "I am taking Jamie with me. He claims to be an expert."

As if to verify his words, Jamie bolted into the room. "Omega, this is famous! I get to help judge the horse show!" He looked at her, his eyes wide. "Omega, you are feeling better?"

"Yes," she said, "if you do not woosh by me again and

make me lose my balance. You may go, of course." She looked at Hugh and lowered her voice. "Please, please keep Jamie close by. Rotherford may be nearer than we know."

He nodded. "I'll be watching."

She smiled her gratitude, and then considered the business at hand. "And now, should I go below and greet the guests? What *does* the housekeeper do?"

"Twinings is serving them some coffee and biscuits," Angela said. "If Hugh is overlong, I will volunteer to sing."

"At nine in the morning?" scoffed Jamie. "Angela, you are daft."

She stuck out her tongue at him and flounced from the room. Hugh turned to Omega. "You will be all right here? We have been invited to be overnight guests at Lord Nickle's manor in Claybrook . . ." His voice trailed off.

Omega grinned. "You are certainly traveling in fine circles, Major Owen," she said, twinkling her eyes at him. "Just remember, always start with the fork that is farthest out and proceed toward the center, and you should acquit yourself admirably."

"Excellent, excellent, Miss Chartley," he said. "You never fail me."

"Certainly not," she agreed. "I have Tildy and Twinings to help me get belowstairs again, so we will do well." Omega sighed. "I expect we will have to entertain Lord Rotherford when he arrives. Perhaps Angela will sing."

Hugh and Jamie went downstairs, while Omega limped back to her room. The pain in her ankle was growing strong again. "This will never do," she said out loud, and hobbled into Matthew's bedroom.

The room was as neat and tidy as she would have expected, nothing out of place. The fragrance of lemon cologne made her sigh. She went to his dressing room and opened the door, marveling at how organized he was, and knowing that if they had ever married she would have been such a trial to him. For I am *not* tidy, Matthew, as you well know, she said to herself.

"And now, sir, do you have a cane?" she asked. "If you ever professed to be a gentleman of the first stare, you must have had at least one."

He had several. They were lined up like soldiers next to his boots and shoes. She found one to her liking, and discovered that it would serve the purpose.

The cane was an improvement, Omega decided as she took herself from the dressing room. She looked about Matthew's bedroom with some interest. She could imagine no other room for him. It was simple, with plain furniture, a narrow bed and an overstuffed chair that looked well-sat-in. She glanced at the book on the table by the chair: Plato's *Apology* in Greek, with his favorite passages underlined. She picked up the other book and smiled. "So you are also reading *Tom Jones*," she said. "How relieved I am that you enjoy a novel now and then."

She replaced the book on the table and her eye was caught by an oval miniature lying facedown. Omega turned it over and tears started in her eyes. It was her miniature, the one she had given Matthew after the announcement of their engagement. She was wearing the pink dress he had so admired, and her hair, wild as ever, was loose around her face.

Omega had almost forgotten the miniature; Matthew had not. She realized with a guilty start that Matthew had given her a miniature in his turn, which she had pitched in the ashcan after her return from the church. And here was her portrait, eyes twinkling up at the artist, still gracing his table after all these years, all this pain. She set the miniature upright and left the room quickly.

Omega descended the stairs and gingerly made her way down to the servants' quarters, where Angela was engaged in helping Tildy arrange some of the clothes from upstairs into the former housekeeper's room.

Tildy flashed her a smile. "Miss Chartley, I took the liberty of taking some of the plainer dresses from the dressing room upstairs for your use down here. And I have loaned you my best apron."

"Thank you, my dear." Omega looked around her at

the other servants, who had gathered in the servants' hall. "And thanks to all of you. I realize what a dither we have dumped you all into. I am sure that things will be back to normal soon, and I will be on my way to Durham before too many more days."

If anyone was delighted with her disclosure, no one showed it. The butler sighed, the footman frowned, and Tildy swallowed and looked away.

"I have a position to fill at St. Elizabeth's in Durham," she said. No response, beyond a sniff from the chef when Angela translated for him. "Someone must educate Britain's young females, wouldn't you agree?"

No one agreed. With an inscrutable expression Twinings turned back to decanting the wine, and Tildy dabbed at her eyes before hurrying into the housekeeper's room again.

There was nothing for Omega to do belowstairs, particularly with everyone so Friday-faced. She resolved to write a letter to Alpha, and then one to St. Elizabeth's, in case anyone was wondering yet where she was. She would keep her letter to Alpha light, describing the national treasures she had seen, and also those she had not. No need for dear Alpha to know that she had strayed somewhat from her itinerary. She hobbled down the hall to Matthew's bookroom, searching for paper.

The room was spotless, nothing out of place. The ledgers and account books were lined neatly according to height in the bookcase behind the big desk. From curiosity, she removed one and opened it, marveling at the careful script and precision of the numbers. Matthew had accounted for everything on the property, and on his other properties as well. She opened another book, and another, not so much to put her nose in his business as to get a better grip on the life he had lived for the past eight years.

Every sum was correctly totaled, no column left unfinished. She ran her fingers down the neat file of numbers. "So this has been your life, dear Matthew?" she asked. "Instead of wife and children, you have lavished your care on records." She sat down and rested her chin on her hands. "And I have devoted myself to literature and grammar that little girls forget the minute they are liberated from the ogre's classroom. How sad we are."

Omega remained a moment longer in contemplation of the sterility of their lives and then closed the ledgers and replaced them, giving herself a mental shake. This would never do. She opened a deep drawer in search of paper, and pulled out a large stationery box.

She opened it and quickly closed it. Matthew had begun a letter to someone, and she had no right to pry. Without looking at its contents, she would reach underneath for a fresh piece of paper. She pulled out another sheet, sucked in her breath, and extracted another and another.

"My dear Omega," headed each piece of paper, preceded by the date, and nothing more. With trembling fingers she pulled out all the sheets and flipped through them. "Dear Omega," "Dearest Omega," "My beloved Omega," headed each sheet. The dates went back to 1808, the first one April 11, the day after she was to have been married.

Hundreds of pages rested in her lap. She was too stupefied to cry, and scarcely remembered to breathe. For eight years, daily at first, and then fortnightly, Matthew had begun a letter to her, to get no farther than the salutation. While she had been agonizing in Plymouth, trying to forget, and very nearly succeeding, he was tearing open the wound every day of his life.

"Matthew, how could you do this to yourself?" she asked as the tears started down her cheeks. She made no move to brush them away, but let them fall on the pages gripped so tightly in her hands. She cried for the waste and the sorrow, and when she was done, she wiped her eyes, gathered up the papers, and threw them all in the fireplace. With fingers that were steady, she struck a match to the whole lot and watched it go up in a blaze.

When all the years were but a pile of ashes, she found one sheet of paper unwritten upon and pulled herself up to the desk. She dipped Matthew's pen in the inkwell and carefully wrote, "Dearest Matthew, I love you." She signed it, dated it, wondered at her audacity, and put it away in the box. He would likely not find it until she was on her way to Durham, but perhaps it would convince him to stop tearing at his insides day after day. It was the least she could do for him.

Omega sat in silence through the long afternoon in the bookroom, shaking her head when Tildy tried to bring her luncheon on a tray. She gazed out the window at nothing in particular, comfortable in Matthew's chair. It had molded itself to his shape, and she felt almost that she was sitting on his lap. It was nothing but pure foolishness, but she felt better when she finally picked up the cane and left the room.

Dinner was another silent affair. Angela had begged permission to share Tildy's half-day at her mother's house, and Omega had consented, wishing to be alone and not have to be clever or wise or accommodating. She pushed the food around on her plate, and then scraped it out the window into the flowerbed, knowing that if she sent a full plate belowstairs, Antoine would be up in a minute, to wring his hands and rail at her in French.

She would gladly have shared the evening with Matthew, and they would not have had to exchange a word. She remembered many such quiet evenings in her father's London house, after their engagement, Matthew with a book, she with her needlework, content, both of them, to leave the plays, operas, and routs to others. A case-hardened bachelor and his little schoolroom lady—how curious everyone had deemed it, and yet how well they had suited.

Omega talked sternly to herself and went belowstairs to bed. There was no point in doing this to herself. Dredging up those tranquil moments was no better than writing "Dear Omega" over and over. "And if this is really and truly over, and it must be, then I must forget him all over again," she finally told herself as she crawled into bed, carefully arranged the blanket around her throbbing ankle, and surrendered herself to sleep.

She slept long beyond a housekeeper's hours, oblivious of the sounds in the servants' quarters. She woke, stared guiltily at her bedside clock, and wondered at the air of tension that seemed to fill the room. She dressed quickly, brushing her hair and then stuffing it underneath her housekeeper's cap. Something was terribly wrong, and she could not identify what it was.

She left the housekeeper's room. The servants all sat at the table, no one speaking. Omega looked around her in surprise. Twinings rose to his feet when she entered the room, all dignity gone. The look in his eyes frightened her.

"Twinings, whatever can be the matter? Has something happened to Jamie or Matthew?"

He shook his head. "Miss Chartley, it is Lord Rotherford. He is waiting in the parlor."

The other servants looked at her. Omega managed a feeble laugh. "Surely he is not a seven-headed Hydra!" she exclaimed. "I trust you made him comfortable."

"A man like that is never comfortable," said Tildy with a shudder. "I won't go back in the room with him alone! I'll leave my job first." She leapt to her feet, clutching at Omega's sleeve. "Miss Chartley, we daren't turn Jamie over to him!"

Stifling the fear that was rising in her, Omega touched Tildy's hand. "My dear, that was why Matthew went to London. He is trying to resolve this thing. I had better go upstairs and face the wrath." She smiled, attempting to put them at ease. "What name have you given me? Am I Mrs. Wells?"

"Yes, Miss Chartley, we thought that best."

"Very well, then. Angela, whatever are you doing sitting over there in the corner? Tell Antoine to prepare a luncheon worthy of a lord."

She grasped the cane firmly and hauled herself up the stairs. No one, she told herself, is such a dragon that he cannot be reasoned with. She would simply have to make it perfectly clear to Lord Rotherford that there would be no discussion of Jamie's removal while Matthew was away.

The hall was empty, the front door open. She closed it and entered the parlor, tucking her unruly hair under her cap.

Lord Rotherford stood with his back to the door in front of the fireplace, contemplating the little blaze that took the morning's chill off the room. He appeared to be of Matthew's age, perhaps a little older. He was dressed as a gentleman, in riding pants and boots, with a coat as elegant as any she had seen. His hair was dark like Jamie's and he was tall and lean. Nothing to disgust one, she thought, and then cleared her throat.

"Pardon me, Lord Rotherford."

He turned around, and she understood.

Her quick glance took in a handsome face with regular features, even if his nose was a bit sharp. But all attraction ended at his eyes, and she could look no further.

They were eyes totally without expression, eyes without any sense of depth to them. Nothing sparkled from them, no warmth, no censure even, no inkling that anyone lived behind them. Omega Chartley had never seen eyes like that before. As she stood in the doorway, and then closed the door behind her, she hoped never to see such eyes again.

She curtsied, leaning on her cane. "Sir, I am Mrs. Wells, the housekeeper. How may I help you?"

He took her in with a long stare, even raising his quizzing glass. Omega felt her blood grow cold, as if chunks of ice were clogging her veins. The hairs on her arms rose and remained upright.

"You cannot possibly be a housekeeper," he said at last. His voice was warm, silky, totally at odds with his unfathomable eyes, which, in their unblinking way, took in every detail of her face, hair, dress, deportment, and character. She felt utterly stripped of all clothing. Even her thoughts seemed to have been scooped from her head.

This will never do, she told herself, and moved deeper into the room, forcing herself to come toward Jamie's guardian. "Lord Rotherford, I am Mrs. Wells and I am the housekeeper."

His eyes flicked to her cane and he smiled. "Matthew has taken to hiring the infirm? I never would have thought him a philanthropist."

Hot words rose to her lips, but she swallowed them and managed a slight smile. "I met with an unfortunate accident on the stairs and sprained my ankle. I do not, as a rule, require a cane, my lord."

He made no move to sit down or suggest that she take a chair, and she remained standing, shifting the weight off her foot, wondering at his ability to put her completely at a disadvantage. She gripped the cane tighter and regarded him with what she hoped was a hospitable air.

Rotherford came closer, and she fought down the urge to step back. "My dear Mrs. Wells—if that is what you choose to call yourself—I am here for my nephew, James Clevenden. Please tell him to come to me at once."

"Alas, I cannot do that, my lord."

He came closer. "But, Mrs. Wells, I insist." His voice was so warm that he practically purred.

Omega raised her chin a little higher. "I cannot produce him, my lord. He has gone to a horse-judging show with Major Hugh Owen, a guest of Lord Byford's. He is not expected back until tomorrow."

"Then I will speak to Lord Byford. Don't tell me that he is not here either?"

"He is not, my lord. He has gone up to London."

"To London? Surely not! And for what purpose?"

She returned him stare for stare. "Lord Byford does not see fit to acquaint me with his schedule. Indeed, sir, I do not ask. I am not even sure when he will return, my lord."

There was no show of emotion on Rotherford's face beyond the slight twitching of a muscle in his cheek. "You, madam, are a singularly valueless housekeeper," he said at last.

She couldn't help herself. "And you, sir, are singularly rude."

The muscle in his cheek worked a little faster. "I cannot imagine why Matthew keeps you on, unless he gets some other satisfaction from your services, madam, and I know that is not the case." He allowed himself a small chuckle at this, and turned back to the fireplace. "I will wait here for James, even if it takes all day and night, Mrs. Wells."

Nails digging into the palms of her hands, Omega struggled to maintain her composure. "I regret, my lord, that our guest rooms are all in use. May I suggest you consider the Ox and Bell in Byford? The food is well-recommended and the sheets are clean."

He turned around to face her again, and Omega stared into his eyes. She knew that her great anger showed in her own eyes, but she was equally determined that she would not be the first to look away. How dare you think to frighten me and the staff of this household, she thought as she gazed at him.

To her intense gratification, Lord Rotherford was the first to look away. He came closer, walking around her, tapping his quizzing glass on one of his waistcoat buttons. When he had completed his circuit, he stopped in front of her.

"You claim he is in London?"

How smooth his voice is, Omega thought. He sounds so wonderful. I wonder if the devil is like this. "Yes, my lord."

"I would not have thought anything could get him back to the city again, Mrs. Wells," he mused, speaking as if to himself, but goading her to reply.

She did not rise to the bait. "I have no notion of his intentions, my lord."

He walked around her again, this time pausing behind her. He let out a deep sigh, and she felt his breath on her neck. "Why is it that I do not believe you, Mrs. Wells?"

"My lord, I cannot imagine," she replied. She turned to face him, wishing that he was not standing so close, but refusing to back down. "We are preparing luncheon, Lord Rotherford, if you would wish to remain. Lord Byford's cook is quite good."

"I will, Mrs. Wells, on the condition that you eat with me," he answered.

He was so close that she could see clearly the pores on his face. Omega managed a smile and a nod in his direction. "How kind of you, sir, but I fear, sir, that you are doomed to disappointment. The housekeeper never dines with the guests. Lord Byford would be deeply chagrined with me. May I show you out now?"

She stepped around him and made her way to the door, wishing that she could sweep out elegantly instead of limping across the room, which seemed to grow longer and longer with each step. She knew he followed, even though he was uncannily silent.

Omega put her hand on the doorknob, and Lord Rotherford leaned his hand against the door, preventing her from opening it. She calmly took her hand away. "Sir?"

"One more question, my dear Mrs. Wells. Does the mail coach stop in this pleasant village?"

"It does, my lord."

"And postal service is rapid to London?"

"Very."

"Ah, that is excellent."

He removed his hand from the door and she opened it, grateful beyond measure to see Twinings standing in the hallway. Omega nodded toward Twinings. "Could you please see this gentleman out?"

The muscle in Rotherford's cheek worked more quickly, but he bowed to her and laughed. He had a pleasant laugh, but it sent waves of goose bumps up and down her back. "My dear Mrs. Wells, I will return this evening and see if you have, ah, learned anything more about your master's bolt to the city. Perhaps you'll find that your memory has improved by nightfall."

"That is unlikely, my lord. And now, let us not detain you any further. Twinings?"

Lord Rotherford allowed himself to be led to the front door. Twinings opened it with a flourish, handed him his hat and cane, and bowed. Rotherford ignored the butler. "Mrs. Wells, one more thing. If you are thinking of sending any kind of a message to James Clevenden, be assured that I do not ever travel alone, and several of my men are quite, quite interested in the architecture of this lovely old home. They may even remain here to observe it."

"You can't do that!" she burst out.

"I would wager that I can, my dear, dear Mrs. Wells. If you summon the constable, Matthew would be so chagrined at your rag manners. Good day, my dear Mrs. Wells. Until this evening? And you *will* dine with me this evening. I absolutely insist."

"Very well, sir," she said through clenched teeth, "since you asked so nicely."

Twinings closed the door and leaned against it. Omega walked as fast as she could to the door and slammed the bolt into the lock. "I hope he heard that!" she said savagely. "God, what a terrible man!"

"Miss Chartley, what does he mean to do?" asked the old man. "I cannot fathom what is going on."

She touched him on the shoulder. "He means to spirit Jamie away. And he means to keep us prisoner so we cannot warn him. The devil take him!"

"What are we to do?"

She took him by the arm. "Twinings, just . . . just go downstairs. I'm going to sit in the bookroom and think. You might . . . you might direct the footman to lock all the doors and windows."

The bookroom was quiet. She sat down in Matthew's chair and rested her aching ankle on an open drawer. "Oh, Matthew, what am I to do?" she said out loud.

Somehow she had to warn Hugh and Jamie. The thought of Hugh brought tears to her eyes. He would know what to do.

"Drat you, Matthew Bering," she said, "it seems you are never around when I need you."

She was ashamed of her uncharitable words as soon as she spoke them, and was grateful Matthew was not within earshot. She opened another drawer and pulled out a sheet of paper.

The letter was soon composed, sealed, and directed. It would startle Alpha and send him up into the boughs, but he would do what she said. On this head she had absolute reliance. Another moment's quiet reflection, sitting at Matthew's desk rubbing her ankle, and she had her answer. She smiled rather grimly and got to her feet. Lord Rotherford was not going to win this time. He had ruined enough lives already.

Twinings waited for her outside the bookroom door, as if afraid to let her out of his sight. "Twinings, you're just the person I need," she said, her voice filled with decision.

"Bring Angela up here. And . . . and if any of you have any money, please let me borrow it."

She sat down on one of the low window ledges outside the bookroom and looked over the flower garden to the back gate. A strange man stood there, hands on his hips, looking back at her. She had little doubt who his keeper was. She turned her back to him.

Angela came running. Omega made her sit down on the floor where she would not be seen from the window. "Angela, we must warn Jamie not to return here tomorrow."

Angela nodded.

"And once he has been warned, we must do something else. He must be taken to my brother Alpha's house just outside Amphney St. Peter."

"I can do these things, Miss Chartley. *Mira*, Twinings gave me all this money!"

It was a paltry sum, but it might provide a meal or two.

Omega smiled and rested her hand on Angela's shoulder. "I have no doubt that you can do all these things I have asked of you. I think the difficult part of your journey will be getting out of this house to take a message to Hugh at Claybrook. Twinings tells me Claybrook is a small village not ten miles from here to the north."

She looked out the window again. The man had shifted his position but was still guarding the back gate. "I don't doubt there is a guard at each gate, my dear. Can you get out without being seen?"

Angela thought a moment and then leaned against Omega's knee. "Do you know, Miss Chartley, that Hugh told me England would be boring and stuffy and not a bit like Spain? But so far, it is very much like campaigning with Picton." She clapped her hands together. "Omega, this is famous!"

Omega threw back her head and laughed. "Oh, I wish Jamie could hear you, my dear! What will you have me do?"

Angela scampered downstairs for her leather campaigning bag and ran up the stairs again, tying it around her waist. She helped Omega to her feet. "Do you know there is a little door off the breakfast room that no one uses? It gives out onto a grape arbor that leads to the gardening shed."

"Oh, but surely you will be seen, Angela! Let's wait until dark."

"No, no. The grape leaves almost cover the walkway. I can get to the gardening shed, and Tildy said her brother will get me out from there and point me in the right direction." She eyed Omega. "Do you think you could create some sort of diversion, just to make sure?"

"What would Sir Thomas Picton do?" said Omega.

"Oh, he would have sent the sappers ahead to pick off a few Frenchies."

"I'll think of something, Angela." She held out her arms. "Now, give me a hug, and don't let anyone see you. Tell Hugh to come quickly, and get Jamie to my brother."

Angela wrapped her arms around Omega, who kissed her and held her tight for a moment. "Do be careful, my dear," said Omega.

They walked arm in arm to the breakfast room. "I wish I knew what to do, Angela, to distract the guards."

Angela twinkled her eyes at Omega and put her hand to her mouth. "Once my mother took off her shirtwaist and washed her hair in a stream while the rest of us escaped. I remember that."

"Oh, I couldn't do that!" Omega said, and then reconsidered. Well, she told herself as she let Angela out the little side door, I've already lied, broken the law, committed assault, and practiced all manner of deceit.

The thought of Lord Rotherford stiffened her resolve. She limped to the door that led out to the garden, threw the bolt, and walked onto the tree-covered pathway. She noticed out of the corner of her eye that the guard was looking her way. She proceeded down the path and stopped before the climbing roses. Taking a deep breath, she allowed herself to stumble into the roses, and soon found herself trapped by the brambles.

"Oh, dear," she said out loud. The guard, still on the other side of the wall, came closer to watch. Her eye caught a flash of movement as Angela started for the gardener's shed. Omega began to cry, loud noisy tears. "Oh, dear," she sniffed again, and then unbuttoned her dress and carefully stepped out of it, leaving it behind on the thorns.

By now the guard was intent. Clad in a camisole and petticoat, Omega turned around and carefully began to remove the dress from the thorns, bending over so the guard would have plenty to look at, and wondering as she did so what Miss Haversham in Plymouth would say if she could see the meek-and-retiring Miss Chartley now.

When the dress was almost undone, Omega looked up and into the eyes of the strange man. She screamed and pointed at him, and then collapsed in a picturesque heap on the walkway. She opened one eye just a crack, watched him scurry away, and sat up, smiling in grim satisfaction. "I hope that was worth it, sir," she said out loud, retrieved her dress, and put it on before the servants came running.

Tildy was quick to see the humor of the situation, but Twinings was not so charitable. "Lord Byford would have been horrified, Miss Chartley," he scolded. "Can you imagine what he would think?"

"Yes, I can," she said, not the least repentant. "I will ask him when next I see him. And now, sir, if you would invite Antoine to prepare a sumptuous dinner, I believe Lord Rotherford will be dining here tonight. Let us show him every courtesy."

"I hope he chokes on it," declared Tildy.

"So, my dear, do I. But that only happens in novels."

14

Omega brushed her hair and arranged it carefully, wondering if it would be quite gray before the evening was over. It shone out, as rich brown as ever, as she tweaked her curls here and there, and then gave up in disgust. Tildy found her a dove-gray silk dress from the closet upstairs and helped her into it, buttoning it up the back. When she finished, she looked over Omega's shoulder into the mirror.

"Miss Chartley, it is perfection!" Then her face fell. "What a pity to waste it on that horrid man."

"Indeed," agreed Miss Chartley. "But it can be worn again, Tildy."

The maid regarded her a moment and then spoke softly. "Begging your pardon, Miss Chartley, but was this dress . . . was it meant for you?"

Omega nodded. "I think so, Tildy." Her smile was a little wan. "Matthew always had impeccable taste." She turned around and took hold of Tildy's hands. "My dear, I know all of you are wondering. It is enough for me to say that Lord Byford and I had a terrible falling-out eight years ago."

"Oh, but could you not resolve it?"

"I . . . I think not, my dear."

Tildy draped Omega's other dress and apron over her arm. "The house will be so strange when all of you leave, and Lord Byford will retreat to his bookroom again, and not speak above ten words a day to us, for all that he is kind."

"I'm sorry, Tildy. Truly I am." Omega squared her shoulders. "There, now. Do I look sufficiently matronly and dignified? No? Well, it will have to do. Let me know when Lord Rotherford arrives."

Tildy went to the door and hesitated. "This is forward of me, Miss Chartley, but do you love Lord Byford?"

It was forward, it was encroaching, but Omega was touched by Tildy's evident concern. "I do, my dear," she replied softly. "I did not think it possible that he could be dearer to me than he was eight years ago, especially after all we have been through, but he is. I wish that I understood such things." She made a small gesture. "Perhaps education and books do not really make us wise, Tildy. I once thought they did."

"Good luck, Miss Chartley," said Tildy as she quietly closed the door.

It was Twinings who summoned her upstairs when Lord Rotherford arrived. "The footman and I will serve tonight," he said. "Tildy is afraid."

"Very well," she said. And I am afraid too, she thought. "Have you shown him into the parlor?"

"Yes, Miss Chartley. Or rather, Mrs. Wells."

Her courage deserted her as she mounted the stairs and approached the parlor door. "Oh, Twinings," she whispered, "do not delay dinner long!"

"No, Mrs. Wells."

Rotherford was resplendent in evening dress. He turned when she entered the room, and bowed mockingly to her. He raised his quizzing glass. "You are magnificent, Mrs. Wells. How honored I am that you have indeed chosen to dine with me."

She nodded in his direction. "It would be rude to ignore my master's relatives."

Twinings summoned them into the dining room. Lord Rotherford offered her his arm and she took it. She could hardly help from noticing how nicely muscled his arm was. Oh, Matthew, I fear you are sadly out of shape, she thought, compared to this paragon. I hope this affair will not come to blows.

Dinner was a challenge. Rotherford's conversation was a smoothly flowing river, a fountain of clever information about London doings and gossip that held little interest for her. He was amusing, he was charming. She listened to his cleverness, forced herself to smile into his dead eyes, and wondered what was going on in his brain.

Course after course came and went, and still Rotherford carried his end of the conversation and hers too, laughing at his own witticisms, nodding at his sagacity. He began to fascinate her in a way that drew her even as it repelled her. Omega decided that listening to Lord Rotherford was rather like running her tongue over an abscessed tooth. It was painful even as it was compelling.

Dinner over, Rotherford pushed back from the table. "Now, my dear Mrs. Wells, my, er, friend at your back gate tells me that you had an encounter with a rose bramble this afternoon."

She colored prettily and looked away. "I fear my ankle is still a trifle unsteady. I should have stayed off that uneven path."

"Oh, come now, my dear. My short acquaintance with you—and I don't scruple to say that I swear I have seen you before—my short acquaintance tells me that you would never do such a thing."

"My lord, you know what a trial roses can be."

"I bow to your greater knowledge. Why is it that I think you may have been attempting a rather clever diversion?"

Omega raised her eyebrows and widened her eyes. "My lord, whatever can you mean?"

He leaned forward, moving almost quicker than sight, and grasped her by the wrist. "If you have somehow alerted James that I am in the neighborhood, it will not be a pleasant thing for any of us."

Just as suddenly he released her arm. Omega remained absolutely still.

"And because I feel some . . . slight suspicion, I intend to remain here all night." He smiled at her. "I am not going to let you out of my sight. And when morning comes, we will see who arrives."

Omega rose to her feet, and Rotherford handed her the cane. "Mrs. Wells, is the parlor more comfortable? Or do you recommend another room?"

"The library, my lord." Her words were calm, even as her thoughts bounded about the room. The library was at the back of the house. Surely one of the servants would alert Hugh before he found himself in the middle of something terrible.

Rotherford bowed and offered her his arm again, which she took. "Lead on, then, Mrs. Wells. We will go to the library."

Omega started down the hall and realized her mistake. That there was a library, she was sure, because Tildy had mentioned it. But where was it? She moved down the long hall as the taste of defeat grew in her mouth, and opened the first door she came to.

Rotherford opened the door wider and peered inside. He looked back at her, his eyes showing absolutely no emotion. "My dear Mrs. Wells, I believe this is the billiards room! Fancy that. Shall we try again?"

Omega tightened her lips and opened the door across the hall. It contained a piano, a harp, and several easels, all in holland covers.

Rotherford laughed. "Mrs. Wells! Such a forgetful housekeeper you are! Let me help you. Could *this* be the library?"

He opened the door and ushered her in, closing the door behind them. Enough daylight remained for him to light the lamp and set the candles around the library winking in their sconces. He raised both arms in a flourish. "*Voilà*, Mrs. Wells, the library! How lucky that we found it!" With each word, his voice grew a little harsher. "Since you have obviously never been here before, you may want to note its location, so you can dust here in the morning."

She said nothing, but sat in a chair gripping her cane. Rotherford quietly pried her fingers from it and set the cane out of her reach. He knelt by her chair. "My dear, we have certainly established beyond all doubt that you are not the housekeeper. Who might you be?"

When she did not speak, he stroked her under the chin. "I have my suspicions, but that is so farfetched that I will not bore you with it. Rather let us remain here and await the arrival of . . . who knows? I am filled with anticipation."

She sat silent, her hands clutched tightly together in

her lap, as Rotherford crossed to the globe and set it spinning. He selected a book off the shelf and handed it to her. "If you read to me, I am sure the time will pass more favorably."

Omega glanced down at the book. It was Defoe's *Journal of the Plague Year*. With fingers that trembled, she opened it to the beginning and then slammed the book shut. "Sir, I refuse to be bullied further by you. We will remain in silence, for I have nothing to say."

He bowed to her and took a seat nearby. He turned toward her and rested his chin on his hands. "I, then, shall study you, Miss Whoever-you-are. Perhaps it will occur to me where I have seen you before."

She bore his scrutiny in silence, willing herself to think of other things. The first hour dragged by, and then she began to conjugate verbs and then to parse sentences in her mind. Rotherford continued to stare at her. When the clock in the hallway chimed eight times, she smiled. It was one more hour that Jamie and Angela were farther away from this terrible man. She could stand anything if only they were even now hurrying toward the home of her brother.

Another hour passed, and another. Thunder rumbled in the distance, coming closer and closer. Soon it began to rain. Omega sighed. Perhaps some friendly farmer returning late from market would pick up Jamie and Angela.

And then, as she was resting her cheek on her hand, struggling to keep her eyes open, she heard voices in the hall. Rotherford sat up straight, but he continued to watch her. He noted her expectancy with that bloodless calm almost more frightening than outright rage. "Please remain seated, my dear. I wouldn't want our latest arrival to think I have been boring you."

The door to the library banged open and Hugh Owen stood there, soaking wet. He opened his mouth to speak to her, but Omega put her finger to her lips and shook her head. Hugh glanced from Omega to Lord Rotherford and nodded in complete understanding.

"Lord Rotherford," he said pleasantly, extending his

hand. "How disappointed Jamie will be to have missed you!"

Rotherford leapt from his chair, all pretense of civility gone. "Where is my nephew?" he roared.

Omega made herself small in the chair. Hugh walked deliberately toward Rotherford until he stood in front of Omega, shielding her. "He is not here. You're not going to find him easily, either, my lord. In fact, I think you may not find him at all."

With a cry of rage, Lord Rotherford slapped Hugh Owen with the back of his hand, slamming the sergeant to the floor like a felled tree. Hugh's check was slashed open by Rotherford's signet ring, and suddenly there was blood everywhere. With a cry of her own, Omega dropped to her knees and reached for the sergeant. Before she touched him, Lord Rotherford grabbed her by the hair and dragged her backward. He shook her like a dog with a bone, bending her back over her sprained ankle.

"Oh, God," she shrieked. "Let go of me!" Little starry lights flickered around her eyes as she clawed at Rotherford's hand, which had a firm hold on her hair.

Dimly she heard someone else screaming in the hall. It must have been Tildy. Omega called to her, but her voice was the barest whisper. As Rotherford shouted terrible things at her that she could not even understand, Omega heard the door slam again. She hung on to Rotherford's hand and prayed that Tildy had run for the constable. "Oh, sir, let go of me!" she begged.

"Yes, Edwin, I suggest that you do as the lady says, and quickly too, before God," said Matthew from the doorway.

Omega tried to slew herself around, but Rotherford held her tight. She sagged to the floor, scratching and clawing to free her hair, when Rotherford let go of her. She crawled to Hugh again and held on to him, afraid to look up.

She felt a hand on her shoulder and cringed. "Omega, it's all right," she heard, and opened her eyes.

It wasn't Matthew as she had ever seen him before,

with a days-old growth of beard, and dressed in the clothes of a farmer. Like Hugh, he was wet from the rain, his hair plastered to his head. She reached for his hand; he clasped hers for a moment, and then stood up again.

"Edwin, I challenge you do a duel," he snapped in a voice she had never heard before. "Tomorrow at dawn."

Rotherford laughed. "Pistols at ten paces then, you fool."

Matthew moved closer to Rotherford until they were almost nose-to-nose. "Make it five paces, please. I don't want either of us to miss."

Rotherford stepped back involuntarily, his eyes holding in them the first glimmer of expression that Omega had seen. It was replaced quickly, smoothly, by that blank curtain. He spoke again in his calm tones, as if he were placating a noisy child.

"My very dear Matthew, you forget yourself. All I desire is that my nephew be restored to the bosom of my family." He moved toward Omega as if to raise her to her feet. She hugged Hugh closer to her and ducked her head over his limp body. "Here, now, my dear, I meant you no harm!"

"Get away from me!" she muttered through clenched teeth.

Rotherford straightened up, a wounded look darting across his face and disappearing. "Really, Matthew, you know you do not wish to duel with me!" He managed a small indulgent laugh. "Have you never seen me shoot, dear boy? I will be pleased enough to forget all this in exchange for my nephew."

Matthew sat down on the arm of the chair close to Hugh and Omega. "I will duel with you, Edwin," he said softly.

As Omega watched in alarm, terrible, murderous anger overtook Rotherford again. He struggled against it, his face growing red and then white. Matthew watched him imperturbably, his leg swinging slightly.

Rotherford took a deep breath. "You forget that I can ruin you, Matthew. And now I will."

Matthew only smiled and looked down at Omega, who stared at him wide-eyed. "Lord Rotherford—Edwin—I would appeal to your nobler instincts, but you have none. You can't threaten me with ruin; I am already ruined. You have destroyed my happiness, and that of the woman I love. What else is there? You can kill me, and welcome to it, Rotherford." He leaned closer. "Who cares?"

Rotherford looked from Omega to Matthew. His eyes traveled to her again, and she curled up closer to Matthew. "This . . . this little scrap is Omega Chartley," he said, his voice filled with a curious combination of amusement and wrath. "Of course! You described her to me that night at Watier's, didn't you?"

Matthew nodded. " 'A waist small enough to span with two hands, and hair like a dandelion puff.' And did I say she was liable to speak her mind? Sorry, Omega," he said, looking down at her with a smile. "But you must agree, it is apt."

She nodded and relaxed slightly, although she did not release her grip on the unconscious sergeant.

"Edwin, she knows everything. I told her the whole wretched story. You can't threaten to tell her, because she knows. So does that very fine man you slapped silly. So does your own Bow Street Runner. I'll run a column in the London *Times* if you choose. I'll stand up in the House of Lords and declare it. You can't frighten me anymore."

"But you could hang for that murder," Rotherford reminded him.

"Could I? I have a signed statement from the ashman at 23 Quallen Lane, and he tells a different story than you do. And besides, whoever said there was a murder in the first place? You hushed all that up." Matthew got to his feet suddenly. "You studied my rather casual courage and *knew* I would do nothing to contest your guardianship of Jamie. You played me like a harp and put me in your *debt*." He spat the word out. "I discovered in London yesterday that I owe you nothing, Rotherford." He looked away from Rotherford then, as if he were bored with the whole conversation. "Tomorrow at dawn on the knoll behind Byford Common. Anyone can tell you where it is." Matthew made a final gesture with his hand. "Now, get out of my sight, Edwin. You sicken me."

Rotherford regarded Matthew for a long moment, rubbing his chin in a meditative fashion. "Matthew, you are overlooking the most pertinent fact of all: I am a wondrous fine shot and you are not. I'll kill you tomorrow."

Matthew laughed and walked to the door, flinging it open wider and gesturing toward the hall. "Edwin, don't you *ever* listen? I don't care! Get out of here."

Rotherford stalked to the door and looked back. "But if you are dead, Matthew, I will have Jamie."

Matthew laughed again and shook his head. "Dear God, Edwin, you have no idea how amusing you are! I place all my trust in Omega and Hugh Owen, even after I am dead. You'll never have Jamie as long as they are about. I do wish you would leave. You're so tiresome, and I am sleepy." He smiled at Rotherford. "I'll see you in the morning."

Rotherford swore roundly until Omega put her hands to her ears, and then left, banging the front door so hard that something in the hall crashed to the floor.

"Temper, temper, Edwin," said Matthew softly, and then got down on his knees beside Omega. "Well, my dandelion puff, you look a bit hagged, but infinitely better than this stalwart soul." He touched Hugh's slashed cheek. "Is that the work of Rotherford's ring? Good Lord."

Omega dabbed at Hugh's bloody face with the train of her dress. "We should summon a doctor, Matthew."

Matthew rested his hand on the back of Omega's neck. "We cannot, my dear. The good doctor would demand an explanation, and scream loud and long for the constable, and there would be no duel. No, Hugh will have to yield himself up to our mercies. He's seen much worse, Omega, I needn't scruple to tell you." He touched his forehead to hers. "Can you walk?"

"I think so." She tugged at his sleeve as he bent over Hugh. "Is Rotherford really such a marksman?"

Matthew nodded, and there was no smile this time. "He is, Omega. I'm probably looking forward to my last dawn. Oh, here, now, don't start that!"

Omega grabbed his arm and sobbed into his sleeve. "At least you're not crying all over my best coat this time," he said softly, and rested his hand on her head while she cried. "Look now, Hugh is coming around. Let's help him into this chair."

Hugh opened his eyes and stared from one person to the other. "I was going to challenge him to a duel, Matthew," he said finally, his words slurred.

"Bless you, Hugh, I beat you to it," Matthew replied. "We're going to get you upstairs and see you to bed. I can't summon a doctor, at least until after . . . after tomorrow morning. Omega, don't you dare start in again."

She swallowed her tears with a great effort and helped Hugh to his feet. In the hall, Twinings took over for her, an apology in his eyes.

"My lord, we were so afraid. I'm sorry." He could not look his master in the eye.

"You were wise not to get involved, Twinings. Rotherford is a nasty customer." He glanced at Tildy, who stood near the stairs wringing her apron through her hands. "But, my dear, I am glad you screamed. It certainly put a spring in my step." He sighed then, and turned Hugh over to the footman beside her. "It has been a long, long day."

He watched the butler and the footman lead Hugh Owen upstairs, and put his arm around Omega. "Let us go into the parlor, my dear. I feel quite old, all of a sudden."

Matthew shut the door and sank down onto a sofa. "Omega, could you pull off these boots? I've been in the saddle since early morning, and everything aches."

She did as he asked, and then sat beside him.

"As the estimable Timothy Platter would say . . . Oh, no, I will not repeat it. Omega, I have added greatly to my vocabulary in the last forty-eight hours. Lord, is that all it has been? But see here, you're not paying attention, my little educationist."

She shook her head as he tried to lift her chin. "And you need to pay attention, Omega. I have a proposition to set before you that would make me most happy, on this last night of my life."

She closed her eyes and leaned against him. Matthew settled himself more comfortably and put his arm around her. "It's a simple thing. I have in my pocket—and it is likely soaking wet—one special license for the marriage of Omega Chartley, spinster, to Matthew Bering, Lord Byford, bachelor. I propose that you marry me this night without any more delay. I have named you beneficiary of my lands and estates, and I mean for you to collect. If it comes to probate, it will be easier if you are my wife."

Omega pulled away and stared at him. "Matthew, I wish you would not talk this way!"

"But I must," he declared, taking her by the shoulders and giving her a little shake. "If Rotherford survives me, as he surely will, he will find a way to get all of Jamie's fortune. Of this I have no doubt. But if you inherit my estates, while they are not as grand, you can at least provide Jamie a comfortable living, and one for yourself too. I'm the author of your eight-year misery, my dear, and it's time to make what amends I can. Now, hush and give me no chat."

Sitting close to Matthew in the early-morning hours, Omega faced what he was saying squarely and without tears. He was right, of course. With his legacy, she could see that Jamie was well-cared-for, educated, and fitted for a position of use in the world. There would be enough for Angela too. And there would be Hugh to manage the estates.

Matthew seemed to divine precisely what she was thinking. "Omega, there will be sufficient money and then some for you to start an eccentric project or two, say, something like providing education for Byford's daughters. Something that will keep them . . . keep them from the streets of London. It's small compensation, but—" He could say no more.

Omega put her finger to his lips. "Let it rest now, Matthew. You've punished yourself enough."

When he could speak, he turned to her. "Omega, will you marry me?"

She looked right back at him, wishing for a small moment that her hair was tidy, her face not tear-spotted, and her dress clean and free from bloodstains. "Yes."

"Very well, my dear. Let us hobble down to the bookroom and—"

"But who is to marry us?" she interrupted as she allowed him to pull her along.

"You forget, Miss Chartley. I am a justice of the peace. I'll do this myself. If I were able to consummate this and we were to live together as husband and wife, I doubt it would hold up in a courtroom, but for now, and for our purposes, it will suffice. We can rely on Tildy and Twinings to witness."

Tildy made an excellent attendant, holding Omega up and taking the strain from her ankle, as Matthew held her other hand and read the marriage lines. His voice was firm. He looked at her with great love, and in the middle of her complete misery, Omega felt a tiny tugging of hope that she knew would betray her at dawn.

She knew there would be no ring, but Matthew surprised her. "I had left this with my solicitor, dearest," he said as he slipped on her wedding ring. "The date inscribed inside says 1808. We were merely . . . a little slow."

Matthew declared them man and wife, and he kissed her to seal the bargain. Tildy wept into her apron as

Twinings inspected the row of ledgers behind the desk as if searching for dust. He sniffed once or twice, and then blew his nose hard.

Matthew closed the book and replaced it on the shelf. He signed the license and handed the pen to Omega, who signed. The witnesses affixed their signatures, and Matthew stamped the document to make it legal.

"I will not . . . not likely be able to register this with the proper authority, Omega," he said. "You'll have to see it is done as soon after . . . as soon as you can. Don't neglect it."

"I won't," she said, her voice tiny.

"And now good night," he said. "Twinings, Tildy, thank you for your services. Twinings, make sure that I am summoned by five o'clock. Come, Omega."

They went upstairs arm in arm. "My dear, this is a shockingly informal kind of marriage, and one that you know I am unable to consummate, as much as I would wish it. But if you please, let us lie together tonight. I do not really wish to be alone." She felt the slight shudder that ran through him. "I confess to some trepidation."

She did not answer, but hugged him tighter around the waist. In her room, she thoughtfully removed her dress as he sat on the bed watching her but not seeing her. Her heart ached and she wondered what was on his mind. She found a nightgown and put it on, crawling into bed with a sigh. The bed was so comfortable. If she were not so numb, Omega knew that she would fall asleep in an instant.

Matthew went into his bedroom and returned in his nightshirt. He stopped at the side of the bed, looking down at her. "You do not mind?"

Omega blew out the candle and settled herself again. "Don't be a goose, Matthew."

She heard him chuckle as he got into bed. He held out his arms for her and gathered her close. Omega curled up against him, resting her head on his chest.

"I always did like the way you just fit under my arm," he said. His voice was close to her ear, and drowsy. "How pleasant this is. How I envy myself." She felt his chuckle again. "Dear God. I have less than five hours until my morning appointment. Wouldn't a sane man spend the time talking and talking, and trying to say everything there was to say?"

"Please, no," she said. "I can't bear it."

"But I only want to drift off to sleep in your arms. To me that is heaven, my dearest, beloved wife. Good night."

She listened as his breathing grew deep and regular, and even the beat of his heart slowed. She knew that she would never sleep, but she did, safe in her husband's arms.

15

The room was cool when she woke, cool and dark. Omega sighed and moved closer to Matthew and then opened her eyes. He was gone. His warm spot in the bed was already turning cold.

She sat up and threw back the covers, hurtling out of bed, gasping when she stood on her ankle, and then reaching for her robe. The hall was deserted. She descended the stairs, moving carefully, feeling for the last step so she would not fall.

Omega limped to the front door. It was still bolted, so she knew he had not left. "Matthew!" she called. "Matthew! Oh, please don't leave me like this!"

He came out of the breakfast room with Hugh. With a sob she ran to him and threw herself into his arms, hugging him to her, grasping all of him that she could hold. Dimly she heard Hugh say something about waiting outside, as Matthew picked her up and carried her back upstairs. He sat down with her on the bed, making no attempt to extricate himself from her fierce embrace. He stroked the back of her neck, his lips on her hair, and she gradually relaxed her grip.

"Better now?" he asked at last.

She shook her head and burrowed closer to him.

"I just sat in the chair and watched you for an hour, my dear," he said, speaking into her hair. "It was the prettiest sight I have ever seen. That was how I wanted to remember you, utterly at peace. I don't think I can bear any more tears, Omega, so please, please don't cry."

She shook her head again but loosened her grip on him, sitting up finally in his lap.

"That's better. Now, kiss me like a good girl and let me go."

Her eyes still closed, she raised her lips to his and kissed him. His lips were soft and warm. Omega put her hands behind his neck. He did not break off the kiss, but continued to taste her warmth and softness, as if he could not get enough. Finally she released him and leaned her cheek against his shoulder again.

"That will . . . last you awhile?"

He smiled. "I think so. Don't follow me downstairs." He deposited her on the bed, putting the blankets up around her shoulders. "It's getting cold again. Soon it will be autumn, Omega." He leaned over and kissed her one last time. "The people here are friendly, my dear. They will help you with whatever schemes you come up with for their betterment. And I think Lord Nickle and Sir Martin will move on that carting route. It is something I have worked for. I leave it for you to see it through."

He went to the door and opened it, looking back just once. "I have a favor, dearest."

"Anything, anything."

"Just this. Put your wedding ring on my little finger after . . . after this is over. Eternity is a long, long time, Omega, and it will be easier if part of you is with me."

"I will," she whispered.

He nodded to her, blew her a kiss, and closed the door behind him. Numb with sorrow, she hugged Matthew's pillow to her breast and listened as they rode away from the manor.

She would have to begin forgetting him all over again, but this time it would be different. Before, she had loved Matthew Bering and lost him. This time, she had loved Matthew Bering and lost him, and lost herself in him. This time would be infinitely more difficult; it would be impossible.

When it was barely light outside, Omega dressed and found her cane, negotiating the hall with more assurance, now that she could see where she was going. She looked out the window. It was still too dark for the duel, but she was sharply aware that the Byford Common knoll would receive the first strong light of morning, and there would be a killing. The thought snatched the breath from her body. It isn't fair, she told herself. It isn't fair.

She went downstairs again. None of the servants came up from their quarters, although she could hear them talking in low tones. She couldn't have faced them anyway. Moving quietly, Omega opened the front door and sat down on the steps, waiting for the sun to rise. She wondered if she would be able to hear the shots.

Omega listened, and heard only a horse approaching, galloping too fast to make the slight curve where the lane circled in front of the manor. She sat up, alert, and sucked in her breath as a horse and rider leapt smoothly over the low stone wall and came to a halt right in front of her.

Omega jumped up, praying that it was not Hugh already, come to tell her that it was all over. "Oh, please, what is it?" she begged.

And then she smelled the cigar and heard the rough voice of Timothy Platter. "Miss Chartley, what're ye doing out here? Haven't you gentry morts a particle of sense?"

She hurried down the steps and grasped the stirrup. "Mr. Platter, oh, please, can you stop Matthew and Rotherford? They have gone to duel."

The Runner swore and threw away his cigar. "Damn fools," he exclaimed. "Where are they?"

"Byford Common, the knoll. But I don't know where that is!" She hurried to the front door and shouted, "Tildy! I need you!"

In a moment the maid stood beside her. Without a word the Runner grabbed her hand and pulled her up behind him. "We're going to Byford Common, miss," he growled. "If you know a short way, don't be shy about it!"

"Across the field is quicker, if you can jump the fences."

The Runner grabbed her hands and pulled them together across his stomach. "Hang on, girl. Tell me the direction as we go. If you should fall off, I'll not stop, mind."

They were gone. Omega shivered and rubbed her hands over her arms. She sat back on the steps. In a few minutes she was joined by Twinings and the footman, and then Antoine, the potboy, and the scullery maid. They were all quiet, and silently she blessed them, drawing strength from their presence.

Omega willed the sun to remain below the horizon, but it rose anyway, with all the promise of a beautiful day. Men would go about their haying, women would continue their preparations for harvest, not even aware that Omega Chartley's heart was broken and would never mend.

"Can we hear anything from the knoll?" she asked finally.

"Depends on the wind, Miss Chartley," said Twinings.

They sat for an hour, until the sun was well up and the roosters had settled down to a new day. Twinings was the first to stand. "I believe I should see about breakfast," he said. "Come, Antoine."

They got no further than a step inside the entrance when Omega stood slowly and shaded her eyes with her hand. A carriage was tooling down the road. Tied to the back of the carriage was Matthew's horse. She sobbed out loud, and then looked again. Rotherford's horse was tied next to it, and overseeing them both was the Bow Street Runner, cigar clenched in his teeth, a big grin on his face. Tildy waved to Omega from her perch behind the Runner, and Omega felt her heart begin to beat again. She walked down the steps.

The carriage swept into the circle drive and stopped by

the steps. The door opened and out stepped the constable, looking remarkably displeased. He tipped his hat to Omega. "I don't scruple to tell you, miss, that both of these gents are too old for this sort of dandified nonsense. And our own justice of the peace, too! Now, how does it look when our betters carry on in such a ramshackle fashion, I ask you? Stand back, miss."

The constable swung down the steps and Lord Rotherford descended, tight-lipped and grim about the mouth. He was followed by Matthew Bering, equally dour.

All of a sudden, it was too much. For the first time in her life, Omega Chartley quietly fainted, caught at the last minute by the potboy.

When she opened her eyes, she was stretched out on the lawn, her head in Matthew's lap. "You're alive," she said.

"Indeed, my dear. And under arrest for dueling, for which I have Timothy Platter and the constable *I* hired to thank."

She turned her head slightly and regarded the two men, who squatted on the lawn close by. "Thank you, Mr. Platter. I don't think you ever made a better arrest, Constable."

The constable merely grunted, but the Runner tipped his hat to her. "Someone had to stop these two fools." He held his hands out in front of him. "There they was, in all their magnificence, already stepping off the ten paces. D'ye know I've never seen a duel before?" He grinned. "I was almost of a mind to let them continue, except I feared our laddie would likely get the short stick." He glanced in Rotherford's direction. "Now, had the wind been blowing the other way, why, I might have been inclined to let them continue. But fair's fair, eh, my lord?"

Rotherford only looked straight ahead, no expression in his eyes. "I'll take you to court for this, Matthew," he said. "You've had your chance to lie low these many years, but no, you had to stir up the water."

"Yes," agreed Matthew dryly, "wretched of me to show a little spine after all this time. Can't imagine what I was thinking."

"I will make you wish you had not."

Matthew shrugged. "Suit yourself, Edwin."

Omega reached for his hand and clasped it to her stomach. He smiled down at her. "I can't say that I'm disappointed Platter showed up."

"You should not be!" Timothy said indignantly. "And me riding all night from Suffolk, with a tiny stop in London." He motioned to the constable. "Sir, you've done a spanking fine job, a fine job. Now, if you don't mind, I'll take over."

The constable bobbed his head up and down. "You'll get no complaint from me. 'Tis the haying season, my lord, and I'll just have to trust the two of you until we are done in our fields."

Platter clapped his hands together as the constable drove off. "And now, Lord Byford, if you would, let us go into the house. I have a matter of business that should prove of great interest to you and your lovely relative over there."

They adjourned to the bookroom, Platter seating himself behind Matthew's desk after a gesture from Lord Byford. Rotherford took his chair as far away from the others as he could. Matthew stood behind Omega's chair, his hands resting lightly on her shoulders.

Platter heaved a sigh and leaned back in the chair, hands across his belly. He took out a cigar, looked at Omega, and thought better of it. He eyed the cigar for a moment, bit off a hunk of it, and started to chew. He regarded Matthew speculatively.

"My lord, do you know what happened the other night in London?"

"I can't imagine, Timothy. Please enlighten all of us."

"A curious robbery. I don't pretend to understand it. A bloke of the thieving population pinched a wooden box from under the bed of a stinking, reeking dustman on Quallen Lane."

"Fancy!" exclaimed Matthew.

Rotherford raised his head, and then elaborately ignored the rest of them.

Timothy sucked on the bit of cigar. "I don't know

what's happening to the thieves of London. Silly man runs straight into the loving arms of one of my fellow Bow Street Boys."

"How fortuitous," declared Matthew, ignoring Omega, who was regarding him suspiciously.

"Indeed. And do you know, there was only an old shirt and cravat in that box, my lord, plus a curious stickpin. I don't know who it belonged to, but it's so distinctive that I'm sure we'll know its owner soon enough." He leaned toward Matthew in a conspiratorial way. "And, my lord, there were the faintest rusty brown stains all over it." His eyes shifted from side to side. "Blood, my lord."

Rotherford appeared more interested. If Platter noticed, he gave no sign.

"Now, why, I asked myself, would a cove pinch something like that, and only that?"

"I'm sure you were curious," agreed Matthew affably. "Pay attention, Omega."

"I was so curious I set a guard to watch that house. He had watched for only a moment or two when a messenger rode up all of a lather and handed the landlord a note." Timothy Platter leaned back and patted his stomach. "That horse was so lathered, why, it could have come all the way from Byford, bless my soul."

"I'm sure it's possible, although we have excellent mail-coach service. Perhaps it just wasn't fast enough. Whatever could the note have said?" asked Matthew, all interest.

Platter clicked his tongue and shook his head. "I'll never know, my lord, for do you know what happened next?"

"No, what?"

"In ten minutes, the whole house was on fire! Why, you would have thought there was something in that message that scared the landlord."

Matthew's hands tightened on Omega's shoulders. "The devil, you say."

The Runner slapped his knee. "What a blaze!"

"And did it all burn down?" asked Rotherford, making

his first contribution. A smile of satisfaction played about his lips.

"Oh, I'm afraid it did, laddie, my lord," Platter said mournfully, but then he brightened up. "But do you know, the Runner watching the house was able to dash inside and save some possessions!"

"Good for him. My faith in London justice grows by the minute. What did he save?" asked Matthew. "Or shall I guess?"

Platter grinned and took another bite off his cigar. "Guess if you want, my lord."

"He saved a mattress, didn't he? From the second floor. One with bloodstains like the ones on that shirt?"

"You've hit upon it, my lord," exclaimed Platter. "And do you know, when that mattress hits the pavement, the strangest little ashman from belowstairs comes up and begins singing such a tune!"

Rotherford slumped forward, his face drained of all color.

"The landlord tried to shut him up, but no, no, the ashman was still talking when I left the place. I wonder what he was saying. Do you think it might have had something to do with the bloodstains?"

"No one believes a drunk," said Rotherford, recovering himself.

Platter nodded. "That's what I say, my lord Rotherford, that's what I say. It would never hold up in a court of law. But do you know, sir, I heard the very same story from Sir Horace Billings of Suffolk. Now, do you think a court of law would believe him?"

Rotherford leapt from his chair and Omega jumped. Matthew stood in front of her, shielding her from Rotherford, who pounded his fist on the desk under Platter's nose. Platter did not move.

"That's impossible!" Rotherford shouted. "Billings is dead!"

The Runner looked at him for a long minute. "Now, how would you know that? Are you friends?"

Rotherford sat down, poised to leap to his feet again. "He is dead, I tell you!"

Platter sighed and crossed himself. "You're so right, my lord. Thank you for pointing that out. I have a bad habit of livening up my tales."

Rotherford smiled and looked around him. Platter pulled open his coat and rummaged among the papers inside, humming to himself. "Ah, here we are. I have a little document, stamped and sealed right and tight, that might be of interest to you, Lord Rotherford, particularly if you were a friend of the late departed."

"He was merely a slight acquaintance. Matthew knew him well."

Matthew nodded. "He was a friend of mine from Oxford. And he is dead?"

"Alas, dead these five years," said Platter sorrowfully. "Died of the damp, he did, my lord. Such a drafty place is Suffolk." Platter rested his elbows on the desk. "But something was weighing heavily on his mind, my lords and lady. Some deep, dark memory." Platter crossed himself again. "Told his younger brother he would sleep better if it didn't weight so heavy."

Rotherford sucked in his breath. Matthew took a seat beside Omega and clasped her hand so tightly that she almost cried out. She squeezed his hand in turn and leaned closer to him.

Platter lowered his voice. "Sir Horace dictated a sorry tale to his brother, a tale of rape and murder, of an evening's jest gone awry, a wedding eve turned sour." Platter turned to face Lord Rotherford, who sat with his eyes closed. "I'm sorry to have to tell you this, my lord, but Sir Horace said some dreadful things about you. It seems you were not precisely the perfect host."

Rotherford rose to his feet slowly and went to the window. He pounded on the frame in sudden violence, and then was silent. The silence stretched into long seconds and then minutes. His voice was soft when he finally spoke.

"Matthew, what will you have me do? I'm too old for a voyage to the Antipodes in the hold of a prison ship, and I don't fancy a noose around my neck."

"Release Jamie to me, Edwin. Sign a statement resigning your guardianship. And then you never, never show your face around my home again. Not ever."

Rotherford did not turn around. "You will discover, Matthew, that there are funds, large funds, missing from Jamie's trust."

Matthew considered this. "I think Jamie's trust can stand the nonsense, as long as this ends it."

Rotherford turned around. "Very well, I agree."

"Then let me encourage you to leave Byford as soon as you can pack."

Rotherford went to the door, looked back as if he would speak, and then thought better of it. He bowed to them all, his eyes still expressionless, and left the room. They waited, silent, until the front door closed.

Matthew let out a sigh. Platter rose to his feet and reached across the desk. "Give me your hand, my lord—we've done the thing." The men clasped hands across the desk. Matthew smiled for the first time.

Platter tucked Billings' statement inside his coat again. "Me for London, then, my lord. Do you know, Maeve is in such a dither. It seems that someone left a box of dishes outside our door. Happens Maeve's name was on it, but she can't imagine who would give her such a legacy." He grinned and took another bite of his cigar. "Particularly since our only company recently was a down-at-the-heels farming laddie without a sixpence to scratch with!"

"Fancy," murmured Matthew. "Some farmers save their money for rainy days, I suspect."

"Happens they do," said Platter.

"Before you go," said Matthew, "could you fetch Hugh Owen back here?"

"Before God," said Omega, "where *was* Hugh all this time?"

"He was my stalwart on the dueling field, offering all manner of advice. Why, I think he was vaguely disappointed when the constable and our Runner materialized out of the gloom. Well, at any rate, he is in the custody of the doctor, who is repairing the damage done by Rotherford last night."

Platter tipped his hat and whistled his way down the

hall. Omega shook her head in amazement. Matthew gathered her in his arms and pushed the door shut with his foot.

"We have one more matter to discuss, my dear," he said. "One that you will find painful, but which I cannot avoid, as much as I would wish."

He released her, sat her in a chair, and went to his desk, where he took out the special license again. As she watched open mouthed, he tore it into small pieces and threw them into the fireplace.

"I will not bind you to a man who wouldn't be much of a husband, my dear."

"Matthew, I don't care about that," she whispered, afraid to trust her voice.

He sat down on the desk. "You would eventually, my dear. You're too young to be leg-shackled to someone who would be an excellent conversationalist but remarkably ineffective in that other kind of companionship. Now, hush, and listen to me! There's likely someone in Durham who will love you in ways that I can't."

When she said nothing, he sighed. "Now, excuse me, Omega. I stink as badly as that ashman. I haven't gone so long without a bath since I took a dare at Harrow. When I am done, I am going to take my carriage to your brother's and retrieve those wandering children."

He bowed to her and left the room.

She sat there until she heard his footsteps overhead and his door closing. With eyes as blank as Rotherford's, she walked slowly downstairs to the housekeeper's room, lay down on the bed, and curled herself into a ball. She ignored Tildy's questions, closing her eyes. She thought she heard Matthew in the servant's hall, speaking to the others. When he finished and went upstairs, no one bothered her again. She wrapped her arms around herself and slept.

When Platter returned with Hugh, she roused herself and helped the soldier to his room. She tucked him in bed, reminding him in her best educationist's voice to lie still so he would not tear his stitches. She bustled about the room, closing the draperies and feeding a small fire on the hearth. The room was cool with autumn. She sniffed the air; fall was here. It was almost time to begin the term at St. Elizabeth's, her first term in a new school.

"Omega," said Hugh suddenly, "I haven't told you, have I?"

"What?"

"When Jamie and I were in Claybrook, Lord Nickle asked me to manage his horse-breeding farm in Ireland."

"Oh, Hugh!" she exclaimed, and her pleasure was genuine. "And will you do it?"

"Of course. Only think of the opportunity . . ." His voice trailed off as the doctor's famous sleeping powders prepared to claim another victim in Matthew Bering's house. Hugh struggled to the surface one last time before sleep overtook him. "We brought your trunk and your valise from the mail coach, Omega. In your room . . ."

She let herself out the door and into the room upstairs. There they were, her shabby trunk, the leather valise that had been Alpha's at Oxford, and her bundle of books. She looked in the valise and sighed with relief. Her money was all there. She untied the cord about the books and sat down, turning the pages of her old friends.

The term would begin in a week. She found a sheet of paper and a pencil and began to outline her first course. The business occupied her thoughts and she almost did not hear Matthew leave in his carriage. The pencil tightened in her hand and her glance wandered to the window for a moment, but then she bent her head over her books again, putting him out of her thoughts.

16

Omega's eyes did not close that night, no matter how hard she tried to sleep. She tossed and turned until the bed was a tangle of sheets and blankets. Toward morning she gave it up and retreated to her chair again, hugging her pillow until her head nodded forward and she slept.

She woke in midmorning, startled by the pounding of feet on the stairs. She sat up, putting the pillow behind the chair as the door opened and Angela and Jamie dashed in. With a happy cry she held out her arms for both of them and they hugged her in turn.

"Oh, Angela, you are such a hand," she exclaimed, smoothing back the child's curls from around her face. "Thank you for getting Jamie to safety."

Angela allowed herself to be held for a moment on Omega's lap. "Oh, Miss Chartley, I got lost once. It was Jamie who found the right road."

"Jamie! You are a complete hand too!"

He dropped his eyes modestly for a moment, and then remembered his news. "Omega, this is famous! Uncle Matthew says I can stay and stay and never leave this place. We have been making such plans."

"I am sure you have," said Omega quietly. She looked at Angela, who was suddenly silent. "And, my dear, has Hugh told you his good news?"

She nodded, but there was no light in her eyes, no indication that her friend's good fortune was anything she wanted. Her eyes filled with tears and she clung to Omega. "Miss Chartley, I don't want to leave Byford! It feels like I thought home would, if ever I had one. What am I to do?"

Omega ached for her little friend. I don't want to leave Byford either, she thought as she hugged Angela closer. She bowed her head over Angela and closed her eyes.

"Angela."

Hugh stood in the doorway. He was dressed in

Matthew's good clothes again, his arm arranged in a sling. How long he had stood there listening, Omega had no idea, but his face was serious.

He came into the room and knelt beside Angela. "*Munequita,* do you want to stay here? Don't . . . don't think you'll hurt my feelings by whatever you say. Just tell me the truth."

Angela rested against Omega. "Hugh, I want to stay here with Jamie and Omega."

Omega winced. Perhaps Matthew could explain it to Angela when she put her own bags in the stage again and left for Durham. She knew she could not.

"It's a home, Hugh," Angela said, attempting to explain something for which she had no words. "Are you really angry with me?"

Hugh held out his arm to her. She came to him and leaned against his knee. "Angry? Why should I be? I've already talked to Lord Byford about this. And do you know what he says?"

Angela shook her head.

"He says he would be happy as a grig if you stay here. Only he promised me that both you and Jamie will spend your summers in Ireland . . . if everyone is agreeable."

Angela burst into noisy sobs. Hugh smiled over her head to Omega. "Now, that's the Angela I know." He kissed her on the forehead. "We've traveled some long roads on foot, *amiga*. We'll get together every summer and refight any battle you say."

"Omega, have you become such a lady of leisure that you sit in your bedgown until noon?"

Omega looked up in surprise. "Alpha!" she shrieked, and hurried to her brother, who whirled her around and kissed her heartily.

He held her off at arm's length. "Such a tale Matthew has told me! And I thought I could trust you on the roadways of England."

"Obviously you cannot, my dear," said Omega. "I've had a world of adventure, even though I missed my whole itinerary and fell in with some of the most *eccentric* people. Alpha, this will keep me warm for many a winter."

"Good. I am here to drag you back onto the straight-and-narrow path and take you directly to Amphney St. Peter, where Lydia awaits with broths and hot packs and good advice, which you can select from at your leisure."

"Alpha," she sighed, and leaned against him. "Let's go as soon as we can."

Hugh stood up. "Not until I leave," he said. "Lord Nickle wants me in London tomorrow for some instructions and information from his solicitors. I expect all of you to see me off this afternoon."

Omega shook her head. "Not I, Hugh. I find that I cannot . . . cannot abide farewells anymore." Her voice broke and Alpha looked at her with some concern. "It is somewhat lowering to see one's friends cast to the four winds."

Alpha hugged her to him. "We'll go in style tomorrow morning in Matthew's carriage. *You* may prefer the common stage, but I think I will enjoy this bit of luxury again."

She dismissed them all, dressed hurriedly, and joined them downstairs for luncheon, served by a somewhat subdued Twinings and by Tildy, whose eyes were red. Matthew presided at the head of the table. He looked tired, and he said little, but the conversation traveled along at a clipping rate from brother to sister, over to Hugh, and back to the children.

Omega could not bring herself to look at Matthew. She steeled herself for the ordeal of eating, and was grateful when the meal ended. If he doesn't come too close to me, or say anything of a personal nature, I can rub through this day and leave with Alpha first thing in the morning, she thought as she stood on the front steps and waved as the others set off in Matthew's barouche to take Hugh into Byford. She blew a kiss to her sergeant and waved both hands until they were out of sight.

The servants hurried down the steps and climbed into the gig that the footman drove. Tildy leaned over the side. "Miss Chartley, Hugh said he would write to me. Do you think I will find something to say?"

Omega touched her arm. "You will find plenty to write

about. I'm so glad. Now, hurry, or you'll miss his good-bye!"

Omega trudged up the stairs, wishing that her ankle did not ache so, and wondering if a visit to a London surgeon was in order, after all. Perhaps Alpha could spare a day to take her there. Her mind a purposeful blank, she knotted her books together, tying a neat bow. Before he left with the others, Matthew had spoken to her quite formally and invited her to take any or all of the clothing in the dressing room. She had decided against it at first, and then changed her mind. If she did not take the dresses, they would only hang unused. There had been too much waste already; no sense in adding to it. She would take only the more useful gowns that would suit in the classroom.

And then when she had packed them, she changed her mind, flinging the dresses from her trunk and putting them back in the dressing room. They would only serve as a reminder, and she was determined to forget this time. She would teach and commit herself to the classroom. Maybe someday there would be someone else. She couldn't imagine such a thing, but perhaps in a few years it would be possible.

Omega was repacking her valise when she heard a noise next door in Matthew's room, the sound of drawers being opened. She stopped and listened. The noises ceased and she continued her packing, berating herself for being such a goose. And then she heard the sound of drawers again.

She frowned. One of the servants must have remained behind. But surely they knew better than to invade his privacy like that. Without a thought in her head, she left her room and went next door on tiptoe, carefully and quietly opening the door.

Lord Rotherford stood before her, one of Matthew's drawers in his hand, the contents spilling on the floor. She gasped and stepped back, and suddenly became aware that she was all alone in the house.

Rotherford put down the drawer. "Miss Chartley, I had no idea you were here."

She was silent, unable to think of anything to say, her feet rooted to the carpet.

"Cat got your tongue, my dear?" he said. "Devilish inconvenient for a teacher, eh?"

"What . . . what are you doing here?" she managed finally.

Rotherford picked up another drawer and pawed through it. "An excellent question, my dear. I thought I would take a look at that letter from Horace Billings. It's not downstairs in the bookroom. I just want another look, my dear, nothing more."

Suddenly she was furious. "Can't you leave Matthew alone? Can't you just go away and cease your meddling? Haven't you done enough? Good God, Rotherford, you are a menace to society!" She wanted to beat him, to flay the flesh from his bones, or at the very least to murder him. She could only stand there in the doorway and rail at him.

He took all of this in, and then began to smile at her wrath. "You are lovely when you are angry," he said. "You would be such a challenge. Not like that little drab on Quallen Lane. You could be such a pleasant farewell for me from Byford. God knows Matthew hasn't any means to do anything with you."

Fear greater than anything she had ever known rose in her eyes. She backed away. "I'll scream, my lord, if you come one step closer."

He crossed the room in a bound. "Scream away, Miss Chartley. I believe we have the house to ourselves." Before she could move again, or even raise her hands to defend herself, Lord Rotherford took the front of her dress and ripped it down to her waist. She screamed as he pulled her sleeves down, pinning her bare arms to her sides.

She screamed again when he touched her. "Oh, scream away, my lovely. That will make it so much more—"

She had no idea what he intended to say next. He uttered a strange groan and a puzzled look pierced his inexpressive eyes. They opened wider, and the look in them was a horror she would never forget. He knocked her off balance as he sank to his knees and then fell forward at her feet, a knife deep in his back.

Struck dumb with fear, Omega struggled to right

herself. She pulled her arms from her sleeves and raised the front of her ruined dress. She crouched in the corner, covering herself as best she could, when she looked up and gasped.

Timothy Platter was sitting in the window, the cigar still clutched between his teeth, his coat covered with pollen again. Without a word beyond a sneeze and a grunt of satisfaction at his handiwork, he tossed a blanket to her. She pulled it around her body and sat there on the floor, her teeth chattering.

"I've been watching him, Miss Chartley," he said finally as he stubbed out his cigar. "Something told me this case wasn't quite over yet, miss. Happens I was right. Maeve always tells me, 'Timmy boy, trust your instincts.' "

In a surprisingly gentle fashion he raised Omega to her feet and sat her down. "Now, tell me, what was he doing here? He couldn't have known you had remained behind."

When she remained speechless, he reached inside his voluminous coat and detached a bottle, which he uncorked and passed to her. She took it without a murmur and downed a good swallow. The liquor made her eyes water, but it put heart back in her.

"Timothy, he came for the letter, you know, the letter from Sir Horace Billings. I think he still intended to do Matthew harm."

Platter nodded and produced the letter from his pocket. Omega's eyes widened. "But didn't you give that to Matthew?"

"I took it back again." He broke the seal on the document and spread out the page so she could see.

The page was blank. Her eyes even wider, Omega took a deep breath and reached for the paper, turning it over and over in her hands, as if she expected to see magic writing suddenly appear. She looked up at Platter. "Oh, Timothy, I do not understand. Not at all."

"I do."

Matthew stood in the doorway. He took in Rotherford dead at his feet, and Omega, white-faced and wrapped in a blanket, and then closed the door behind him and locked it. "It wouldn't do the children any good to see this," he said, and then touched Omega's cheek. "He didn't hurt you, did he, my dear?"

She shook her head. "Timothy . . ." She couldn't collect her thoughts.

Matthew bowed to the Runner. "I remain in your debt, sir," he said. He plucked the paper from Omega's nerveless fingers and handed it back to the Bow Street Runner.

"There never was a letter, was there, Platter?" he said.

"No," Timothy said simply, "although that part about Sir Horace and his nightmares was true. His younger brother told me how deeply troubled he was. I merely supplied the text."

Matthew sank down on the bed next to Omega and stared at the Runner. "You broke the law for me?"

"Happens I did," said Platter gruffly. "Happens sometimes you have to bend the law to preserve it. Don't stare at me like that!" He put the paper back in the envelope. "Was it a bad idea?" When no one said anything, Platter looked Matthew in the eye. "And I did it for Millie Platter."

"You knew," Matthew said simply.

"I knew. She wasn't a good girl, but she was my sister, Lord Byford."

A curious range of emotions passed across Matthew's face, a mixture of sorrow and shame, coupled with respect. The expression yielded to a quiet calm that Omega had been wishing to see for eight years.

"Timothy, thank you. Thank you from the bottom of my heart. For everything."

Platter nodded, and coughed, wiping around his nose, with a swipe at his eyes. "Too much of that treacle, Lord Byford, and I'll not be fit for duty. Give me a hand with this rascal. Let's wrap a sheet around him. No sense in giving the little ones the blue devils. Miss Chartley, Omega, my dear, I suggest you find another dress. You'll catch your death in that one."

By the time the house was cleared of the constable, the doctor, and the undertaker, and the Bow Street Runner had at last taken his leave, dinner was long over. Omega left Matthew and Alpha in the dining room discussing the events of the day over brandy and what remained of Antoine's mousse.

She had to complete her packing. She and Alpha would be away at first light for the drive to Amphney St. Peter. She would see her nephews and Lydia would laugh and cry over all her misadventures, and then it would be Durham for her.

After she had finished, Omega took one last look in the dressing room, running her hands along the frocks, wishing there had been time to try on the really elaborate ones. She closed the door then and put them from her mind.

The window was open and she went to it, leaning out for a last smell of roses. Winter would sweep over this lovely land, and then spring. Her life would go on with the same regularity as the seasons. The thought brought Omega no pain now. She was almost content with the way things were. Matthew would have the children to comfort him, especially since he would likely have none of his own, and she would be busy enough. She would not think of him beyond four or five times in an hour, and with any luck, by the time another eight years had come and gone, she would only recall him to mind once or twice a day.

She closed the window and shut the draperies. She turned back the coverlet, aching for a good night's rest. Someone knocked. Her heart rose for a moment, and then resumed its normal rhythm. It was not Matthew's knock.

"Alpha?"

"May I come in?"

She opened the door and drew him in. He surveyed the trunk and books, all tidy and bound together. He rubbed his hands. "You can almost smell winter in the air already." He flopped on her bed and put his hands behind his head. "Well, dear heart, you remind me of something."

"What?"

"I have become a reader of nursery rhymes. You may

credit your nephews. Remember the one about St. Ives, and the kits and cats and sacks and wives?"

"And 'how many were going to St. Ives?' " she finished for him, a smile on her face too. "I confess I feel that way." She sat down beside him. "A soldier, a runaway, a Spanish orphan, a Bow Street Runner, a true villain, an almost-husband . . ." The light left her eyes. "But I was the only one going to St. Ives after all, wasn't I, Alpha?" she asked, her voice small.

He took her hand. "I'm afraid so, my dear." His voice was soft. "We're teachers. What did you learn from all this?"

She lay back next to him and he put his arm around her. "Alpha, I learned to toss away itineraries and just let things happen. I feel as though I haven't looked at a clock in years. Is that enough?"

She sat up. Suddenly it wasn't enough, not nearly enough. "Alpha, it won't do."

He watched her from the bed, his eyes bright.

"Alpha," she said slowly, "what would you say if I went to Matthew Bering's room tonight?"

He considered the question. "You're old enough to make your own decisions, dear heart."

"That's no answer," she said crossly.

"It's the only answer you'll get from me. I just don't want to see you hurt any further, Omega. You mean too much to me. So there."

"Won't you give me some advice?" she pleaded. "Alpha, I don't want to leave him. I simply don't know what to do!"

He got up and kissed her. "I think you do know what to do. You want advice? I'll tell you this: nothing is worse than regret. There's no hell greater than asking yourself: 'What if I had done this, or that?' Good night, Omega. Pleasant dreams."

"Alpha, you are worse than useless," she said after he closed the door.

Omega climbed into bed, examined her ankle, decided that she would likely limp for the rest of her life, and pinched out the candle. There was no comfortable spot anywhere in the bed that only two nights ago had felt so wonderful. She might as well have slept on rocks or sharp-pointed sticks. She folded her arms resolutely and willed her eyes to snap shut.

They would not. She listened to the clock in the hall as it chimed, and then chimed an hour later.

"This is impossible," she said at last, and got out of bed. She paused with her hand on the doorknob. "Oh, I can't do this," she said out loud.

It sounded almost like whimpering. She berated herself and almost retreated to her bed. Courage, Omega, she thought, and let herself into the hall.

There was no light showing under the door of Matthew's room. He had probably been asleep for hours. Heaven knew it had been a tiring day. She raised her hand to knock, and then lowered it again. I can't possibly do what I'm contemplating, she thought, and started back to her room.

She was almost back to her door when she thought of Alpha's words and turned around. Matthew could tell her to go away. But if she never knew for certain what he would do, she would only spin out her hours and days and years in endless circles of regret.

She gritted her teeth and knocked on the door, steeling herself, already turning to go.

"Come in."

She opened the door slowly. "Matthew?"

He didn't say anything, and all heart left her. The tears welled in her eyes and she started to back out into the hall. But then Matthew lit a match, and a small point of light shone in the room. She couldn't see his face, but he was there and he had lit a candle.

"Matthew, I would like to stay with you tonight."

Again the long silence. Again her heart failed her.

"Omega, don't you remember anything I've told you? I'm impotent. That's as plain as I can make it."

And then she was angry with him. She came into the room and shut the door behind her. "Matthew, you cod's head, I love you! Did those . . . those ladies—"

"Scarcely ladies," he interjected.

"Did those ladies you tried—did they care for you?"

"Hardly."

"Then I wish you would take a chance with someone who loves you!" She gestured in the dark, warming to her subject. "And I've been feeling in the last week that you're not entirely indifferent to me."

"That's true enough. Good God, Omega, I love you. I never quit doing that."

"Then you'd better show me, Matthew, or I'll just go on being a teacher who never takes a chance, and you'll wither away."

"Omega, you are absolutely daft."

"Oh, good night, Matthew!" She blew out the candle and went to the door.

Her hand was on the knob when he spoke again, and this time his voice was softer. "Omega, it's a narrow bed."

"The most paltry excuse," she said, and leaned her forehead against the door.

"But it's comfortable, my dear, if you don't mind sharing a pillow."

She smiled to herself. She was silent, waiting.

"And the floor is cold, and you're not getting any younger standing there."

She laughed. "Neither are you."

She heard him sit up and light the candle again. Her smile deepened as he pulled back the coverlet. "Come on, Omega. Let's . . . let's throw out the itinerary."

She got in bed, feeling a tingle of fear mixed with her joy. This was different from the other night, when they had clung together for solace. She needed something more this time, and so did he.

Without saying anything, Matthew touched her tentatively, running his hand down her body. She relaxed and moved closer. In another moment they were in each other's arms, and Omega couldn't tell where she ended and where Matthew began. She was afraid for a moment, but no more than he was. Without a word spoken, he gave himself to her, and she welcomed him into herself, her hands tight across his back, loving him fiercely as she had always wanted to do.

He was her lover, and she was his, and there was no room for regret or pride. They were the only two people in the world, and it was a world they knew they would never tire of, now that they had found it.

Omega refused to let go of him.

"See here, my dear, I'm not going anywhere!"

"Promise?" she whispered, and then ran her tongue inside his ear until he groaned with the pleasure of it.

"Good God, Omega, I fear we are going to be exhausted by morning. And you have to leave with Alpha. Hold still, we're going to fall off."

She giggled. "Silly, I'm not leaving with Alpha."

"Oh, yes you are! In a week's time I will arrive at Amphney St. Peter with another special license clutched in my hand. And Alpha will give you away, and Lydia will cry, and Jamie will say, 'Oh, this is famous!', and Angela may give you a Waterloo souvenir, for all I know."

She considered this. "No more than a week. If something should result from this evening's sport, and heaven knows, it could, I wouldn't want your—our—neighbors counting the months back on their fingers."

He settled himself beside her. "A distinct possibility, now that you mention it. Two days?"

"Much better, Matthew."

"Excellent. Oh, do that again. Good God, Omega. Where was I? Oh, yes, we will leave our darlings with Lydia and bolt to the city for a week or so. I want to renew some old acquaintances, and I have a proposal for Mr. Timothy Platter."

"Which is . . ."

"The constable, I fear, is sorely displeased with me, and in truth, he has been thinking of retirement. Do you think Timothy Platter would give up London's beauty and safety for the boredom of Byford?"

"Oh, Matthew, I love you."

"And I love you. Of course, the Platters will have to get used to the birds yelling, and fresh water, and all manner of evils, but I will put it to Maeve."

He kissed her. "And there was something else. Omega, you are such a distraction! How can I think? Oh, yes. Dear Omega, it has come to my attention that you are not entirely indifferent to me. Can I . . . oh, have I reason to hope that—"

"Yes," she interrupted, and kissed him.

"Hush, Omega, I'm not through, and I'm only going to propose this last time in my life. Do I have reason to hope that you might consent to joining your life with mine?"

"Yes," she said again, and touched his face. "Matthew, you're crying."

"I am. Older men get funny. Omega, you'll have to send a letter of regret to St. Elizabeth's."

"It will be my only regret, dearest."